The Wom

The Woman in the Trees

GERRY WILLIAM

NEW STAR BOOKS
VANCOUVER
2004

New Star Books Ltd.
107 – 3477 Commercial Street
Vancouver, BC   V5N 4E8
www.NewStarBooks.com

Publication of this work is made possible by grants from the Canada
Council, the British Columbia Arts Council, and the Department of Cana-
dian Heritage Book Publishing Industry Development Program.

Printed and bound in Canada
First printing, September 2004

LIBRARY AND ARCHIVES CANADA CATALOGUING IN PUBLICATION

William, Gerry, 1952–
  The woman in the trees / Gerry William.

ISBN 1-55420-013-X

1. Okanagan Indians — Fiction. 2. Vernon Region (B.C.) — History —
Fiction. I. Title.

PS8595.I544W65 2004   C813'.54   C2004-904613-6

Acknowledgements

I would like to thank the following people:

Carol Barrett, M. Willson Williams, Joseph W. Meeker, Douglas Davidson, Marilyn Dumont, Georges Sioui, Bob Henry Baber, Cheryl (Sue) Ware, Catherine Copley-Woods, and Kathryn Rickert for their wonderful support, suggestions and comments.

Darrell Jones and the Spallumcheen Indian Band for their financial support of the beginning of this whole thing.

Lynn Phelan of Sn-Klip Theatre Company in Vernon, B.C. for her always-present spiritual support of what I write.

Stan and Chris Cuthand without whom this novel would not have been completed.

Mourning Dove and Chief N'kwala for whom they were in the wonderful history of the Okanagan people.

Last, and most invaluable, my wife Beth Cuthand, who is the center of my world.

The Woman in the Trees

Prologue

•• ● ••

The wind blew through Coyote's fur, ruffling his grey fur and perked ears. Coyote ignored the wind, knowing that it wanted to speak. He had no time to listen to the wind's endless dialogues.

Instead, from where he sat, Coyote looked down and over the bluff. He could barely see the split in the cliff below him. It ran a black vertical line double Coyote's length. Coyote's memories of that break in the cliff went back many lifetimes.

"Many lifetimes." The wind repeated Coyote's thoughts. Coyote yipped at the wind, which paused to study his demeanor. Satisfied that Coyote had other things on his mind, the wind curled around his form. It saw what Coyote saw, and swirled down into the crack, spilling into a cave whose power drove the wind back to Coyote.

"I'm scared," the wind whispered.

"Scared?" Coyote sneered.

"Stones of water," the wind whispered. "Stones of water."

Coyote yelped back, "Stones of sky." He flipped his head towards the deep blue lake that lay near the foot of the cliff. "The caves hide the future. Caves are cold. I could tell you stories, wind, of what is to happen."

"You don't scare me," the wind whirled back its bravado.

Coyote ignored the wind's defiance. His mind heard the voices from other times and spaces. Around his form the unearthly cold formed a blanket impervious to wind gusts.

"Mole would know what to do," the wind said.

"Leave my wife out of this," Coyote growled. "She and I will meet again, but not here and now. Now belongs to the people coming from where the sun rises."

"I know these people," the wind proffered. "They have been a long time coming."

Coyote rose and shook his fur. "No," he said. "They were always here. They are the syilx, and they will know me by my great wit and wisdom."

The wind giggled.

"Careful or I'll fart at you and, as the wind, you'll have to carry the smell everywhere. People won't like you then."

"Tell me a story only you can tell," the wind held back another giggle.

Coyote sat back on his haunches, pleased with the wind's wisdom. "I will tell you many stories. None of them end, but you will know the story from the mark I give it."

"What mark? Your poop?"

"No, this mark."

And Coyote stepped into the story.

The Father of British Columbia

•• ● ••

The center fire burned large. As the cavalcade rode into the campsite, Major Robinson, the brigade leader, directed that the fire be fed more wood, saying, "We don't need to fear these Indians. No reason to hide. Word is that they're pacifists. They won't be any trouble. We should reach Fort Hope and the gold mines in good order."

Some of the three hundred men from the six companies began drinking as soon as they rode into camp. Others quietly went about raising tents, making sure that none of the tents were too close to the ever-growing fire. Smaller campfires quickly dotted the campsite. Men drew together in their own brigades, the French staying away from the Americans. Many went to sleep without food, too tired to want more than falling into dreams. The ones who stayed up formed a rough circle around the small fires, their eyes hidden by their hats.

Despite the center fire's size, voices were kept low as men ate from their tin plates. They drank the bitter sludge, which once had been coffee. Between gulps, they chewed on their jerky or dried salmon, the latter eaten discreetly to avoid the ridicule of the ones who saw salmon as fit only for dirty Indians. The drinkers, mostly the Californian miners, gradually grew more boisterous. However, they continued to avoid the center fire.

"It's been a hard ride from Fort Simcoe." A company captain, a Frenchman who had worked with the fur brigades of old, stared into the fire's flames. He spoke over the sound of the crackling wood. Red sparks frequently sprayed up from the wood as the flames took new hold of each log.

A Californian miner and Indian hunter was the next to speak, "We're better off splitting into two groups. We'll travel faster through Indian country. My men can handle the Indians."

Another Californian miner said, "I agree with the Major. These Indians are sheep. Not many of the buggers left. By this time next year this land will be empty."

Robinson spoke up. "Like I said, we've nothing to fear. They touch us, the cavalry will hurt them bad. Border or not, they'll give these Indians the same beating they've giving Chief Joseph and his Indians, British Empire be damned."

A volley of soft grunts gave Robinson support. He waited, knowing what was coming.

"I don't care much which way we go, in two groups or one. Either way, we'll do what we want. These Indians are whipped. Word has it that their chief is an old bugger, and he's a Company man."

Another volley of soft grunts lent support to the Californian. One captain protested that breaking the brigade in two made both groups more vulnerable to Indian attack. The Californians snorted their disagreement, and then a silence descended. Robinson waited. When no one spoke for a time, he looked at his six captains. He knew he couldn't fight the Californians. "We'll break camp at first light. I'll take one group up the Okanagan Lake. The other group will go through the Similka-meen Valley west of the lake. We can cut our travel time by a third. Are we agreed?"

●●●●●

Several days after the brigade broke into two, a group of syilx children were playing near the food caches at Okanagan Lake. They heard the first volley of guns, and several camp dogs fell, one of them still kicking its hind legs at the empty air, its bowels exposed by a bullet. The children ran north a hundred yards, where the adults were scrambling to get their canoes. The children and dogs jumped into the light boats, and the boats were off into the lake. Within moments they were out of range of the guns. The brigade of Californian miners whooped and hollered as they spilled onto the beach, some of them watching the canoes speed across the mile-wide lake. Others ripped apart the food caches, uncovering bushels of berries, on which they began to gorge. Several brigades on the nearby ridge looked down at the carnage taking place. The French felt sick for the syilx who had spent the summer preparing and storing food for winter.

Robinson watched, smiling grimly. This made up for his previous expedition, which had been stopped north of Fort Simcoe by an Indian attack. The attack had left several of his men dead. The rest had no heart to go on. He knew that the French hated what was happening; many of them had Indian wives from their years as fur traders. But these were different times. Mining, Robinson was convinced, made for harder men, men who did not allow sentiment to color what needed to be done.

As the miners dumped the remains of the food caches into the lake, Robinson looked into the distance. The Indians had reached the other side of the lake, where a larger group met them. "Not this time," Robinson thought. "This time we'll be ready for you buggers. We have more men, and the U.S. Cavalry knows where we are."

That night, by the center fire, the brigade captains decided to travel quickly along the west side of Okanagan Lake. The Californians disagreed. They wanted to trick the Indians. For the past week, the scouts who trailed the brigade as it moved north noticed that the Indians waited until the brigade was on the move, and then scoured the remains of the campsites, looking for leftover canteens, pots, plates, and other items. When the Californian leader told the other companies of his plan to ambush the Indians, half of the captains left the center fire. The others questioned the miner. In the end, they agreed that he had a good plan. What finally convinced them was when the miner, sensing their reluctance, had said, "You know that what we did today will make them angrier than bees defending a hive. Now's the time to get the buggers. They won't be expecting an ambush. We can get them good before they get crazy ideas in their head, like attacking us. My men can take them. We've fought tougher Indians than this."

Robinson, itching for revenge, agreed with the miner. "Boys, we've got to take the fight to them. Knock the tar out of them before they get too strong. What do you say?"

A captain asked, "How do we lay an ambush? They'll be watching every move we make from now on."

The miner grinned. "My men have already thought of that. Tomorrow night we'll have our men hide, so that at daybreak no one will see anything more than the brigade breaking camp."

The syilx watched as the large party of sha-mas broke camp and filed north in a long line that extended two miles. Close to five hundred horses and two hundred men raised dust into the air as they moved north along the lake. The syilx waited until the last of the brigade had left the campsite before they canoed across the lake. Syilx scouts quickly searched the empty campsite. They signaled that all was safe, and the rest of the syilx beached their canoes.

The food caches were beyond recovery. The headman keened for their loss; many families would go hungry that winter. But little could be done. The brigade was too large to attack. The headman sent runners up the Valley to warn the other syilx of what was coming. The syilx then returned to their camp on the other side of the lake, where they traveled north to set up an overnight camp. The next morning, as the brigade continued its journey, the syilx once again paddled across the lake to the deserted campsite.

The first round of bullets from a nearby gulch took three Indians down. The gunshots echoed from the fifty-foot limestone cliffs that loomed over the lake. The Indians ran, scattering once more along the lakeshore, some dropping into the water, which grew red with blood. The guns continued firing until the last of the Indians was either out of sight, or away from the shore, beyond the range of the bullets.

The miners emerged from their hiding places. They whooped and hollered and danced into the water, attacking the bodies of the Indians, clubbing them into pulpy masses. Robinson, as he watched, clenched his left hand into a fist, feeling the strain of the past two days. His men, already driven to distraction from keeping constant vigilance since Fort Okanagan, vented their fury on the Indians. When the orgy of violence subsided, the miners gathered together, bees to honey, and after only a few celebratory whoops and slaps on the back, rode north to join the rest of the brigade.

Four days after the ambush, the brigade stumbled on good fortune when two Shuswap Indians met the brigade's advance scouts five miles from the main body of travelers. The Indians were traveling south and hadn't heard of the brigade's attack. The older warrior was preoccupied with meeting his wife in Colville; he wanted to be there in three days, a hard ride even though he traveled light.

Robinson watched as his men led the two Indians to the center fire. The Californian group was more subdued, although still

9

somewhat feisty. The Indians had taken to following the brigade, and each day their numbers grew, although they kept their distance. Drums sounded each night from all sides of the brigade's main campsites. Often the night was clear enough so that the Indian songs were clearly heard by the brigade. Robinson, sensing the fear among his men, doubled the guards at night.

Now Robinson stood in front of the two captives, who waited silently. Robinson had the prisoners' wrists bound tightly. When that was done, Robinson turned his attention to the many men who circled the fire. "Boys, I think these two buggers are our ticket to Fort Thompson. Keep them safe, but keep them secure, as well. It's still three days to the fort."

The leader of the French company stepped out from the mass of men. "Sir, our company objects. We didn't like the ambush, and we don't like what you're doing now."

The entire camp grew still. In the distance could be heard the cadence of the Indians as they sang and danced in preparation for battle. Robinson felt his men closely observing him. He looked up at the nearby trees. A cold gust of wind sent sparks leaping from the fire. He had never liked the French traders, but he couldn't fight two fights at once.

"What can you do about it?" Robinson threw the challenge back at the French trader.

Without hesitation, the French leader raised his voice for all to hear. "My company is going ahead. We're breaking camp now, and will meet you at the Fort."

Robinson watched as the French trader returned to the larger group of men around the campfire. Soon he saw the French traders separate themselves from the main camp.

"Any other Indian lovers want to follow them?" Robinson asked the men who still stood at the fire. When no one else moved, Robinson nodded towards the two Indians. "Keep watch over them. Make sure they're at the head of our brigade tomorrow. I want the other Indians to see what we have."

•• ● ••

Walking Grizzly Bear slept uneasily that night. All day he had watched syilx, Secwepemc, Similkameen and others ride into camp. Headmen from every important family for two hundred miles south and east of Fort Thompson asked for Walking Grizzly Bear's permission to set up camp. There was no choice in this ceremony. Each headman could barely contain his anger against the sha-mas, who would be at the fort by the next day.

Many of the families, including Horse and his family, Walking Grizzly Bear had not seen for years, and yet each greeting was from a family whom he knew intimately. The headmen brought only the warriors from their families, the women and children being left to the safety of the surrounding hills where other camps sprang up.

Walking Grizzly Bear felt his age. His half-son, Chief Tonasket, had been pressuring his stepfather for years to give him formal leadership of the Sinkaietk, the Okanagans south of the newly placed border with the Bostons, the name syilx used to call the Americans. Now Walking Grizzly Bear (the sha-mas called him Chief Nicolas, or Inquala) questioned again whether he had made the right decision in not giving his half-son the control he wanted. It would have been so easy to do.

One of Walking Grizzly Bear's sixteen wives spent the evening preparing the clothes Walking Grizzly Bear would wear when he greeted the American miners the next day. Walking Grizzly Bear knew that to some, perhaps many, of his own people, his leadership was in question because of his close ties to the Hudson's Bay Company, known simply as the Company to everyone. He had heard the talk, and it sent pain straight to his heart, pain which he showed to only his family.

Even the choice of clothes for tomorrow's epic meeting would be questioned by those who challenged his status among his people. Within his tent, Walking Grizzly Bear watched as his

11

wife carefully laid out his blue jacket. Each medal given to him
in trade over many years by the sha-mas was carefully pinned to
the jacket. The firelight made the medals glitter. The wife laid
out a set of new deerskin leggings and his finest pair of moccasins, their soles stitched for extra cushioning. The stovepipe
hat was placed at the top of the laid-out jacket. His wife had
cleaned the hat and carefully inserted an eagle feather to give it
distinction.

Walking Grizzly Bear examined his outfit, and told his wife
she had done well. He sent her away. He wanted to sleep alone,
to have his dreams speak of what he would do tomorrow.
Although his family enforced a zone of quiet around the imme-
diate area of his tent, he heard the arrival of warriors as they set
up camp. Perhaps strangest of all, and something that set both
the fort and the distant brigade on edge, was the lack of drum-
ming or singing. Despite hundreds of warriors, the sounds
within the camp that now surrounded Fort Thompson were
ominously subdued. Walking Grizzly Bear hardly knew he had
lain down before he was asleep.

Coyote, Sn-klip, entered through the tent flap. He took a seat
opposite Walking Grizzly Bear. For a while he nibbled at his tail.
Walking Grizzly Bear waited.

"So now your dream begins, old man." Coyote's black eyes
glinted in the low fire. "What would you have me do in this
dream of yours?"

Before answering, Walking Grizzly Bear thought for several
minutes. "I'm scared," he admitted. "My people would slay
these Bostons when they arrive. I know of no way to stop them
from doing this."

"You could just step aside and let them do it," Coyote pointed
out.

"If I did, their justice would be swift. It was for this reason that I asked my people not to get involved with our brothers and sisters who fight the blue-coats on the other side of the new border."

Coyote stared at Walking Grizzly Bear. "What makes you fear the Bostons?"

Walking Grizzly Bear shrugged. "I met my brother, Chief Joseph, several years ago. He asked for help, but he also told me that if I did so, I would have to lead my people all the way. The Bostons would not ignore the killing of their own people."

"You do have a problem there," Coyote admitted. "I'm glad that I'm not in your moccasins."

"Is that it? Is that the only advice you can give me?"

Coyote grinned. "You mistake me for Snee-Nah, the Owl. She gives what you seem to look for. Me, I'm content just to watch."

"Not much help," Walking Grizzly Bear complained.

Coyote sat for a few minutes, and Walking Grizzly Bear thought the talk was over. He was about to get up and leave the tent, when Coyote's eyes blazed. Walking Grizzly bear felt his heart grow warm, almost as though Coyote's gaze had pierced his chest. "I cannot tell you the future, " Coyote said. "What I can tell you is that this is where your life has led. Everything you have been, you must be for tomorrow. Your people will follow you only if you speak from your heart."

"Many people have told me what to do," Walking Grizzly Bear said. "My people have given me many good words to think about."

Coyote nodded. "Yes, and many angry words. Words spoken in pain. But they are not your words. You do not own them. They are not yours to give to others. The words you speak tomorrow must be your words. The future of your people, and the future of the sha-mas who begin to fill these valleys, will come from what you do and say tomorrow. Love and hate cannot be taken back once they are spoken."

Walking Grizzly Bear felt the words reach into his soul, each one taking him places no one else knew. Through his pain, he saw Coyote grin. Coyote spoke a final time. "This thing you do tomorrow, it will be your last gift to your people. It is time you and I spent time together. Let others carry on with life. The Woman in the Trees, the one you know from your childhood, she will bring you to me. You will know her by her greeting. I'm leaving; there are other stories I must tend to."

Robinson's brigade of two hundred men and five hundred horses rode through the narrow valley to Fort Thompson. They were bunched up, no longer strung out as they had been before. The two Shuswap Indians walked twenty feet ahead of Robinson, their hands still tied behind their backs. A mile from the fort, the brigade met up with the French traders, who waited for reinforcements before risking the final journey into the fort. The Thompson River flowed past them, unusually swift and full for this time of year.

Surprisingly, the Indians did not block access to the fort, and the brigade set up camp under its walls. The next day they continued on to Kamloops Lake, where they set about building rafts to cross. It was here that the Indians met them.

Near noon, the brigade saw a solid group of Indians heading their way. The Indians were stretched across the valley, a mile-long group of warriors ten to twenty deep. Several men, including an old man, rode at the head of this column of warriors.

Walking Grizzly Bear had woken early that day. He bathed in a shallow part of the river before returning to his tent. Here he dressed in the clothes his wife had laid out the previous night. When he stepped out of the tent, he saw a line of syilx warriors. Walking Grizzly Bear rose to his full height. Although he was not tall, this movement silenced the low murmur of voices. A cousin of Blue Dreams stepped from the group of headmen, and said, "The Bostons are at the lake. It is time we attacked. I speak for the syilx. Justice must be done."

Walking Grizzly Bear stepped to the side of the headman so that he faced everyone. "Listen. You say we must have justice. Is justice the killing of these Bostons? When the blue-coats come from the south, they will come in great numbers, and they will not leave. They will seek justice, too. They will seek revenge for the killing of three hundred of their own tribe. Our Great Mother lives across the waters. She will not stand against these blue-coats. She has lost one war with the Bostons, and she will not risk losing another. Who then will stop the killing of our women and children?"

Walking Grizzly Bear's eyes were the eyes of a bear, fierce and unyielding. His voice, usually low, could be heard by every warrior in the great throng that surrounded him. "I seek release of the two Secwepemc, but that is all I will do. The taste for blood is sweet, but I will not see my children pay that price. To those who wish otherwise, I say this. If you kill the Bostons, you also kill me. My heart is small. It cannot watch our women and children pay the cost of your anger. We live on the edge of a great lake, a lake that lies deep and strong in the number of Bostons who come our way. Perhaps Coyote can stand against the waves from such a lake, but I am not Coyote."

"Listen, yesterday I heard from the families of the two Secwepemc. What they said about my brothers made me weep. I promised that I would do everything I could to have the Bostons let the two go. I could promise no less. If any syilx wish to lead us, you must do so now. I will step aside and let your wisdom guide us."

Walking Grizzly Bear stopped speaking and waited, his head bowed to the ground. No one in the great collection of warriors spoke. A silence ensued, broken only by the occasional sound of horses moving about. After a time, Walking Grizzly Bear looked up and began the walk to where his horse stood. After he had mounted, the syilx drew aside to let him make his steady unhurried way to the front of the line of warriors who now filled the valley. Walking Grizzly Bear led the war party down the valley to Kamloops Lake.

Major Robinson waited as Walking Grizzly Bear, flanked by the Okanagan headmen, approached. Behind Major Robinson, the two prisoners stood. The miners and fur traders formed a line of defense behind the Major, their guns loaded and brought to bear on the Indians.

Walking Grizzly Bear stopped a dozen feet from Major Robinson. The warriors also stopped. The dust slowly settled, and Walking Grizzly Bear waited, his eyes scanning the miners before him. When he spoke, his voice, clear, strong, and full of scorn carried through the still air.

"You sha-mas come to our land. You travel through, and we let you do so. But look how brave you are. Three hundred great, strong, well-armed Bostons. How powerful must be my two brothers from the Secwepemcin Nation, that it takes so many to capture them. They must surely be the greatest warriors we have ever seen. It is well that we syilx are their friends and allies, for who can fight against such men? Even Coyote would stand aside for them. How can I say more? You Bostons must let these two go, or they may turn on you."

Robinson heard the Indians behind Walking Grizzly Bear chuckle, and his own face burned. But he also felt the stillness in the air. A false move, a wrong word, and his brigade would be in for the fight of its life. Nor was victory assured. The Indian warriors were as well armed as the brigade, and there were many more Indians than miners.

Walking Grizzly Bear dismounted. A warrior held the horse's reins while Walking Grizzly Bear walked up to Robinson. Sunlight glinted off Walking Grizzly Bear's medals, and Robinson smelled the strong clean scent of the Indian's new leggings. More than this, Robinson felt the physical force of Walking Grizzly Bear as the Indian drew close. Old as the Indian was, Robinson felt threatened by him.

"I ask you this one time only. I want my two brothers let go. If you do this, we will go in peace. But know this also. I am only one man. I cannot hold back my people for long. You decide."

With those words, Walking Grizzly Bear stood, his hands at his side and his eyes looking into those of Robinson. Not a tremor passed through the Indian, although more than fifty rifles were pointed directly at him. His eyes, while shaded by the rim of his stovepipe hat, were clear and strong. What frightened Robinson was the lack of any threat in those eyes. Walking Grizzly Bear had become a force of nature. Robinson had met a grizzly like this man, and knew why the chief had earned his name. The grizzly, just before attacking Robinson's party, had reared onto its hind legs, and gazed at the men without fear. Before it dropped down onto all four paws for its charge, the bear had stared at the men, and Robinson had seen the attack in the bear's eyes, a look that carried a promise, not a threat.

Robinson walked back to his captains. The Californians wanted to fight, but the French and other companies said that they were supposed to get to the gold mines at Fort Hope. Everything else was a distraction, and they had not come to see their trip ended this way. No one had to say that they might lose the battle. Despite the Californians' protests, Robinson made his decision. In three quick steps, he was in front of the two captives, his knife in hand. Seconds later, the two Indians were free to walk away. As Robinson watched them go, Walking Grizzly Bear smiled, sending a chill down Robinson's spine. "When I give to you, I give myself," the Indian said. And then the Indians were gone, riding east in an unhurried fashion. Robinson watched them for several minutes. Although the day was not hot, sweat trickled down the back of his shirt. He turned to his waiting captains.

"Which fool said that old Chief Nicolas was toothless? You should watch your words. That old man has the devil in him."

Storytelling: Part One

•• ● ••

The Woman In the Trees

Enid Blue Starbreaks looked around. The great river flowed by, its surface sparkled by the rising sun. The air was cleaner than any Enid had smelled and felt in years. Her hardened body moved into the trees bordering the river. A camp of her people was a short fifteen-minute walk upstream. Her long legs carried her over the uneven ground. The few people who knew of her came from a long time ago. To them she was the star person — the woman from the other side of creation. They feared and respected her, generally avoiding her where possible. Still, Enid kept her senses alert as she strode along the riverbank towards the rising sun.

•• ● ••

The boy crouched at the edge of the swift flowing Swanetka (the sha-mas would later call it the Columbia River), reaching for a floating twig, when his gasp drew his sister's attention from the nearby mound where she played. She turned and saw her brother's head rise to the surface; he was already a dozen feet downstream. She hesitated, but her brother's panicked cries galvanized her. She dove in, her small arms and legs churning as she felt her body tighten against the cold spring water. The water carried the weight of silt, and the objects that flowed downstream in this heavier water made swimming in it difficult. The young girl could not see underwater and in moments she struggled to the surface. The river tugged at her small body, carrying her inexorably from the shore. Although she came closer to her brother, and saw his eyes turn towards her, the cold reached into her. She tried not to scream or shout, fighting her panic, knowing, as her mother had taught her, that struggling took energy from the struggle itself.

When she reached her brother, he was floating on his back to conserve energy. She was about to do the same when she saw the driftwood a dozen feet away, near the center of the river. She nudged her brother. The two swam until they were beside the half-hidden log. With her longer legs and arms, the sister clambered onto the log. She pulled her brother up beside her before she began to shiver. Her brother, also cold, hugged her from behind.

Walking cleared Enid's thoughts. She had spent many years in the wilderness, so she read signs everywhere of animals passing through or stopping at the water's edge for drink. Animals didn't worry Enid. People did.

She followed a deer trail around a tree grove and back to the swollen river. At first glance, she didn't see the children. But when they moved to secure their hold on the log, Enid looked up, saw that she was clear of any overhanging tree limbs, and launched herself into the air, spinning as she rose. She leveled off above the treetops, long practice making her flight over the water easy. As she neared the children from above, she automatically banked towards them.

•• ● ••

The girl sensed her silent approach and looked up just as Enid's arms wrapped around her and her brother. The girl froze in the woman's arms, fearing that this was the end, and that she was being taken to the spirit realm by a ghost. Her brother was as frozen with fear as she, and so neither dared to move as the spirit holding them flew towards the camp where the children lived.

The boy watched the river below, following his sister's example. Her face was inches from Enid's, and she stared wide-eyed at the woman holding her. She was entranced by the scar that ran the length of the woman's left cheek, and had seen the same type of scar, long and narrow, on the faces of the grownups in her family. She knew the scar, then, to be a knife wound. The woman's grip on both children also spoke of a warrior's strength, confusing because the person holding them was a woman and not a man.

In less than two minutes Enid saw the smoke curling above the trees. She kept to the treetops, her six-foot figure a shadow that sped northeast faster than any horse could gallop. Enid was in the camp before the adults even knew she was there. She released the children and was up and away as the six adults gawked at her, the children forgotten. Leaves and pine branches stirred in her wake. Then she was gone.

Time Immemorial

Time whispers. It tells no secrets to those who seek too long; tells no secrets to those who think they have the answers. Time folds back on itself, a single being whose soul wraps around Old Coyote like the winter robes he once tore into pieces.

"You're talking about me again."

"Can't help it. You're part of the story."

Coyote looks at the monitor. "Time, eh? I don't think she'd like to be referred to in that way."

"She?"

"Don't tell me you didn't know! Thought you knew everything."

"Not everything. Tell me what she's like."

"She's a smoothy. Into everything. Sometimes I see her hanging out at the mall. A mall rat. Small and fevered. Scurrying around. When she's bored, she'll reach out like this," Coyote extends a paw towards me. "And then that's it. Whomever she touches, their time is up. They're gone before they hit the floor."

"Sometimes I see her curled up under a tree, just breathing it all in. She can stay like that for days. When she gets up to go, that's it, too. The gig is up. Summer's gone. The leaves shake and fall."

"It's all one to her. Means everything, and nothing. We're so caught up in it all, and she's just meandering. Can't blame her. She knows what's going to happen, what is happening, and what has happened. It's all one to her. She doesn't do anything that isn't meant to be. The rest of it she leaves up to me."

"Why you?"

"Why not me? Everyone else takes her too seriously. Big mistake. Where are you going with this story?"

"I don't quite know yet."

"Well, if you don't know, how about another story?"

"I need to talk about time."

"Oh, part of your history stuff?"

"Yes, but there's more. I need to know about those words we used to know. 'Time Immemorial.'"

"Your grandfather used to use that phrase a lot."

"What does it mean?"

Coyote smiled. "Thought you'd never ask. Time Immemorial belongs to the syilx, to you and me, to your grandfather and grandmother, to Wolverine and Horse. Let me tell you a story."

• • ● • •

Wolverine walks away from the priest, the priest's words ringing in his ears.

"God loves you," said the priest. The priest's energy burns, for he draws strength from his trip across the lake. Once he was flexible, but no longer. The priest felt the cold deep in the lake's depths as he crossed over; afterwards, with the Indians watching him, he had staggered onto the beach, where he became deathly sick for several minutes, choking up the food from earlier in the day."

This memory turns the priest's fury into words. He says, "He cares for all of us, even the red man. The universe with its countless stars are tiny compared to God's love. He is everywhere, and He is everything."

"The seasons are His to give, and He wants you to plant potatoes in His name. He wants you to stop hunting and living an aimless life. He wants you to stop dancing in the winter, stop telling stories about beings who do not exist. About beings who blaspheme the ground they walk on, for they are God's unclean."

"He wants you to become good Christians. There is only One God, and all others are cast from Heaven, thrust into the scorching loss and despair that is the Universe with no God. It is not too late to change, to grow under God's love, to renounce your wicked ways."

"Why do you think so many of you have died in the past three generations? Because your gods are powerless before the One God who is the Christian God. He smites those who do not believe, afflicts them with the seven plagues of Egypt. Because you sin in His eyes, he has given you the unmerciful kiss of forgiveness, that slays as it saves. Your elders could not stop the wrath of God, who saw your ways as wicked."

"God lives outside of time, but He knows everything, even the thoughts that crowd your spirits. He forgives those only who repent of their sins, who abide in His name, who sleep under His angel's wings. He forgives those who cherish His commandments, who leave their own sinful ways to place their trust and their souls in His care, who trust in no one but the One God who is the Christian God."

Wolverine feels hurt, dizzy as he walks the trails on his day-long journey to the Winter Dance. The priest had said, "The One God. He who smote the elders, made them powerless before His might. He who sent the smoke of despair, the fog that wrapped itself around the Indians and ate into their faces and spirits, burning them with the fire of the One God who cared enough to both kill his people, and save them.

"Lot stumbling away from a doomed city, his family trailing behind him, wailing and gnashing their teeth, leaving so many others behind. And then the heat of the One God lights the sky, makes their robes billow and their ears ring. One wife turning her eyes towards the wrath of God, turning to salt as her face and body are scorched black and then become white powder, white salt, before the loving touch of God's fury."

Wolverine hears the drums echo within the long narrow home where his grandfather Horse holds his Winter Dance. He stumbles in, a despairing Lot whose soul is riven by fear, whose feet no longer are in touch with Toom-Tem, Mother Earth. His younger brother, who worships him, looks on helplessly, a boy too young to do anything but watch. Wolverine feels lifted away and borne on the winds away from his own people.

His cry rings true, bringing the Dance to a shocked stillness. Wolverine moves to the center pole, looks around at his family. False Sun rises to his feet and bows towards Wolverine. Wolverine sees the mocking smile, the hard eyes.

"Where were you elders when the white breath took us away? Why did you let so many die? Is the sha-ma's One God so strong

He could make your wisdom useless? Is the priest right? Do we worship the wrong gods? Perhaps there is only One God, and we worship Satan."

With one hand, Horse moves his son effortlessly to one side and goes to the spot where his grandson stands. Someone passes Horse a drum and stick.

"Since Time Immemorial Coyote has shown us the borders of right and wrong. Since Time Immemorial Coyote has directed our paths."

The drum beats.

"Since Time Immemorial we have walked in Toom-Tem's steps. She leads us as she leads Coyote."

The drum beats.

"It is not good for us to say that the white man's God is wrong. It is not for us to say that the white man's God is good."

The drum beats twice.

"Since Time Immemorial we have listened to the spirits around us. Since Time Immemorial we have feasted on the bounty given us by the Creator."

The drum beats twice again.

"I have watched my father die under the breath of the white smoke that came before the first white man. I watched as his spirit left, and I knew that he was going to a good way."

The drum is silent.

"Our people are not as once we were. Our families have shrunk. Many of the elders I knew just two hunting seasons ago are now gone where my father lives."

The people are silent.

"We cannot fight these white men. They are too many, and they come too swiftly. What we have left is Time Immemorial."

The drum rings true.

"Time Immemorial is the land we live in, the spirits we move among, the thanks we give the Creator. We are simple people, but we are good in our way."

Horse feels his grandson's shoulders sag.

"Time Immemorial is the way we will come back one day as strong as we stood in my father's time. Time Immemorial is the heart we all see in our children, who carry us forward into hard times. Time Immemorial is the dance we share tonight, for the creator does not promise us tomorrow, yet we must always live for the next day."

Horse pauses long enough for his grandson to be led to the seat that waits for him. The people move aside and then embrace Wolverine, who wails as he feels torn by the darkness of the new spirit that moves inside. He wails as he feels this spirit displace his love of his own family. Horse begins to dance around the pole, knowing that his grandson has begun a journey as old as Time Immemorial.

Fever

On the second day of the hunting trip, the syilx rounded a bend of the mountain. The land was still save for the chirr of grasshoppers jumping from the path of the nine horses and their riders. The heat was constant. But it was also light, a reminder of their height above the valley. Horse knew the country well, and rode easily, letting his horse follow the lead of the riders ahead.

Every so often Horse would turn to look behind. It was instinctual. He had to know the country they passed as well as the country they rode into. He also knew enough to watch for any signs of pursuit from either animals or from the Secwepemc, whose lands were very close.

Horse also had his mind elsewhere. Last night, just before setting up camp, Horse had watched as Coyote — Sn-klip — sat on a mound half a bowshot from the riders. Sn-klip's boldness, always there, was different this time. He ignored the other riders and stared at Horse, their eyes meeting and locking. "What are you trying to tell me?" Horse asked.

Sn-klip cocked his head to the left, his ears flapping forward. Another rider, seeing this, grinned. "I think Sn-klip likes you." Horse grinned back. "I guess he has good taste."

This set up a round of humor that lasted until the headman chose a camping site. By the time Horse looked around, Sn-klip had faded into the low underbrush, his lingering yip the only mark of his presence.

Sn-klip's bold stare was a message. This every syilx knew. The other riders also knew that his message was directed at Horse, and so left him to puzzle over what that message might be. The headman had spotted elk less than an hour's ride ahead.

Horse, being the last rider, paused at the bend. The steady, low hoof beats of the horses ahead quickly became distant. Horse saw the far blue ridges across the valley. Many days' ride away, the mountains glinted with streaks of white. Below, the valley arced south, briefly hooked right, and then faded out of sight straight south. The lake shimmered in the heat, its edges colored a lighter blue where the water lapped ashore. The lake's surface was mottled with whitecaps, a contrast to the still warm air that hovered higher up the slopes.

Horse couldn't shake Sn-klip's mocking gaze of last night. Something silent called to him, and he turned to look back. The shock of seeing Sn-klip so close, and without any warning snicker from his mount, startled Horse. Sn-klip was again staring at Horse.

"What are you telling me, old one?"

Sn-klip was crouched on all fours, his head tilted forward and his long ears laid back in a posture Horse hadn't seen Sn-klip assume before.

At the moment their eyes met once again, a wind from the south brought a quick chill to the air. The tree branches all around remained still while the gusts of air made Horse's mount nervous. Sn-klip had disappeared by the time Horse regained control of his steed. Horse suddenly felt the air and sun spin around him, and he held onto his mount's mane while the dizziness first swept over him, through him, and then was gone as quickly as the return of the still air.

On the fifth day, the hunters returned victorious. The camp knew of their coming, and the hunting party was greeted well before it came within sight of the twenty lodges. While most of the hunters were joyful, Horse was quiet. None of the other riders had felt the wind that blew through him, but neither had the trees. The headman told Horse he had had a vision but couldn't explain Horse's uneasiness.

"What you have seen and felt you must bring to our elders. They will know what signs to read."

Horse entered the lodge through the tule mat cover. He accepted the fact that four elders were waiting as though for him alone. He took a place near the fire, and thanked the Creator for his health and the health of the camp. Then he sat staring into the low flames until an elder spoke from the opposite side of the fire.

"It was a good hunt."

Another elder spoke. "The elk were large and swift, but not as swift as our young men."

"Yes, our young men can run fast."

The subdued laughter that followed trailed into the sounds of the wood as it burnt, sending shadows jumping against the tule mat walls. Although still daylight outside, it could have been any part of the day or night. Horse waited, his eyes glowing in the fire's light.

"How is old Sn-klip?"

Without looking away from the fire, Horse answered, "Sn-klip tried to tell me something."

"Only you?"

The voice, being low, could have come from any of the elders.

"Sn-klip looked at me twice from close up."

"Aiyee. It is a sign, a dream."

"The second time there was a wind. It came and went without warning, and I felt sick. Like I was both warm and cold at the same time."

Another silence, while someone threw a piece of wood into the flames.

"We must move camp soon. Some of the families will go root and berry gathering, while others will travel south. The fish are coming."

"The signs are good. It will be a good year for our people."

"Sn-klip talked with only Horse. Perhaps the message is only for him, not for our people."

"We should think on this. Sn-klip's boldness means something. I will talk to our shaman, the tl'ekwelix. When we gather again, I will have some answers."

The fire came on the wind, twists of flames spiraling north like the breath of the wild Woman in the Trees. Red tongues licked up everything in their way. Horse saw the syilx fleeing in groups, scattering towards safety. But the flames increased, sweeping people off their feet and hurling them into the sky, where they disappeared within ravenous walls of fire. Other syilx, panicked beyond all reason, dove into the river, only to be swept away by its rushing torrents.

A black shape took form in the sky. From its gaping mouth, a tall woman strode towards Horse. She was one of them, a syilx, and yet so strange in her clothes of shimmering colors. She moved as the wind moved, a wave of motion and heat. Horse experienced her coming like the early syilx must have felt at the coming of the first horse. The land shifted around the woman. Behind her loomed a floating object, larger than the great peaks east of the valley.

The woman bore the carriage and marks of a warrior, a scar running down her left cheek.

"I welcome you to our land," Horse managed to say to the stranger.

The woman smiled, and warmth flooded through Horse that had nothing to do with the tongues of flame that continued to consume syilx everywhere.

"I have looked for you all my life." The woman bowed. "When I give to you, I give myself."

"Good words. How may I help you?"

"I am your future. The future of your people. You cannot help me. I come into your dreams, as I must."

"I understand. Can you help my people?"

The woman turned to gaze at the devastation around her. For a long time she stood motionless, the winds of flame brushing against her blue iridescent clothes without scorching her or the cloth. She turned back to Horse as the screams of the syilx faded into the distance.

"Help isn't here. I cannot give you what you ask. But I am here as proof that we will continue."

Horse stared at the great object that hung in the sky. "Is there anything I can give you?"

The tall woman laughed. "Our people are dying around us, and you ask whether you can help me. No, you cannot help me. I bring you a simple message. 'The future will be yours when you own it.'"

Then the woman faded as she returned to the floating object.

"I cannot say what the dream means."

The tl'ekwelix nodded, his dark eyes unreadable as the sweat lodge steam poured from the lava rocks. The heat rolled over them, cleansing Horse's body and grating against something deep inside, a dark object that refused to budge.

The tl'ekwelix turned to Horse. "I know this woman. She has appeared in my visions before, and in the visions of others. We cannot say who she is. She has power, but that power does not help us. She is not from our time."

Horse waited, his body a river of sweat burning down his skin. The tl'ekwelix threw another ladle of water onto the rocks, and a cloud of vapor obscured them from each other. When the vapor became heat, Horse could once again see the small wiry tl'ekwelix. The shaman was again staring at him.

"We have been told of strange things coming our way. There are people whose skins are the color of the clouds, and more numerous than the grasshoppers along the hillsides. Our brothers down south tell of empty villages and bodies floating down rivers. Spirits roam this land now — angry spirits, strange spirits. In the last moon, one of our villages disappeared. Five Hearts found the empty village and felt sadness as he approached, but something held him back from going in. He saw an untended campfire in the middle of the village, but there were no dogs anywhere. Just ghosts, pushing through the empty land. Not even the cry of babies. It was the strangest feeling of Five Heart's life, and half of his hair turned white. He ran for two days, forgetting even his horse."

"Aiyee. Are we then to die without a fight?"

"We cannot fight ghosts, spirits. They are the land itself. They are the woman of your dreams, something not here. Something we cannot touch."

It came in the first cough. The young hunter had returned from a trip to a village southeast of the valley. Over the last day of travel he felt light-headed, and he moved as if he waded through water. A pleasant lethargy filled his body, and his hands turned red from warmth. By the time he reached his village, his hands contained a rash that burned. He scratched the red blisters, unable to help himself. The young hunter took to his tule mat as soon as he arrived, and it was there that he coughed for the first time. His woman daubed his face as the fever took hold.

The tl'ekwelix whom she brought in to look at her man used bitterroot medicine to soak the young man's body. When the fever raged on, and red pustules began to dot the man's face, the tl'ekwelix tried to get the hunter to drink bitter tea, but the fever and cough continued.

On the third day the tl'ekwelix was exhausted, and the wife was near hysterics. Her weeping filled the teepee and the surrounding area, where a good number of syilx hovered, both in support for the young couple, and puzzled by the young man's fever and outbreaks. None had seen its likes in their lives.

The death rattle came when the tl'ekwelix left the teepee for more medicine, leaving the feverish man and his exhausted woman alone. She was sleeping, but the tl'ekwelix's motions as he left gradually stirred her from her sleep. A strange sound woke her — a sound that sent chills down her spine. In the low firelight she could barely make out her man wrapped in blankets. The moan came from the wind, or so she thought at first. But the rattle from across the fire, and the way her man's body seemed to heave into an impossible arc, made the young woman stiffen with fear and bolt upright off her mat. Horrified as she was, the wife screamed for help as she scrambled towards her husband.

She heard an awful pop, as though her husband had broken his back As others raced into the teepee, they heard his throat rattle. He unbent like a twig. As he released his final breath, his body relaxed until he was once more stretched out on the mat.

The gathering of family and friends was enlarged by those who had heard of the man's strange death, and came to support the village in its grief.

Horse rode down the gentle slope towards the village. He had followed the tl'ekwelix's words and had spent the last twelve suns alone, beneath a waterfall where he regularly bathed between sweats. He was eager to be with his family. The strange Woman in the Trees had appeared to him the previous night and in soft tones urged him to return home.

Horse's mind was on this woman and he almost didn't see the body in the stream until his mount shied away. Startled, Horse found himself staring at a corpse that lay face down in the gently flowing water. The corpse's arms and legs moved as though the boy was swimming. Horse didn't immediately do anything, secretly hoping for the boy to stand up or to move.

When neither happened, Horse felt every hair on his arms rise up in the warm air. Through the trees, smoke spiraled up. Horse knew something was not right, and five minutes later he rode into camp. The first things he noticed were the blankets. They were strewn throughout the camp and among the pine trees along the ridge. Horse dismounted and let his cayuse go. A cool breeze stirred the leaves that fell into the smoldering ashes. Small flares briefly flamed and then subsided. Horse limped to the nearest pile of blankets. He noticed the acrid smell of death as he drew closer. Beneath the blankets lay the great seer of old, Wolverine, his eyes now eternally staring into the overcast sky. His face was ravaged by marks that Horse had heard the fur traders call the pox.

Horse forced himself to gather some foliage. Leaning over the naked Wolverine, he closed the mystic's sightless eyes, letting go of his own grief with a song that took Wolverine into the world where Coyote waited for his children. In another time, perhaps even in this lifetime, he would meet Wolverine's soul again. East of the camp the river flowed over more bodies, also naked. Women, children, old men, and warriors had stripped their clothes off in a frenzied attempt to cool the fires that burned their skins.

Time changes everything but memories, and the leaving of the geese, the falling of the leaves are with the Okanagans forever.

Priest Magic

The ghosts of the past return. They burn into his dreams, and he wakes every night with the room shifting its darkness. They pull him forward, tripping him, taunting him, cackling. Whispering in ceaseless voices.

Their shapes are many, and none. His cross is ignored. His pleas are corroded into rust at the back of his throat. Savages twist in their tracks and aim shale arrowheads, their bows bending, their lips pulling back to reveal bloodstained teeth.

Their god lopes across empty fields, ears bent back. An animal lower than humans. An animal that circles the pole during their winter dances. Diabolical. Evil. Satan's curse. Satan's child. Spawn of whores.

His soul twists. He sweats and screams gibberish that goes unheard. Soaked into a wilderness so terrifying he cannot believe the dreams that show gardens thirty years from now.

"My God, hear me. Answer my prayers."

The Moon of Souls. Gone. Fled before the savagery of people who mock the One God, the One Son, the One Holy Spirit. The trinity of eternity. The earth, the moon, the sun. All gripped in a dance through the cloudy stars that speckle the heavens in a swathe from one horizon to the next.

One shape comes to him again and again, her blue-green eyes indifferent to his tremors. She spins through the room when he's alone. She treads through the edge of the trees at night when he travels. She brushes her long fingers through his hair when no wind stirs the high grasses through which his horse passes.

She is tall, willowy, dark-haired. A savage. The stuff of dreams and nightmares. He yells at her, but she never breaks stride, never pulls up, never turns her piercing eyes towards him, never gives him the satisfaction of recognition.

The people call her the Woman in the Trees, the TsEatlEmOx, for she moves with the wind. They hear her hands as she pushes branches aside. They hear her scuttle through groves too thick for humans to penetrate. They feel her presence in the crack of trees as they fall into the lake called Okanagan.

Her stories inspire awe. The priest has witnessed entire camps become still and quiet under the spell of one of her stories. Children look into the bright pupils of their parents to see whether this is real. Old women keen. Warriors stomp around the pole, dancing in a rhythm that reaches far into mother earth, and that shakes the ground around them. The elders hesitate, their voices spinning words that pull the woman from the dark skies above.

Against this the priest tries reason. He uses logic, sharp words meant to pierce belief. He says that the children want stories, that the warriors grieve for a time once theirs, when they were ten times what they are now. He whispers to the women, the gatherers, pointing out that their medicines, their foods, their knowledge of the hills — these are mere shadows of what they once knew and will know no more. He tells the elders that their words were powerless to stop the white fog of death that crept into the valley seventy winters ago, and then again forty winters ago.

He tells his own stories of a man who gave himself up for god-head, and of the sufferings he endured for them all — for the weak, the poor, the ill, the old, the crippled. A man whose only magic was his father's love for everyone. A man the likes of whom could not survive the trash of humanity. A man whose eyes knew God. A man who had stared into the fury of Satan, had been promised the world, and had walked from the desert purified by his encounter with evil incarnate.

This language meets stony silence from the start. As time wears on, and the Okanagans watch more elders die each winter, watch more medicine people go to the next world with much of their wisdom intact and untouched, the spirits waver, and first one, then two, then many children are sent by their parents to listen to this black robe who seems to have the Creator on his side.

His power grows, even though his dreams of the Woman in the Trees drain more of his energy every day. Even as the children, sometimes with the help of their parents, sometimes drawn by the other children, sometimes just curious, flock around him, he feels that he may be an opportunist, elbowing his way into the camps in a time of anguish and despair. But he never lets his voice betray his fears. His superiors in Victoria goad him on, pushing him to "convert more heathens to Jesus."

Storytelling is the way. The priest modulates his voice when reading from the text. The story of Moses crossing the desert with his people following him becomes a tribute to conviction and fortitude against great odds. Let the Okanagans know the power of these people from far away, feel the futility of resisting those who would cross deserts with armies at their heels.

David and Goliath becomes the fight of good and evil. As Jesus stares down Satan, David stares down the Philistine. The gods are with the black-robed people.

Noah, knowing the one way into the center of a new world, leads his family and all the creatures that walk, crawl, and fly into a ship the size of the next world.

Pillars of fire, plagues of locusts, sandstorms. In the early evenings the priest holds captive growing numbers of Okanagans on his travels around the lake. Word spreads of this story-teller who personally knows the Creator.

When the black robe wakes one day, he knows what to do. He begins building a small abode. The two brothers with him chop down trees. The Okanagans watch from the nearby hills, their eyes studying each move the three men make. Over the next few weeks, a log house rises from the earth. When it is finished, the men begin to fence in a property line that draws more Okanagans to the spectacle.

The Okanagans wait for the Creator to punish the black robe, who has offered nothing when his men chop the trees down, nor when he begins to pound posts into Toom-Tem's soul.

And still the Woman in the Trees remains silent at nights as he sleeps restlessly in the hot interior of the house. She remains with him, a spirit whose existence he will take with him to his grave.

The more Okanagans come over, the more she is the desert wind that blew the pillar of fire towards the pharaoh, the rock that sailed over the battlefield towards a transfixed giant, the wall of water that rushed inland towards the man who stood at the helm of the ship larger than the flood itself.

The cross has no meaning to the Woman in the Trees. She holds it, spinning its silver mass in the low light, attracted only to its glint and glitter. She leaves it on the rough table. Once, he reached for the cross and it burned his hands with a cold so chilling that almost stopped his heart. His fingers ache with the memory of that chill.

At his age, the doctors say he cannot have what he has; the chill does not run in his family. But on the hottest days his blood seems to run slower than glacier ice. Although he stokes the fireplace, the cold reaches deep into his skin, into muscles that clench in pain. He feels the Winter Dance in the way his feet shake. He hears the old voices around the fire, that pillar of flame that taunts his soul but cannot get past the frigid heart. Without effort, her eyes sink deep into the nightmare of his days, gripping his heart with a viselike hold that makes him tremble.

His confessor tells him that unless he speaks of his fears, there is nothing to be done. They hear his confessions. He stammers; words falter. Deceptive words. At the bottom, lies Satan.

In his denial, he drifts closer to the blue-eyed woman of his dreams. In the end, as his sight fades and he stares at the log ceiling above him, the Woman in the Trees stares down at him. She smiles and reaches for him, her hands of ice reaching into his heart, freezing it. He struggles, tries to scream. But she holds his heart effortlessly despite his fierceness, and his soul begins to weaken. His body stiffens. And although a black robe speaks the last rites above him, it is not that voice he hears. Instead, at the edge of his life, as he sinks further, grows smaller, he hears the woman say "My people welcome you into their fold. Coyote is here to greet you."

And he stops resisting. The pain vanishes, and her hand turns warm on his heart, flooding him with relief. "After all of this," he thinks, "I was wrong."

Wild laughter fills the room. A coyote laugh.

Wolverine

•• ● ••

Coyote begins a new story.

This story is about Wolverine.

Wolverine is not one person; he is many.

Wolverines are short and stocky. Two 's' words in a row isn't good for anyone, so you know it's not going to be good for Wolverine.

Wolverines are fearless because they can't see worth a damn. But short sight isn't what makes a wolverine stubborn. Lots of people are shortsighted, and easy to share a drink with.

No. What makes wolverines fearless, what makes them cranky as hell, is that they can smell pollen on a butterfly's wings a mile away. They feel the ground beneath their feet sing a language as old as Coyote. They hear the heartbeat of a squirrel five miles down a gulley. The sweat from a horse in the next valley over makes the wolverine's lanky fur quiver.

If you could do all of these things, wouldn't you be cranky as hell, fearless as steel? Wouldn't your hair turn white, your fingernails break off, your teeth grind to a nub, because even coyote laughed at your weak eyes?

Okay, so wolverines are pissed-off little bears with attitude.

But this story is about a wolverine whom isn't any of this.

Our wolverine can see a Class M star in the Andromeda galaxy. He can spot the wind shift six hours before the air begins to move. He can see the skin growing on a rabbit a month before the rabbit is born. Nothing wrong with his eyesight.

Stubborn confidence marks all wolverines — except ours.

So this is the story of Wolverine, the story of Pietro, the gardener of hate; the story of the Woman in the Trees. The straight-line story is the story of the sha-mas. The story that moves like a rabbit is the story of the syilx. The two stories don't really meet, because they haven't met yet in our world. They may never meet.

We start at point A, the sha-ma's story, the story of the Coming and the Contact.

Ricardo di Jesus reigned in his horse. The riders behind followed suit, grateful for the break in the long ride. Di Jesus glanced back at his twelve soldiers, who looked around, their postures reflecting the nervousness of the raid four days ago.

"If the Lord wills it, we will succeed," di Jesus assured his men. "We are in the land of infidels, and we must guard against their Satanic ways."

The nearest rider, a short and stocky man whom di Jesus trusted completely, spoke for the rest of the men. "Perhaps we should have used our two spare mules. Our prisoners are slowing us down."

Di Jesus sensed their fear, and he thought about the last three months. Since losing their way, his soldiers had followed him as he tried to map these new lands for his King. Late fall was making way for winter, and his men were in no shape to undertake the three-month trip due south to their rendezvous point with the other members of the expedition.

Di Jesus had raided the Indian camp on the spur of the moment, driven by his need to find carriers for the equipment and to ease the work on his men and horses. He had been rash, but he could not look back. It was done, and he had to make the best of it.

For a moment, his eyes rested on the five prisoners, each carrying fifty kilograms of equipment and food. They were mostly silent, their feet beating a familiar rhythm as they trailed the main body of soldiers by some thirty paces. Behind them rode two guards, bored with the endless duty of keeping watch. When di Jesus stopped his men, the prisoners continued walking until they stood five paces behind the horsemen.

The raid four days ago went swiftly, the camp scattering when his soldiers fired their rifles. During the raid, arrows had glanced off their mail. Di Jesus charged his horse to the center of the camp, where his steed stopped so quickly that dust ploughed into the fire pit, almost dowsing it. Then spun his horse around and charged towards the largest group of Indians. They tried to hold their positions, but the sounds of his horse's hooves, together with di Jesus' blood-curdling screams, sent the men scattering before di Jesus could reach them.

His men followed suit, and soon they had corralled the five prisoners, all young, healthy-looking men. They rounded up the Indians and were away before the camp could overcome their fear of the rifles; but even so, it had been close. Di Jesus kept his men moving the rest of the day until the quarter moon shone its light directly overhead. None of his men were wounded, but in the raid itself the Spaniards had killed or wounded ten Indians.

The prisoners spooked his men, for they seldom spoke, not even to one another. Instead, they continually glanced along the ridges and slopes that fell towards the lake to their right. Clearly, they expected help. Di Jesus sometimes cursed at them, trying to get them to walk faster, but the prisoners kept up a stolid pace, making it difficult to make quick progress.

The terrain along the west side of the lake also made their travel slow. They couldn't go south, for the Indians to the south probably knew of the raid by now. Di Jesus cursed again, for the energy spent on the prisoners kept his men from mounting any serious hunt. They would have to settle in for the winter without the food they needed.

As darkness came, di Jesus stopped in a sheltered cove. A fifty-foot cliff rose above the camp. The ground sloped down to the lake one hundred feet away, and here di Jesus' men bathed. The brush and trees around the camp made it a natural fort, easy to defend. Di Jesus' men drank from the creek that ran along the base of the cliff. The scout returned, as the others made themselves comfortable for the night.

"Did you see any Indians follow us?"

The scout shook his head. "None that I could see, but they know this country better than I do. They want their men back."

"Perhaps. But we have the rifles."

Later that night, di Jesus outlined the options to his soldiers. When he finished, his men sat quietly for some minutes, pondering his words. The five prisoners sat under guard at the edge of the firelight, their seated figures casting bizarre shadows onto the cliff behind them.

"So long as we have the horses and rifles, we can fight the Indians. They won't attack us too vigorously, for fear of our prisoners being hurt. So long as we don't mistreat our prisoners, their people should leave us alone for the time being. After all, they have to stock up for winter, too."

"That may be so," di Jesus' corporal admitted. "They are our prisoners. I think that any concerns about mistreating them are gone."

"We aren't savages. The Indians are pagans, but they are also God's creatures. If we make it through the winter, we won't need them."

"I say we kill them now and make our escape south. Without them to slow us down, we could still make it if we travel by night."

"Corporal, we are Christians. We have our souls to worry about."

"Perhaps." The corporal's skepticism warned di Jesus that he hadn't completely convinced his men. He promised himself to tread carefully during the next few months. He thought of the prisoners, and realized for the first time how much energy they'd take to keep alive.

•• ● ••

Snow swirled down the slopes, striking the makeshift log house where di Jesus and his men huddled. Earlier, the scout had left the cabin to check the area. Now he returned, snow spiraling after him as he hurriedly entered and shut the door behind him. He dumped his load of wood by the crude stone fireplace and eased onto a makeshift log seat, where he pulled off his boots. The others had finished eating, and huddled close to the fire. Their eyes followed the scout's every move.

Snowdrifts everywhere. I've not seen its likes in my life."

"Any sign of Indians?"

"Plenty. But just like our commander says, they won't risk the prisoners' lives. They left me alone pretty much to go where I wanted."

"Have you seen any of the bastards?"

The scout shook his head, water dripping from his hair as the snow melted. "They're good. They stay out of sight, but their tracks are there, fresh. I've come across five of their campsites, but they were gone by the time I got there. Kind of spooky, walking into a camp like that, knowing that they're watching your every move."

"What's the lake like?" di Jesus asked.

"Frozen over. A horse could walk across it without fear."

Di Jesus nodded. "Maybe it's time we went ice fishing."

It was early afternoon when di Jesus led three of his men to the lake's edge. The snow had stopped, and a cloak of stillness lay over everything. Their voices carried, and so they unconsciously spoke in near-whispers until di Jesus asked them to stop whispering. "They know we're here. We've nothing to hide."

It was as the scout said. Ice stretched for a mile, to the eastern shores of the lake. As di Jesus studied the surface, a loud crack marked where the ice moved. Di Jesus chuckled at his men's nervous looks.

"Don't worry, men. The scout's right. We could ride across the lake on our horses. Let's go fishing."

Punching a hole through two feet of ice took the better part of an hour. When that was done, di Jesus had his men drop lines into the dark swirling waters.

"We ought to catch something with those meat baits."

Di Jesus left his men and walked back to shore, where he climbed the slope to the cabin. Halfway up, di Jesus felt eyes on him, and looked to his left. An Indian stood fifty feet away. Di Jesus stopped. The Indian looked from di Jesus to the men ice fishing a hundred yards from shore back to di Jesus. Then the Indian slowly and deliberately looked towards the cabin. Di Jesus followed the Indian's gaze, and saw the footsteps leading up to and around the cabin, a single set of footprints that were clearly those of the Indian. Di Jesus looked back, but the Indian was gone, his silent ghost a presence that cut through the bitter cold to give di Jesus the shivers.

In the cabin, his men had neither heard nor seen anything. Di Jesus told them of the Indian, and had one of his men stand guard outside the door. If there were to be an attack, they would be prepared.

An hour later, as evening came, the men returned from ice fishing with six small fish. This food served to lighten the mood within the cabin, and soon several men were playing with a deck of cards, while others sat around the fireplace reminiscing about home, two years and uncounted thousands of miles from where they now sat.

Di Jesus kept an eye on the prisoners, but they simply sat in a circle, away from the fire. Perhaps they talked at night, although neither di Jesus nor his men had heard them do so. Before he went to sleep, di Jesus saw the still forms of the prisoners cast against the walls of the makeshift log home. Their dark eyes were unreadable; whatever thoughts they had, they kept to themselves.

The first signs of spring swept through the valley from south to north in the form of warm winds. Di Jesus had his men prepare to leave, and within a day he stood outside the log house that they'd called their home for the past five months. His men formed a straggled line in the snow, and the Indians, as always, stood silently to one side under the watchful eyes of two soldiers.

"If we leave, we leave now. Spring is coming, and we need to try to leave this cursed valley to the Indians. Are there any questions?"

"Why don't we just leave the Indians behind?" one of the men asked. "They'll slow us down."

"Those Indians are the only reason we aren't already dead, di Jesus said. "Without them, their tribes will have no reason not to kill us on the spot."

Di Jesus got the go-ahead signal from his scouts, and led his men south, their senses alert for danger.

When it came, it came on the fifth day, at a point in the valley between two lakes. Di Jesus leapt from his blankets, but the battle was already over. Most of his men lay sprawled around the campfire, their eyes staring sightlessly into the night sky. The sound of escaping horses faded into the night. Di Jesus fired his rifle at the shadows that circled in and out of the campfire's light, but the sounds that had woken him from the deep sleep of exhaustion no longer frightened the Indians. As he turned to fire again, di Jesus felt a burning sensation in his lungs. He looked down at the arrows protruding from his chest, and reached up to touch the shaft of one of them. He felt the warm stickiness of his own blood and looked up to the shadows, now a solid circle of Indians who stood at the light's edge, their eyes on him. His last memory was of the prisoners, who had joined the attackers. For some reason, his eyes focused on a freed prisoner, whose flushed face made di Jesus remember his own childhood and the time his grandmother had soothed his burning brows with a cloth to soak away his fever. Di Jesus smiled as the ground rushed towards him.

•• ● ••

In his dreams, he slipped into the world of daylight. It was the fifth day of his fast, and today he stood at the edge of the flats above the valley floor. North and south of him the valley curved away, almost as though it touched him, but only just.

A single hawk gently wheeled below him in search of food. The lake's northern head lay southeast of him, its green-blue colors sparkling in the bright heat of the sun. He shivered as he felt the cool, dry wind move through his thick, long hair.

A faint tremor passed through the valley floor. Then he felt it through the soles of his hardened feet. It was a drumbeat. It flowed into his blood, but he saw no movement below him to account for these feelings.

In the way of his people, he waited. Time passed. The hawk shifted in its flight and then banked into a steep dive towards the valley floor. In the space of ten heartbeats, it completed its dive, arching back up with a small field mouse in its claws. The drumbeat grew, not steadily, for there were times when it faded into a whisper or disappeared completely, like the movement of many animals moving together. The sounds were different than the sounds of elk or deer herds.

As the drumbeat neared, he waited in the open clearing. If this was danger, he would meet it before deciding a course of action.

The drumbeat pounded to the edge of the clearing, and stopped. He saw the four-legged animal stare at him, and for all the warmth in the air, he felt a chill reach into his bones and travel the length of his body. The animal's shoulders were as high as the man's head. Its chestnut coat was sprinkled with white.

For an endless moment, his eyes met those of the animal. It shook its head and snorted. The animal then wheeled about and disappeared into the woods. He heard their thunder as the animals moved into the gully on the valley floor.

He could still hear their movements when he at last saw them emerge more than a mile away. They moved towards the lake, and the one who had looked him in the eyes moved ahead of the pack. It stopped and turned once, staring towards the spot where he stood. Although he couldn't see its eyes, he knew that its spirit had forever changed the valley.

The dance went on to the pounding of the drums. Dust rose from the shuffling feet of the people. Blue Dreams had finished his dance, and watched as his father, the one they called Horse, moved slowly inward to the center of the circle of dancers. His father moved with caution, his feet starting the pattern that dominated his life.

Pound, pound, pound.

His footsteps, though light, silenced the other dancers. They turned inward and joined hands to complete the circle, ringing Horse in. They watched, as he had watched the first horses fifty years before.

Pound, pound, pound.

His footsteps deepened, and he gave a shaking of his head. His glazed eyes, that until now had stared downward, moved up and focused as he swept his people with a proud look.

"I have a story to tell," he said in his whispered way.

"Aiyeee!" his people urged him on.

Pound, pound, pound.

The people swayed together, and their feet began the rhythm of the horses. Pound, pound, pound.

"My story begins where my life began. I had a dream."

"Aiyeee-yah!"

"I saw life come into the valley. New life. The life of the horses. They came to me, and they sang the song of the hooves."

Pound, pound, pound.

The people danced the horse dance, as they moved sideways together in the way of all dancers.

Blue Dreams watched them, as he watched his father. The elders had met, in the syilx way, and soon Blue Dreams would be chief of the hunters, leading them to hunt for the coming winter, that the people knew would be harsh.

It was the way, letting everyone speak before the decisions were made. Letting everyone speak and have their say, down to the young adults. Showing respect, and letting the group decide. A way of life bred into the hearts and minds of the people. Blue Dreams hoped it would always be that way, but his dreams troubled him, and he turned from the dance of his father.

As he walked towards the nearby creek, behind him he heard the drums sound the horse beat, following the lead of the people's dance.

Blue Dreams stumbled, and one foot went into the creek to break his fall. As he regained his balance, Blue Dreams felt odd. A sickness lay in his stomach, something that gnawed at him, and had made his eating over the last several days a chore. Now, as he stripped down to bathe, Blue Dreams fought with all his will to keep the darkness and dreams away. He could not let his people see him this way, for they depended upon him.

The ice water closed his lungs as he dove towards the center of the deep pool. The men had dug it when Blue Dreams still played with the other children. Blue Dreams felt the cold waters fold around his body. His skin tightened against the cold, but he fought the urge to scramble for the banks. Instead, Blue Dreams forced himself to tread water for what seemed an eternity of time. The drumbeats in the distance gradually soothed his tensions enough for him to float on his back.

The pale blue skies stared down at Blue Dreams. A small cloud streaked with grey moved from north to south across his sight, and he followed the cloud's path until it moved beyond his vision. The cloud meant something.

By the time Blue Dreams waded ashore, five more songs from his people had been sung. Blue Dreams felt the familiar knot in his stomach ease, although it never completely receded. He chose a small alcove, where he laid down on a flat rock in the sun to dry. The alcove faced away from the dance, and away from the pool of water. Its privacy was something he cherished. He came here often to think.

Today he thought of the hunt that lay ahead. Twenty young hunters would go with him, and their excitement already blanketed the camp. They had waited for such a moment. Blue Dreams was not about to let them down. His path was set, and he welcomed the coming days.

At the barricades, he studied the patterns of each horse. One was too quick, its nervousness spreading to its neighbors. Another was distracted by the shadows of the others. A third plowed in one direction, its stubbornness felt by Blue Dreams, who was in no hurry to choose which horse to ride to the hunt.

The sun dragged towards its resting-place before Blue Dreams chose the one at the far side of the barricades. The horse studied him, its ears pricked forward in curiosity. No matter the energy of its comrades, it held its ground, refusing to sway from its stance.

Blue Dreams remembered the horse well, for it had once thrown him when he hadn't paid it the respect it deserved. One minute he had been thinking of his woman, and in the next minute he was in the air. He landed hard, knocking the wind from his lungs. While he struggled for air, his horse stood right where it had stopped. As Blue Dreams climbed to his feet, the horse whinnied, and the other riders had chuckled, one of them saying, "Blue Dreams, your horse owns you. Look, he waits to lead you."

Blue Dreams watched as the horse waited, and saw its calm spread to the other horses standing near this stubborn and proud animal.

"You will do," Blue Dreams said, and the horse understood as it shook its mane and walked to him as if beckoned. It stretched its neck over the barricade, and fed from Blue Dreams' open hand, in which he held some grass. As his horse ate, Blue Dreams stroked its neck.

"You have the trickster's mind, and the bear's patience. We will hunt together."

•• ● ••

On the second day, the rains fell. Blue Dreams fed his mount and settled in for the night. A guard stood over the horses, although the party hadn't sensed another human in the last two days.

The party of hunters now relaxed. The tracker walked into the lean-to as the others pulled off their top clothes. The heat from the fire curled about their wet steaming clothing, which they hung along a pole to dry.

They ate in silence, each listening to the light sound of rain against the woven branches of their lean-to. The nearby creek's flowing waters soothed their ears, and the day's events slowly left them, relaxing their bodies.

The tracker told of his travels. He knew that a herd of thirty deer moved through this valley three hours ahead of them. By tomorrow, that distance would be half a day. The deer knew enough to be nervous, but not enough to take full flight. They would reach the flatlands just above the Valley and halfway down the western lakeside before the hunters caught them.

Blue Dreams waited until the others had gathered the information they needed. In the silence, he spoke.

"Are there signs of the Secwepemcs?"

The tracker looked into the fire. "None that I could see, but we move in their territory. We must travel carefully, for they know this land as we do."

"Perhaps better," Blue Dreams agreed.

The tracker looked sharply at Blue Dreams' profile, and Blue Dreams waited until the tracker looked back at the fire.

"Do you know something?" the tracker asked at last.

"No. Only a feeling. We must be careful. It was only ten springs ago that we last fought with the Secwepemcs. They're good warriors, and they still claim this land as their hunting area."

"Let them come," a younger hunter said. "We'll show them what we can do."

Blue Dreams waited until the bravado had stilled. "We must be careful. My brother once felt as you do. We know the cost of pride."

"Tell us the story," a hunter asked.

"It happened in this way. Ten springs ago we traveled through this land. My father, Horse, led us. I was twenty years old and full of strength and courage, but not much sense, and definitely not much more than my brother, who was two years my elder. We had agreed that my father, being so old, would lead this, his last hunting party."

"My father warned us as I warn you. We are never as good as we think we are. Life is precious to the land, but so is death. We scoffed inwardly at Horse's words. That night, while the others slept, my brother and I decided to travel ahead, and be the first to eat of deer."

"Perhaps if my father had not been so old, he might have felt us leave, and stopped us. I don't know, but I do know that we were far ahead of the others by the time the sun rose."

"A day's travel down the other side of the lake we came upon the deer's spoor. We were both excited, and never saw the Secwepemcs until it was too late. My brother was drawing his bow when the arrow pierced his stomach. Before he fell from his horse, two more arrows struck him."

"I turned at the sound of his fall, and that saved my life, for the arrow aimed at my heart hit my shoulder. I never felt the pain. All I saw was my brother, who lay on the ground, his eyes staring up at me. I began to climb off my horse, but my brother's last cry was to my horse, that began running at my brother's command. Even then I might have jumped, but for the sound of the victory call from the Secwepemcs who sprang from cover to get better aim at me."

The tracker nodded. "I knew your brother. He was a good hunter."

"Yes, he was a good hunter. But that day he also proved to be a good brother. If not for his call, I would not be here to lead us now."

Another hunter spoke. "It is said that your family is close to the horse clan. I know that few other families have such understanding of how horses think. I watched you choose your horse for this hunt. You have a gift."

"My gift is none better than the gifts we all have in our family ways."

"That may be so, but don't lose your gift, or we'll all be walking after the deer."

The hunters laughed, and the last tensions of the day eased from the lean-to into the growing darkness.

Blue Dreams, as the oldest one there, decided to tell another story. The story went thus.

Sn-klip, Coyote, walked into his home, where Mole busied herself preparing their supper. Because it was spring, their supper was small, for plants were just beginning to sprout from the ground, where snow still covered much of the land. Sn-klip saw the small supper, and growled.

"Mole, we have so little to eat. We deserve better. I am Coyote, king of all the peoples of this land."

Mole sat across from Sn-klip and ate her food without a word.

"Have you nothing to say?"

"Sn-klip, my dear, I can say little. It is early spring, and we must be patient."

Sn-klip gave a small bark of scorn, and stuck his head out of their small but warm cave to sniff the air and check Sun.

"It is still light outside. I will ask Sun to hurry up and bring summer."

"Sun is strong," Mole admitted, "but I don't think he's that strong."

"What do you know? All you do is root for our supper and keep our house clean. I, on the other hand, make this world what it is. I am so busy these days."

"My dear, you're getting excited. Remember the last time you got excited? It's not good for your health."

"I'm going. I'll be back before nightfall."

With that, Sn-klip left his cave and hurried to the top of the nearby hill. He stared at Sun until, feeling his stare, it turned to Sn-klip.

"What is it, little one?"

"I am not little. I am Sn-klip, king of all that you shine upon. I may even be your king, for all I know."

"That may be so, little one, but I do have to keep my routine."

"Where do you go when you leave me? You're always gone for half the day, sometimes more."

"It's a big world, little one."

Sn-klip yawned with boredom. He sniffed the air again and then, below him, he saw the deer. They gave him an idea.

"Sun, I think I will follow you on your travels. We need to spend more time together, get to know one another."

Sun smiled at this thought. "Little one, you have such small legs, and I travel so very fast."

"But I can fix that. I will become like the deer. My legs will become long, and I will then be able to keep up with you in your travels."

"Do what you will," Sun said. "I must go now."

Sun began to disappear over the distant hills. Coyote gave a single bark of surprise, then made his legs longer, until they were as long as the legs of the tallest deer below him. Then he began running towards where Sun was getting lower.

At first Sn-klip thrilled to the way his long legs easily carried him over the ground. He was swift, and he moved like the shadows. In no time at all he was over the hills where Sun had disappeared from view. He was surprised to see that Sun's last rays gleamed over the lands far to the west of him. In all his life, Sn-kip had never thought Sun could move so fast.

After some time, and running as fast and as hard as he could, Sn-klip reached the far hills where Sun had dropped behind. It was dark, and when Sn-klip reached the hills, he looked forward to seeing daylight, and talking with Sun. This time, Sn-klip was even more surprised, for darkness lay over the lands to the west of him. Nowhere could he see Sun.

"No one can run as fast as I," Sn-klip thought. "I will look for Sun, because he must be hiding somewhere close by."

With that, Sn-klip began to forage about, looking under every rock and tree he could find. For a long time he roamed, until at last he tired out and tried to sit back on his haunches. He fell, his long legs awkwardly struggling for balance. Sn-klip then remembered that his legs were those of the deer, and not his own short but comfortable legs. Disgusted, he made his own legs come back. After that he sat down on his haunches to think this out.

"How could Sun have outrun me? I had the swiftest legs in all the land. He is hiding somewhere. But he can't fool me. I'm going to wait until he tires of this game, and then I will catch him."

Sn-klip waited, but before he knew it, he was asleep. He woke up to find Sun staring down at him. He got up and yawned. He scratched his back and behind one ear before he looked up.

"So, Sun, where were you hiding?"

"I hid nowhere. I traveled the world. Other people need me, you know. I cannot hurry things just for you."

"But I am Sn-klip. If not for me, then for whom do you work and obey?"

"Little one," Sun laughed. "I work for and obey no one. It is my pleasure to shine for everyone. Including you."

• • ● • •

After Blue Dreams finished his story, the hunters slept, each of them taking an hour to stand guard.

Blue Dreams also slept, and in his dreams he felt the shadows chase one another, stirring spirits awake. At one point he was sitting by the flickering fire when a pale shadow loomed from the dark. He knew its shape. His people, the syilx, had heard stories of the pale ones from other tribes farther east. The stories of these sha-mas were fantastic. Some said they were the ones who brought the horse, but how could that be? His father had seen the first horse before the stories of the sha-mas reached the syilx.

"I know you," Blue Dreams spoke.

The tall pale shadow of the sha-ma hovered on the other side of the fire, its form never solid enough to distinguish.

"What would you have of the syilx?"

Upon this question, as always, the sha-ma's ghost faded and Blue Dreams woke up with the familiar knot in his stomach. He lay there for awhile, until his breathing steadied and the sweat stopped.

Down the hill, the horse riders pounded after the deer. The sun stared directly down on them, leaving no shadows to spook the powerful animals. The riders formed a crescent shape a quarter-mile wide. Ahead of them, deer shadows leapt and bounded from cover to cover. Horses were no match for the deer in this rough terrain, and the deer pulled ahead of the riders.

The lead rider slowed his horse to a trot, and the others followed suit. The wind at their backs held the pine scent of the trees, which often hid the riders from one another.

The deer ahead of them hurried down the hillside to escape the danger they sensed. Their hooves beat a different rhythm than their heavier pursuers, but fifty deer cannot run in tandem without leaving their own thunder.

The tracker marked the place where the deer would have to scamper through a narrow ravine or have their herd split. He and a dozen other hunters waited in the clusters of thick brush that lined each slope. Blue Dreams had six men on each side, spaced out over five hundred feet.

The sun made a small trickle of sweat run down Blue Dreams' face, but he ignored it. Any gesture, however small, could change the air around him, enough to spook the nervous deer. Blue Dreams would leave nothing to chance. An hour earlier he had found this place, a small clump of brush that sloped halfway down the hillside. Behind him, farther up the slope, a flat sheet of rock raised the air temperature by several degrees, keeping Blue Dreams from being chilled.

The other hunters were well hidden, and Blue Dreams had difficulty seeing them, although he knew where each laid waiting. He had been staring occasionally at one spot for several minutes, when a chill went down his spine. In the distance, he could hear the sigh of movement from the horse hunters who chased the deer towards his ravine. But Blue Dreams had eyes only for the spot that lay ten yards below him. A ring of rocks surrounded the bare spot of earth; in the middle of this patch of earth, he saw the grey ashes of a recent campfire.

Around this campfire, Blue Dreams felt and saw the strangeness, the alien nature of a campfire that neither his people nor the Secwepemcs would have left in such a way. The grass was beaten down in odd patches around the fire, as though the fire makers cared little for where they moved, or perhaps they thought little of their movements, for the patterns of their leave-taking were careless.

Blue Dreams closed his eyes for balance, and the odor of the fire-people made his nostrils flare with disgust. There was a rotten meat smell, and something else that he couldn't place, although it seemed as familiar as it was strange. The humans who had moved through this valley and left the campsite below were neither of the syilx nor of the Secwepemcs. And, as he heard the sound of the deer approach, Blue Dreams knew this place was all wrong; the oncoming deer would know this, too. Without thinking further, Blue Dreams stood and called to the other hunters. In doing so, he upset the balance of the hunt. The other hunters rose from their hiding places, as there was nothing else they could do but to follow his lead. With a quick and terse command, Blue Dreams had the hunters run for the top of the ravine to avert the deer.

They were almost too late, for the first deer were already bounding along the ridges. The herd had split in half at the head of the ravine. Each group of deer ran along the two sides rather than dash down into the ravine, as the syilx had first expected.

Blue Dreams drew his bow and steadied his aim, letting loose his arrow and reaching for another without breaking his stride. He abandoned the strange feeling of only moments ago, and all of his strength and energy directed itself at the deer, which flashed through the trees. In a state of total concentration, he released the first arrow and saw it strike just behind the deer's front shoulders. The second arrow glanced off the back of a second deer, while a third lodged into the stomach of another. Blue Dreams felt sick, for this was not a clean kill, and he'd have to run down the deer as it bled to death. He hoped he could catch it soon, to kill it properly instead of having it endure hours of pain to a slow death.

He signaled to another hunter before he began running along the ridge, following the deer's blood path. The amount of blood told Blue Dreams that the deer would not outrun him for long, and within minutes he heard the buck thrashing through the trees and bushes, its flight now dominated by panic and pain.

Then he saw the deer just above him on the ridge. It turned to see its pursuer, and the sudden movement threw the usually agile creature off balance. Blue Dreams kept running, even as he watched the deer scramble for footing, its two hind hooves digging into the loose soil for balance. In slow motion, the earth gave way, and the deer toppled backwards.

Blue Dreams was about to loose a final arrow to the deer's heart when his ankle twisted against a hidden tree root and he fell against the ground, his head hitting the base of the small trunk hard enough for him to see stars. And then he was falling down the steep slope, every roll bringing him closer to the small stream that made its route through the gully's center.

The slope was too steep for Blue Dreams to check or slow his tumble downhill, but he had enough presence of mind to twist away from the tree that lay before him. That was Blue Dreams third mistake of the day, and it was the last he remembered as his body hit another tree farther down the slopes.

Blue Dreams winced with pain. Sky Woman took the birch leaves from his wound and replaced them with fresh ones. She threw the old leaves into the fire. He watched the flames lick and hiss at the edges of the leaves, curling them before they blackened and charred. The splint prevented him from moving closer to the fire's heat, so he lay back to let the warmth soothe his aching muscles.

Horse, holding a stout walking stick, entered his home. Sky Woman looked up as the wind whipped through the open entrance; Horse, seeing her look, hastily closed the bear-hide flap. Sky Woman continued treating Blue Dreams, tightening his splints and wrapping his leg with herbs given to her by her mother.

"Whi," Horse said in greeting.

"Whi."

"We took a count. Winter lies one full moon away, and we need more food. The winter will be long and cold."

Blue Dreams gestured at his splints. "I am not going anywhere soon. What would you have me do?"

Horse fed more wood into the fire, his wrinkled face calm. "We talked about this. We need your words to complete the process, or begin it again."

"I cannot help you in your hunt."

Horse smiled. "We do not want you on the hunt. You would slow us down."

"It is not I who would slow you down. The quick can sometimes defeat themselves."

Horse looked at the splints, then into Blue Dream's brown eyes, before he laughed. "I see this is something you learned in your last hunting party."

Blue Dreams sank back onto the bed of intertwined branches and hides. "There is something you should know. Something that troubles my sleep."

Horse looked into the fire again. "I know. I have seen it."

"I do not like this. It comes before its time."

"The campfire left its mark on the land, and on your body. We gathered there to talk about the hunt."

"When I saw the camp, I lost my balance. There was a strangeness there, as if the people who made it did not know the proper ways to live in this land."

Horse nodded. "We felt the same energy. For the last two days we have talked by that fire and in our own village. The tracker says that the fire makers made no attempts to disguise their way, nor did they leave offerings of friendship."

Blue Dreams felt honoured, for Horse seldom talked at length.

After waiting to see if either man would continue, Sky Woman spoke, "The women say we must think of leaving here. The shamas, the white men we have heard much of in the last ten summers, are the only ones who would not respect our customs."

Horse nodded in agreement. "We have felt the same thing — sha-mas are here. But where do we go? The stories say that they are like the grasshoppers. One day there is a single grasshopper, and on the next there are countless others. "

Blue Dreams interrupted. "You came here to ask me something," he said to his father.

"You cannot come with us on the next hunt, but we feel that the camp needs a headman while we are gone, someone who will know what to do if something happens. Someone to look after the young, the elders, and the women."

"How many syilx can you leave with the camp?"

"Five young warriors and three older hunters."

Blue Dreams thought about the camp's layout. "Before you leave, we must tighten up the shelters."

"That is already being done."

"I will do this for the camp, then."

"You are a fine son. We will be gone for nine suns."

Sky Woman spoke again. "My husband is only one syilx. What if the sha-mas come this way?"

"My son will know what to do. He does not have the brashness of the younger warriors, and the elders and hunters will follow his lead. We have agreed on this."

"My husband cannot run very fast."

Horse smiled. "We will leave twenty horses with the camp. Blue Dreams will know what to do in case of trouble."

"I fear for our future. The sha-mas do not have the ways of our people. Neither do they respect the Secwepemcs."

Horse looked sharply at Sky Woman. Then he turned to the fire and stirred the coals and small logs with his walking stick. Blue Dreams waited, sensing that Horse did not want to answer Sky Woman's fears. Horse smiled again. "You can feel my spirit, Blue Dreams. Don't lose that gift. I've said enough for one night. You two should spend time together. There is much to say."

After Horse left, Blue Dreams studied the flames, and sank

into a comfortable state. The ache in his broken leg eased slightly as long as he kept it close to the edge of the fire pit. As his mind drifted into reveries of a former hunt, Sky Woman's words broke through.

"Blue Dreams, we're going to have a child."

Five full moons later, as the tribe moved north following the winter, Blue Dreams watched for landmarks. They walked or rode along the ridges. Younger hunters joked about Blue Dreams and the way he always rode back to check on his wife, but Blue Dreams would only smile and continue on.

The syilx had been traveling for a week, and they all sensed the changes in the air that told them that they were close to the great lake that filled the Valley for more than two sun's travel to the north of them. They traveled slowly, their minds filled with the strangeness of the news that came from the tribes who lived south and east of them. Hunters from other tribes had actually seen sha-mas. These stories were the constant talk of the hunters every night, for the sha-mas brought with them a strangeness that Blue Dreams already felt. No one knew how to deal with the sha-mas, for their violence filled many stories. Their ways were outside the ways of any syilx, and Blue Dreams' stomach clenched when he remembered the empty camp six full moons before.

The break in Blue Dreams' leg had left him with a permanent limp, and the syilx began comparing him to his father. Horse relished the comparison. He often made the syilxs laugh as he imitated Blue Dreams' limp, but the joking was gentle and meant no disrespect. Everyone knew of the story behind Horse's own limp, for he was the first syilx to ride a horse, and those stories also filled many nights around the campfire. Blue Dreams was asked several times to tell the story of the hunt that left him with his limp. He retold the story to different families and tribes, until it was known around all the campsites. People watched him as he limped by, their eyes full of speculation and thoughtful study.

Horse-trading rapidly replaced other means of trade, and the number of horses measured the value of a family. The syilx had all left the huge encampment, and many feared that they would never again gather as a tribe. The tribes east and south of them were at war with the sha-mas, and stories of the blue-coats who slaughtered women and children filled everyone with dread. What type of human would kill innocent people simply for the right to live on land that belonged to everyone? No one owned the land; didn't the sha-mas know this?

The stories east of the Swah-netk'-qhu, which is the syilx name for both the Columbia River and the falls which the sha-mas call Kettle Falls, were different. Red-coats apparently thought that land was theirs, and fought to keep the blue-coats and their followers out. No syilx knew the quarrel between the blue-coats and red-coats, but figured it must be a matter of honour for them to act in such odd ways about Mother Earth. Trusting sha-mas was not wise, no matter what side of the river they were on.

Horse, as a headman, automatically gave respect to others until they proved themselves otherwise. Among the other tribes, Horse drew respect for his role among the syilx. Many elders nodded in agreement as Horse calmed the fears he knew were lurking within the great camp. His policy of trust made sense, for it was the basis of the way so many tribes treated one another. Should not the sha-mas receive the same trust as any tribe? They were humans, too, were they not?

Blue Dreams shuffled around the campsite. Over two thousand tents were set up along the northwest banks of the Swahnetk'-qhu. More groups arrived daily, swelling the camp and bringing their own energies and excitement to that already growing every day. It seemed that everywhere he went, Blue Dreams heard strange and hard to understand stories about these odd sha-mas.

So many stories of the sha-mas traveled the campfires that few could remember the details of them all. Horse tried to fIght off his sense of growing uneasiness; as headman, he could not allow himself to cede to his fears. Others looked to him for guidance in his role as a leader of the syilx, and he knew if he said the wrong thing panic could fly through the camp like startled sparrows. So he kept his misgivings to himself, talked to the elders, and tried to calm as many other families and campsites as he could.

Blue Dreams felt the now too-familiar knot grow in his stomach, too. Each night, he woke in a sweat and Sky Woman sought to calm him by stroking his brow. But she had her own matters to worry about, and one night she left the tent, leaving him to his restless dreams. When he woke up with the sun, Sky Woman came into the tent, holding their new child tightly to keep him warm against the cold winter air.

For days, Blue Dreams and Sky Woman kept to themselves, lost in the beauty and wonder of their newborn child. Finally, busy as he was, Horse noticed their absence from the larger campfire. After a few quick questions to others, who laughed as they told him the news, he felt foolish, for he was now a grandfather who hadn't yet named his grandson.

Horse came into his family's tent. As he sat down, Sky Woman handed him his grandson wrapped in blankets. Horse stared at the small face, and he became like his grandson, lost in the feelings of love for this young child. Sky Woman smiled and looked at Blue Dreams. They spoke to each other without words and quietly left the tent to Horse and the child he cradled in his arms.

New snow lay thick on the ground, but Blue Dreams felt that the air was warmer than he had left it just days before. The smoke from a hundred fires curled into the air, and Blue Dreams heard the drums of late winter fill the air. He hugged Sky Woman close to him, and they walked slowly to the nearest gathering of syilx. As they came near, a dozen heads looked up. Then the women streamed towards Sky Woman, their joy filling the air with talk as they led her to the far side of the fire.

Blue Dreams greeted the men, who studiously stared at the fire and waited until Blue Dreams made himself comfortable on a log.

"Does your child have a name?"

Blue Dreams blushed. "He does not, but my father is with him now."

"What have you been doing since your son was born?" a hunter asked, and the other syilx laughed.

Later, after Blue Dreams finished his meal, he heard Horse call them to the tent. He and Sky Woman hurried to obey, followed by many curious syilx, who stood at a discreet distance to wait for the news.

After they were in the tent, Horse held the baby in front of Blue Dreams and his woman.

"Look into his eyes."

Blue Dreams looked into the dark coals of his boy's eyes, eyes that flickered with something Blue Dreams couldn't guess. Puzzled, Blue Dreams looked up at his father.

Horse touched the child, who stopped wriggling in Blue Dreams' arms to stare at his grandfather. The intensity of that stare, almost as if the child studied Horse with old eyes, surprised and troubled Blue Dreams.

"His eyes are old and cunning. His energy is deep, but steady. When I sat with him he looked at me as he looks at me now. When I gave him some soft food, he refused it, but ate a tiny piece of dried deer meat with great relish."

"But how could he?"

"Look into his mouth."

Sky Woman opened the child's mouth and stared, her own eyes becoming rounder as she saw what should not be possible in a newborn. The child looked at his mother, his small front molars gleaming softly in the firelight.

"But he doesn't cry," Sky Woman said. "A child cries when it teethes."

With a shaking hand, Horse touched the child's brow. "This

63

child means something. I have to consult the elders. But his name is clear to me. He will be called Wolverine."

•• ● ••

As Blue Dreams saw the first gleam from the northern lake, he remembered the past winter as something that might never happen again, in more ways than one. Wolverine was as strong as Horse said, and grew rapidly, his stocky body seeming to fill out with every passing day. Well before his time, the baby took his first steps, walking across the tent floor with a grim look on his face, as if to challenge the world to tell him he was too little to be walking. When Blue Dreams reached out to steady the child, Wolverine grabbed his extended finger with a strength that made Blue Dreams wince.

Sky Woman was confused. She loved Wolverine with a mother's fierceness, but she also watched his accelerated growth with trepidation. Wolverine seldom smiled, but his loyalty and love towards his mother and father showed in the way he always moved around them in their tent. Circling and touching them frequently, his parents became comfortable with the way he looked at them and listened to their every word. It also took time before Blue Dreams grew used to having Wolverine's eyes always on him.

When Wolverine first saw the lake, he was in his mother's arms. She felt his tug and let him down, where he stood on the bluff and watched the waves cross the lake in endless patterns. Gusts of wind rippled over the dark blue surface of the water, carrying with them the cold feel of melting ice.

The syilx set up camp in an alcove clearing, out of sight of the lake. But from the campsite, they could keep an eye on the neighborhood. Trees sheltered them from direct sunlight, and their shade settled even the most restless.

A creek flowed down a small gully south of the camp, and

here Wolverine spent many hours over the next few days, his squat, stout frame hunched over the water. Every so often the small child would dip his hands into the creek, drawing his hands out to stare at the water as it flowed between his fingers. Sky Woman, whenever she could get away from her tasks at the camp, would sit beside her son and relax with the sounds of the flowing creek and rustling trees.

The time came when the hunters decided to go into the hills to get more food, as their winter supplies were getting low. The families sat around a fire one evening, the younger children running in and out of their circle. Older children strained to hear the talk around the fire, where decisions were made for the good of the syilx.

Blue Dreams, despite his limp, felt strong enough to ride over long periods of time, so he was placed in charge of the hunt. The younger hunters, most of them the same ones as in the previous year, seemed to be more uncertain about having Blue Dreams as the headman for their hunting trip. No one disputed Blue Dreams' abilities, but everyone thought of the events leading up to Blue Dreams' finding of the sha-mas' campsite, the botched hunt, and Blue Dreams' broken leg.

Blue Dreams went down to the same creek he had bathed in before the last hunt, but he did so with a heavier heart, and his journey to the stream took much longer to complete. Night was closing in, and Blue Dreams felt grateful for the solitude darkness afforded him. Early in his life, he had found that people took energy from him, and while he didn't begrudge being with others, he also enjoyed moments like these. When the sound of the creek filled his mind with its flow, it took him away from everything for the short time needed to regain his balance and energy.

The cold water swirled first around his ankles, then rose to touch his legs, the cold biting into the scar where his broken bone had healed. The pain made Blue Dreams wince. He enjoyed the way the cold water cleared his mind, and he sank until only his head was above water, his legs stretched out and curling against the current.

The camp became quiet, with only a few people talking in low voices around the fire. Blue Dreams saw the sentry nearby. There was a renewed caution to the way the sentry moved; not knowing what to expect, the sentry expected the worst. The syilx knew what Secwepemcs could do, but sha-mas were another matter. If half the stories told around the fires at the Swah-netk'-qhu gathering were true, the sha-mas posed danger for everyone.

Blue Dreams' mind felt clear by the time he returned to his tent. Sky Woman slept with Wolverine gathered in her protective arms. Blue Dreams saw Wolverine's eyes shine in the low light as the child followed his every movement. The child never stirred in his mother's arms, but Blue Dreams wondered again about his son. People already talked about Wolverine with puzzlement. They knew of no child like him, and the naming generated its own stories that were told until the entire nation of syilx, every tribe and family, knew of Blue Dreams' precocious youngster.

In the last moments before he slept, Blue Dreams, lying beside his woman, thought he felt a caress, as though Wolverine's small fingers brushed against his arm. Blue Dreams opened his eyes halfway to see the still form of his boy. Wolverine's eyes were shut, and his face looked as serene as his grandfather's.

The hunt went well, and the hunting party came home with a full weight of meat and hides, which the women took as the hunting party rode into camp. Blue Dreams felt tired, but jubilant, for the hunt had gone without trouble. They hadn't seen a sign of the Secwepemcs, not even campfires. It was as though the Secwepemcs had gone into hiding, or moved farther north.

During the ten-day hunt, Blue Dreams found himself missing his child and woman. He struggled to keep his mind focused, for the hunters depended upon him to lead them to game. Every night Blue Dreams rubbed his bow with leaves and let the juices soak into the wood fiber. The bow became saturated with moisture squeezed from the leaves. This kept his bow flexible and strong. He sometimes notched an arrow and launched it at a nearby tree. His aim stayed true, and he could hit a thin trunk from forty paces, five out of six times. He was, by far, the best marksman of the group.

Still, despite Blue Dreams' duties, he often found his mind wandering back to his family. He saw Wolverine's eyes on him, following him on the hunt. The child's spirit made Blue Dreams wonder what lay in the future for his son. Such strength meant something that Blue Dreams would have to figure out in the next fifteen years, before Wolverine came of age.

Blue Dreams first sensed the camp's pensive mood after he settled his horse in the corral and saw to its feeding and water. He walked to the fire, where Horse and the other elders talked. They became quiet when Blue Dreams and the other hunters circled the campfire. Blue Dreams knew enough not to ask until the elders were ready. He soaked in the fire's heat and gave a heavy sigh as his bad leg felt relief at its warmth. In the distance, the women gathered in small groups to work on treating the meat and working on the deer hides from the hunt.

As Blue Dreams waited beside the fire with the other hunters, he suddenly felt small fingers curl around a finger of his right hand. Blue Dreams looked down into his son's eyes from where Wolverine tottered. Startled, Blue Dreams looked for Sky Woman, who stood a dozen paces away, her face lit by a large grin.

"Our child walks with his father."

Before Blue Dreams could say anything, an elder stood up on the other side of the fire and called for everyone's attention. The children, and those women who could spare a few precious moments, together with the hunters, headmen, and elders of the Syilx, all formed a large circle around the fire. Blue Dreams knew something important was about to happen, and waited for the elder to speak.

"We have come to this spot for many springs now."

Everyone nodded, their minds going back to past times and memories of other years.

"We have become comfortable coming to this place, for its spirits are strong for our people." The elder paused to gather himself for the next minutes. The syilx waited in trust. "We must now choose new ways. The first sha-mas have asked for an audience with us."

Blue Dreams felt a shock go through him as though he had been hit by lightning. "While our hunters were gone," the elder continued, "the sha-mas came to us. They wait for our answer."

"They have killed many families from other tribes. Can we trust them to speak true?" a hunter asked.

"No, we cannot. They do not believe as we believe. They do not live by their words beyond the time in which they speak them."

"Do we have a choice?" another hunter asked.

"We have the choice of telling them 'no.' But there are more sha-mas coming, and we cannot ignore them forever."

Blue Dreams watched his father for signs, but Horse stood with his head bowed in thought, not letting anyone read his face. Horse let the elder speak for their group, but Blue Dreams decided to ask, "Then we have to choose the time and place of our meeting with the sha-mas. Is now a good time?"

The elder looked calmly at his people gathered around the fire. "I cannot choose for our people. We must do this together. First we feed our hunters, our children, and ourselves. Then we gather to choose the path to follow. The sha-mas are a quarter day's travel to the north of us, and they will wait for our answer."

And so it was that, three days later, Blue Dreams saw the first sha-ma he'd ever seen walk calmly to the center of their camp. The sha-mas' long black robes flowed in the steady winds, which warned of a change in weather ahead.

•• ● ••

The lake stretches some eighty miles, north to south. It bends in the middle, like someone kicked it in the stomach, folding it over. This bend is the result of a fault line that lies twelve miles beneath the Okanagan Valley, intersecting another fault line running its length. Neither has caused significant damage to the cities that now dot the landscape, although minor tremors occasionally shake parts of the Valley.

The lake is the people and life that come to it. The syilx knew the lake when it stretched for one hundred twenty miles north to south, and when its shores lay three hundred feet above where it now resides. The lake was blocked in the south by an ice bridge. This held the huge waters at bay until the climate warmed enough to melt the bridge in a series of devastating steps, each one ending when the bridge gave a little. Billions of gallons then poured south along the Valley bottom, devastating everything in its path.

The syilx told stories of that lake, and of its larger-than-life creatures: fish bigger than men, waves that capsized rafts in still waters, winds that picked people up and sucked them into the sand-filled air. Travelers along each side of the lake left stories with the families they found, as well as through petroglyphs in hard-to-reach (and therefore more lasting) places.

The lake created its own weather. During late fall, spirals of water vapor above the lake formed countless funnel-shaped formations. These joined to form clouds that darkened the land and water for days at a time.

As old as the syilx were, no human witnessed the earlier history of the Valley, when volcanoes spewed forth ash tens of thousands of feet into the atmosphere. Lava flows left behind traces that are still found in the surrounding hills.

Glaciers, a half-dozen in all, spent a million and a half years scouring the Valley until they reached bedrock. The volcanoes that once lined the Valley were worn to the knobby hills they now present to the world.

In this Valley the syilx made their world. Blue Dreams' ancestors spoke of game so plentiful that a day's journey netted families meat enough to last a full winter. But when the lake grew smaller, the Syilx gradually found themselves hunting along the slopes and plateaus above the Valley, even in winter. Hunting trips led by the headmen took longer and longer, until sometimes they took a full moon's journey to complete.

Coyote, Sn-klip, once fat and heavy, became lean and clever. He was the symbol of the syilx — an animal that roamed freely, led only by his curiosity. But his troubles were the troubles of the syilx, and his ingenuity became a survival tool for them.

The plateaus above the Valley held game during the winter, but the terrain of ravines and slopes made hunting difficult and treacherous. Rarely did hunting trips happen without broken bones and, sometimes, worse. Yet the syilx had no choice. They were part of the land; their souls the souls of all animals, plants, and non-organic beings that dwelt therein. It was no land for the squeamish or the timid.

From the time he could walk, at the age of one, Wolverine began exploring this Valley. He showed no fear, and the animals accepted him as one of their own. Sky Woman found him one day; sitting on the grass. His small right fingers were curled in the short fur of a squirrel that blinked and ran upon Sky Woman's approach. Wolverine smiled at his mother, and in the syilx language told her the story the squirrel had just spoken.

From the beginning, Horse spoke to Wolverine with the same words and tone he used in talking with the adults of the family. Horse, when asked by Blue Dreams why he did this, simply said that Wolverine was already a man with an old spirit.

The syilx knew of Wolverine's spirit, for such a spirit lived among them every tenth generation. Like the animal of the same name, Wolverines were loners, preferring to spend their time in their own company. Yet their wisdom was second to none; having such a person as part of one's family counted as an honour.

Wolverine knew nothing of this. He watched his parents, studying the way they went about their tasks. Blue Dreams seemed to Wolverine to be the more distant parent, for often his father would stop whatever he was doing and stare into the distant hills, his dark eyes unfocused in his reverie. Sky Woman kept her distance during these moments, which became more frequent over time.

His mother made sure that Wolverine was fed at all times, until he had to ask her to stop feeding him so much. Wolverine hated the sensation of being full, of being weighted down with food that slowed his walks.

Sky Woman had the habit of pausing before each gesture of her hands, whether in picking up firewood, or in cleaning hides. These pauses reminded Wolverine of his father's reveries; his mother reflected, in her own way, the same mind as his father. Perhaps it was this that kept her from saying or doing anything to bring her man from his world of dreams. How could she, when she was so much like him? Did she even know her soul was so similar to Blue Dreams?

Wolverine thought about this, sometimes while staring at reflections of himself in the water. At three, Wolverine's accelerated growth stopped, and by five he was small and stocky, unlike his parents, who were slim and light. Many family members within the tribe talked of Wolverine's spirit, a spirit that could be so strong and yet so different from his parents.

At seven years of age, Wolverine got into his first and last flght with another young syilx child. The child, eight years old at the time, saw fit to take a piece of dried meat from Wolverine. Wolverine listened to Cats Willow's taunts, and studied the four other children who stood behind Cats Willow. He knew of Cats Willow — every child did. Cats Willow "led" a group of children, and was thought to be a possible headman when he grew up.

Cats Willow was strong, and open. He fought with the ferocity of his namesake, gaining the respect of every child in the village. He lacked subterfuge, preferring instead to deal boldly with everything in his way. Already some children and elders pointed to Wolverine with a measure of respect that threatened Cats Willow's position among his young followers. Taking Wolverine's deer meat was his way of establishing his superiority.

Cats Willow expected Wolverine to protest, and stood ready to face Wolverine down. Wolverine, a head shorter than his rival, paused, his face blank, just like his father's. Cats Willow waited for Wolverine to speak, but watched in stunned amazement as Wolverine charged him. Before Cats Willow could move, his feet flew out from under him, and then he felt himself being thrown to the ground. He landed hard, the wind knocked out of his lungs. As Cats Willow tried to catch his breath, Wolverine reached down to take the chunk of dried deer meat from the grass where it had fallen from Cats Willow's hands. He straightened himself and stared at the other children for several seconds. Then he returned the dried meat to his brother and walked away.

●●●●●

Blue Dreams sat beside his oldest son, who was perched on a log beside the fire. "I heard about Cats Willow. His father spoke to me today."

Wolverine looked up, his eyes curiously placid. When his father said no more Wolverine returned his gaze to the fire. The two sat in silence for a long time, listening to the fire's crackling.

To Wolverine, the flames transformed into the screams of many syilx, but his father sat beside him, silent to the horror Wolverine saw and heard from the spirit world.

When the terror of the visions became too much, Wolverine reached out for the comfort of his father's hands. His body shook with the power of what he felt, and his father drew him closer to hug him. Blue Dreams felt the small boy's ribs tremble, and he looked down at his son, seeing the sweat beaded on Wolverine's brow. He stroked the boy's head, feeling his son relax into his protective hug.

It was in this position that the black-robed man found them. Black Robes frowned, his anger almost palpable in the warm haze that separated him from the father and son. Black Robes warned Blue Dreams of his presence by coughing politely as he drew near. Blue Dreams looked up at the approaching figure. He kept his son shielded within his arms as the priest stood over them.

"I'm looking for Horse. What's wrong with the boy?"

Blue Dreams hid his surprise at the priest's fluency in the syilx language. The man had learned quickly in the two years he had spent traveling up and down the Valley.

"My son is well. He just tired himself out playing today."

The priest looked at the small boy, who said nothing. His dark eyes troubled the priest, who felt uneasy even with the father's assurance. Wolverine's confidence and open curiosity threatened the priest's desire to have the pagan Indians see the world his way, to want to have Christ come into their lives. But so distorted were they by their own barbaric beliefs, it paid to be cautious. The lessons of the Jesuits, and their hasty and ill-timed attempts to convert the tribes back east, forced the Church to be more circumspect in its approach with the more recently discovered Indians. The Oblates had said to "work from within, not from without"; the priest felt the sting of these words hold him back from making more pointed comments. Learn the language first, he thought, and then he'd understand the Indians' world view.

"My father has gone to fast for three days. He should be here by tonight," Blue Dreams told the priest.

Black Robes, as he stood over the two, noticed for the first time the resemblance between Blue Dreams and Wolverine. They both stared at him as though they read his thoughts and knew what he felt. But their faces betrayed nothing of their own thoughts; their eyes were too steady, too analytic. The priest understood the father, but the boy's self-assurance was unseemly, somehow unnatural. The priest vowed that one day soon he would crack through that facade and wrench the boy from his heathen beliefs. How else could the boy be saved from his parents' and elders' stories?

"Tell Horse that I want to see him tomorrow," Black Robes said.

Later Horse listened to his son. Once Blue Dreams finished, Horse sat before the fire to think about what he'd been told. The priest stirred something among the syilx that they'd never felt before. Horse had seen it before he left for his fast. A headman had told the story of Sn-klip's southern journeys, and for the first time Horse saw the younger ones lose their attention. Several had gone so far as to leave without permission, not to return. Horse remembered the headman's look of shock and disbelief at this obvious break with custom.

The headman finished his story, but something of his culture drifted away with the smoke, never to return. The headman was confused, uncertain, and his story became incomplete, unfinished in spirit. The young ones were later reprimanded, but an air of defiance remained within the camp, separating the elders and headmen from the younger ones, who began asking questions in the same sharp manner as the priest.

Blue Dreams watched as his father became lost in his own reveries, and he waited patiently. Horse straightened his legs towards the fire. He had been on a fast, but rather than renewing his energies as in the past, he felt light-headed and empty.

During his fast, Horse had thought about his people, and about the priest.

The syilx had been exposed to other tribes and other ways of thinking and speaking. The Secwepemc to the north had different ways, yet for the most part respected the syilx, often waiting for them to leave an area before making use of it for themselves, a custom that the syilx returned in their own fashion. The tribes had lived in peace for as long as anyone could remember.

Black Robes, the priest, was a sha-ma, and his way of thinking troubled the younger members of the five thousand syilx who lived around the lake. He represented forces larger than the priest. The headmen and elders tried to extend to the priest the same respect they paid to other visitors, but it was hard to maintain this welcome in the face of what the priest brought with him.

Horse was only one of many elders who fasted in order to try to understand the priest's reasoning. For three days he had fasted, but he saw no visions or dreams to guide him. Once, he thought of the dreams Blue Dreams shared with him two summers before. He thought of the emptiness within his son's dreams, an emptiness he still saw within Blue Dreams' eyes and way of moving.

As a young boy, Horse remembered a syilx who troubled his tribe, a man consumed by something evil that the elders and spiritual healers tried to cure through a ceremony of cleansing. Four days after the ceremony finished, on a bright afternoon, the man had slain his woman and children, a crime so unthinkable and evil that the syilx had banished the man from within their midst. Shunned by everyone, the man had taken to the plateaus above the Valley, where his bones were found at the bottom of a steep ravine four summers later.

Black Robes was not as direct in his actions, yet his murderous ways seemed to seep into families in the same way as the strange cough that had appeared in the tribe over the past twelve moons. The priest's public words were different from the words he shared in private with those who listened more closely to what he said. When asked about this, the priest did what no syilx would consider doing, he denied his own private words. The thought of such a twisted mind made Horse weak in his legs, just as he felt helpless now.

How could he and his people deal with such a man? Good manners demanded respect to others, but never had their customs been tested in such a way. How could Horse ignore thousands of years of experience for the sake of one man? There had to be another way.

Looking at last towards Blue Dreams, Horse made his decision. "The families will meet tonight."

The fifteen families who shared this one site gathered around the fire as the sun stood just above the western ridges. The fire was large, allowing everyone to sit or stand within easy speaking distance of one another. Following the opening ceremony of thanking the spirits of the air and land, the elders, by chance most of them women, moved forward to sit on the logs placed around the fire. Those who next moved forward were the headmen not already among the elders. The third movement was from the children and family members, including hunters, food gatherers, and the berry pickers. In the syilx way, each family member had his or her place around the fire. Each had their say. As each spoke, the others listened.

"Black Robes brings us a message. We must listen, for he speaks for all sha-mas," one headman said.

An elder, her hands shaking with the energy it took to speak, whispered, "Black Robes does not seek our approval. He speaks and listens only for himself. Nor does he count the cost of his words, for his words are only a tool to be used to bring us his message, not for him to hear and understand us."

"I don't believe that Black Robes can be only a messenger," Horse said at last, after hearing the two sides of Black Robe's presence talked about by the elders and headsmen. "The sha-mas must want to know us so that they can begin talks with us. They do not treat us like they treat our brothers in the south."

Everyone had heard of the killings and massacres of women and children, as well as warriors and hunters. Such a thing lay beyond the syilx's comprehension; no humans could act in such a way, so the stories must surely be exaggerations. The chill these stories left among the syilx and their neighbors resulted in their trying hard to discount what they heard from other tribes.

As Horse continued, many syilx were swayed by his sonorous voice. They remembered other times of need, when Horse lent an air of calm to the fevered talk of younger syilx.

"We have no dead among us, no blue-coats ambushing our women and children while we are away, no unwashed sha-mas killing our animal spirits for no reason. Black Robes does not speak like us, but he has never raised a fist against us. He has not brought soldiers to our camps. We must continue to give him our welcome," continued Horse.

After an hour of such talk, the syilx agreed to leave the priest to his travels.

"You spoke well," Blue Dreams said to Horse.

Horse turned at his son's voice. "I spoke what I had to. When other sha-mas come, they will give us the same courtesy and respect. If we mistreat the Black Robes, they will have reason to fight us."

"I hope so. They do not think like us."

"We have no choice here. It is our way. Our ways would not be very good if we changed them for a single man. We made our customs through many generations."

Blue Dreams walked with Horse down to the lake that stretched to the south, and then out of sight. Horse walked into the lake and sat with the water rising to his chest. For some time he was quiet. Blue Dreams, who sat beside him, enjoyed the lake's cool currents. Small waves lapped at their chests, gently lifting their bodies an inch at a time with a soft, swaying motion.

"Do you see the benches on each side of the lake?" Horse pointed to the flat lands that stood a hundred feet above them. These mesas ended at the edge of the lake, where the land dropped in cliffs whose clay shone white and grey in the last remnants of sunlight.

"The lake once rose to the top of those lands, where they meet the hillsides. There are stories of caves within the hills that our ancestors once used for ceremonies. Those caves, many of them, were sealed off when the land shook many years ago."

"I have heard of those stories," Blue Dreams replied. "It is hard to think of the land moving."

Horse laughed. "Yes, it was a time of change. The land moves when change comes. My father said that when the land moved, the lake also moved, becoming smaller by a man's full height within days."

"And we stopped using caves."

Horse nodded. "Some of our elders were in those caves when they closed. Since then, our families have stayed away, partially from respect, partially from danger. The caves that still exist often move without warning, and we fear being trapped. Our children are warned to stay away. It's been so long since that happened that the locations for most of the caves are hidden by time and lost memories."

"They were good times."

"I am getting old, Blue Dreams. One day I will travel into the hills to one of those caves and I won't return."

As he bobbed in the cold waters, Blue Dreams thought of the dust-covered Black Robes. He reminded Horse of the Black Robes' demands to talk with Horse. Horse nodded. "I had a vision of him. He brings confusion, but I see nothing in him beyond the shadows around him. He troubles me, and whenever I see him, I feel tired."

Blue Dreams watched a nearby bird hover over the stream as

it flowed into the lake. The bird sank into a riverbank tree, where it perched to preen its feathers.

"Wolverine's dreams of fire and death trouble him," Blue Dreams said.

"Just him?"

"When he speaks, I feel something beyond his words. Something he cannot yet say. I think it's important."

"Your son's visions must be heard. Listen to him when he talks of them. Our people may yet have to understand what Wolverine sees."

"You've decided, then?"

"Yes. I must start him into our stories. He knows, and he listens. Our family needs him to carry on."

"He's so young."

"I was his age when my father took me aside to teach me."

The next morning, upon rising, Blue Dreams saw Black Robes' angular shape standing over Horse. He was speaking as Horse listened. Blue Dreams frowned. He didn't trust Black Robes, but he respected Horse, and the syilx had backed Horse's suggestions. Blue Dreams would not break their decision, not even for the feeling of doom Black Robes generated within him.

The northern end of the lake splits in two, one arm reaching farther north, while the other arm, some five miles long, reaches to the northeast. The great plateau that stretches to the east and north of the lake is here jogged farther east. The Valley that lies parallel to the lake has its own milder climate, and here the syilx often camp for weeks at a time, sheltered along the small creek that flows west to the lake.

This year, warned by Horse and several other headmen, the syilx moved to this shelter earlier than usual. They took two days to reach the site, and spent the next several days making their camps.

Wolverine, now ten, watched his parents dig a large pit some fifteen feet across. Blue Dreams then laid four logs across the top of the pit and wove many smaller branches across it. Next, he covered the tight structure with a mixture of dirt and leaves, making the lodge blend into the terrain. When he finished, Blue Dreams had a comfortable winter dwelling whose two entrances were sealed by deer hides attached to the lodge's central poles. Blue Dreams placed the smaller hole at the lodge's center; from this hole, smoke from the fire within the lodge could make its way to the outside. The second entrance was as wide as two syilx, wide enough to enter and exit comfortably.

Sky Woman picked berries with the other women, some of the elders, and many children, who were cautioned to watch for the Kee-lau-naw. These large bears sought the same berries as the syilx, and must be paid proper respect. Wolverine, although too young to help, watched from his vantage point higher up the slopes from the lake. He kept an eye out for the Kee-lau-naw, but none came down while the syilx picked berries.

After watching the adults for a while, Wolverine got up and began climbing the south hill. Through long practice, he scaled the hill quickly, his small figure clambering up the various slopes towards the round top.

A large flat rock lay along the eastern slopes near the peak. Trees and brush separated this slab of granite from the peak, and gave it shade from the relentless sun and heat of the day. Wolverine stopped to lie on the rock. He stared into the sky, watching idly as small clouds drifted overhead. Last night, while his father built the lodge, Wolverine had another dream of blood. Blue Dreams had listened to Wolverine's dream before he left with the berry pickers, but he was at a loss about what his son's dream meant.

Wolverine heard the small sounds of animals nearby. Birds darted in and out of the bushes and trees, while squirrels chattered to one another, oblivious of his presence once they saw he posed no threat. Once, a deer peeked out at him from the edge of a clump of trees below. Its ears twitched as it hesitated. Wolverine ignored it, so it resumed its feeding on the grass. Its small figure soon disappeared farther down the slope, although every so often it lifted its head to look his way.

Wolverine was almost sleeping when he felt something shift in the air. His nose sensed something new to the land. Puzzled, Wolverine sat up to look around. Halfway down the hill, he saw horse and rider weave in and out of the brush and trees. Even from here, Wolverine knew the priest's black robes. The priest rode his horse slowly across the steep terrain, letting his mount find its own footing. The priest's shadow lay long across the slope.

On an impulse, Wolverine cut across the slope along a path that would intersect the priest's direction a half mile ahead of where he rode. Wolverine got to the spot five minutes before the priest came into sight around a sharp bend in the hillside. From his perch high in the tree, Wolverine kept still, knowing that any movement would spook the horse and warn the priest.

The priest sang something strange, barely audible over his horse's hoof beats. Wolverine heard each word clearly, but the language was strange. The priest sang with conviction, his bass voice rising and falling to the cadence of both the song and of his horse's steps. His long angular face, pale against the black robes, was flushed with the late afternoon heat. As Wolverine watched, the priest dabbed his gleaming forehead with the sleeve of one arm.

Horse and rider passed beneath Wolverine, and soon disappeared around the bend that led to the syilx camp. For several minutes, Wolverine puzzled over the priest's song. Try as he might, he could not understand the words that were stranger than the words of their Lakota cousins to the south of the syilx. He had watched the priest enough to know that the words were in a language called anglaise, or anglasse, depending on that pronunciation the priest used.

Later, after he rejoined the berry pickers on their way back to the camp, Wolverine told his mother of the priest. Sky Woman frowned. "That man worries me. He talks of things that we know nothing about. Be careful. You were right not to talk with him. He has a temper that is short."

"He spoke in his own language."

"Yes. He's teaching this anglaise to the older children. We haven't decided yet whether this is good or not."

"Do all sha-mas speak like this Black Robes?"

"Son, I don't know."

"I think I will talk with him."

Sky Woman gently bit her lower lip. "I won't stop you, but please be careful when you do. Black Robes brings his own spirits into our lands."

Wolverine nodded. "I felt them. They scared the animals around me."

Sky Woman smiled. "No bears were around today. They never are when you come with me."

"I saw a bear once, close up. He stared at me for a long time, then walked away. He was nice to me."

"You never told me."

"It was a small bear."

Sky Woman studied her son as they walked along the grassy slopes. "You aren't afraid of the animal people, are you?" she asked him.

"They don't bother me. I like talking to them."

"Horse tells me the same thing. All the same, young one, do not be too brave."

"Grandfather says that I should talk more with the animal people."

Sky Woman was startled. "Why?"

"He finds out things. I ask the animal people, and they tell me things that I tell Grandfather."

"How long have you been doing this?"

Wolverine frowned, his small dark face tight with concentration. Finally he shook his head. "I don't know. As long as I can remember."

On a hunch, Sky Woman said, "There were wolves last winter."

"Those big dogs that came near our camp in the snow?"

"They stole meat from many camps around the lake."

"They were nice, mother. But they were hungry. They didn't want to harm anyone."

"Promise to be careful?"

"I will."

The priest sat on an old log at the edge of the camp. Several older boys of around ten summers stood or sat in a semi-circle in front of his gaunt figure. Wolverine came up as quietly as he could, and sat between two larger boys. From where he sat, Wolverine could see the priest's face. The priest said in syilx, "Say the following words." Then the strange tongue, "Hower Fahthard, who arked in heven."

In unison, the older boys tried to recite the strange words, their tongues tripping over the harsh sounds. Wolverine listened carefully for several rounds, before he softly mouthed the new words.

On Wolverine's third try, the priest suddenly turned towards him. "You there. Speak up."

Wolverine, feeling the other boys' eyes on him, said, "Our Father, who art in heaven."

"That's good. What's your name?"

When Wolverine told him, the priest scowled. "Blue Dreams' son. Did Horse send you to watch me?"

"No. I want to learn the language you talk."

"How old are you, Wolverine?"

"I'm ten summers old."

"Ten years old. The boy talks better than you older ones."

The way the other boys looked at him made Wolverine nervous. He felt their disapproval, and his stomach ached. Whenever young syilx excelled in anything, they were normally encouraged by their playmates to become better, for they might become headmen. Competition improved the families' chances of survival during winter, for the better their food gatherers and hunters were, the more food they had over the winter moons. But Wolverine's small size, his precocious mannerisms, and his preference for solitude made the children around him nervous. He was a pariah in their midst, and so the scowls the other boys now directed at him when the priest turned his attention elsewhere hit Wolverine like a fist, making him dizzy. They were like the priest's scowls, and went against everything he had been taught by his elders.

Wolverine was so disoriented by the strange responses of the older boys, that he couldn't hear the priest's voice any more. He staggered away towards the nearby creek, where he found a small cove hidden in the brush. There, in the dark, he shivered, as tears flowed down his face. He curled into a ball in the soft dirt.

His mother's voice brought Wolverine out of his shaking long enough for him to say, "I'm here." Then his mother's arms wrapped around him, a soft cocoon into which he sank and slept.

Horse listened to Wolverine. The other elders and headmen sat in a semi-circle around the campfire, their faces reflecting nothing of their inner feelings. Every so often they asked Wolverine a question. After Wolverine finished, Horse looked to his grandson. He missed the gatherings which had once filled the Valley with energy. He missed the laughter that used to ring out from camps now shunned because they contained the spirits of the ones the pox had taken. He missed the fires, the stories told around them, some to the dozens of children rapt with attention, others of a distinct grownup slant later in the night that drew the ribald guffaws of an appreciative adult audience.

So many elders were just memories, and so many more were names he had forgotten, knowing that each name that slid from him into the spirit world carried priceless stories and knowledge that would never be regained. Who now listened to old men like him? What children aside from the one who sat alongside his father and grandfather cared to listen to his memories? Black Robes now held the syilx spirit in his hands, and most of the elders had already passed their power to that man.

Still, the syilx were a proud people, and might have yet put up a struggle. But all the Black Robes held a magic that none could resist. They knew how to stop the pox, and when they infected the people in a massive inoculation drive, some syilx died, but most lived, and with their survival ended the hold of elders who clung to the traditional syilx ways. At this campfire, on this night, Horse witnessed another loosening of the elders' hold on their families. And this time it grieved him to support the Black Robes, but his mind wavered between his beliefs and the survival of his people.

"How often has your son seen or talked with Black Robes?" an elder asked Blue Dreams.

Blue Dreams put aside his misery long enough to look at the circle of elders. "My son spends his time in the hills. You all know that. We have found his gifts valuable. He has had no time to spend with Black Robes."

"And yet the older boys, those not of age yet, spend time with Black Robes."

Another elder spoke. "Until now, we have never told our young what to do with their time when they aren't learning from us."

Blue Dreams' mother lifted her head. "Black Robes came to me last night after Wolverine left their circle. He asked me questions about my grandson."

"Did you tell him anything?"

Runs with the Sky looked miserable. "I didn't know what to

say. I saw no harm in talking about Wolverine. Black Robes seemed interested in him."

Blue Dreams saw his mother's misery. "It's not Runs with the Sky's fault. I should have watched over my son better."

Horse spoke, his heart twisting in his chest. "No one is laying blame here. We're not sure whether harm has been done or not. Black Robes thinks differently than us. Perhaps in his world, he means well. We must decide whether what Wolverine saw and heard is enough for us to worry about."

A quiet woman who sat on the edge of the circle spoke the unthinkable, shocking the circle into silence. "Perhaps we cannot trust Black Robes to have our families in his best interest."

Horse, as did others, tried to wrap his mind around not giving a guest complete trust. But the words had been spoken, and had to be talked out. The darkness surrounding the fire seemed to deepen, and Horse took several deep breaths. He looked towards his son. Blue Dreams stared into the fire, his eyes glittering and unreadable.

"Words like this must be owned. Trust is the root of our relations with our neighbors." Horse looked miserable as he completed his thoughts. "Yet the words ring true. Can we trust Black Robes to do the best things for our people?"

"I have dreamt of the darkness that my son sees in his blood dreams each night." Blue Dreams looked at each person around the fire. "I have a knot in my stomach that goes back to the deer hunt five summers ago. It sits there, eating at me. I lose sleep, because the dreams I have grow from my stomach. Lean years lie ahead, years of blood like my son dreams."

"He is young to have visions," a headman spoke.

"Age has nothing to do with visions," Horse pointed out.

The headman spoke again. "What you say is true, Horse, but it is not everything. We need help to decide how to deal with Black Robes. He speaks to our children, teaching them this anglaise. His words are strong, because they teach our children different things. Some are good, but we are not here to speak of the good things. There is unrest among our children. They are no longer happy to learn from us. They speak of other ways of doing things, ways coming from the sha-mas."

"My son is confused. His hurt is felt by the other children, and they make fun of him."

Sky Woman spoke in a hesitant voice. "The children speak of something called fath, or fathe. It is what Black Robes believes in. Black Robes speaks from a strange thing called a buk. The thoughts in this buk are awful. They terrify the children, and they listen to Black Robes more from fear than understanding."

"The children need direction. Perhaps we should have someone with the children when Black Robes is here."

Several headmen and elders nodded their heads. Horse thought hard, but saw nothing wrong in the suggestion. It was agreed that Blue Dreams would sit in on the children's meetings with Black Robes, and bring back what Black Robes spoke of.

"God is mighty. He looks down on you all."

The children looked to the skies, their eyes filled with fear and wonder. Blue Dreams sat entranced. North of where the lodges were built, the first winter storms threatened the Valley. Grey-black streaks ran through the clouds, almost as if Black Robes' god was angry at them. As Blue Dreams followed the children's looks towards the sky, a cold wind from the west swept through the Valley. Wolverine, who huddled in his father's arms, shivered and drew closer.

Black Robes, who called himself Father Kennedy, stared at the small group. His eyes sparkled in the low light. He lowered his voice so that the others had to lean closer to hear him.

"God loves you all. His anger is held for those who do not believe in Him, who believe in other gods, gods who are devils to tempt you, to lead you from the flock of God's son, Jesus Christ."

Blue Dreams held one of the books that Father Kennedy had passed out to the group. For the past forty days he had sat and listened, quickly learning the anglaise spoken by the priest. He pondered the words spoken every day. They troubled him. Although the priest never directly attacked the ways of the syilx, his voice often reflected a criticism and mistrust of them. His god seemed to have power — power and anger.

Horse cautioned Blue Dreams several times to remember the strength of the syilx, who had lived among these valleys for more generations than could be counted.

"Black Robes, this Father Kennedy, will pass through. Sha-mas travel through countries, so all the tribes to the south say."

"I have heard that new sha-mas follow the first travelers, and they make their homes along the rivers and flat lands," Blue Dreams said to his father.

Horse shrugged. "It will take many generations for enough sha-mas to move here before the syilx need to worry. We must welcome them, and not make the mistake our cousins to the south made. Everyone who fights the sha-mas are attacked by the blue-coats, who care little for women or children when they kill."

"My son has nightmares about this god that Father Kennedy speaks of."

"Is Black Robes an enemy?"

Blue Dreams frowned, his smooth brow furrowing with the effort. "I don't think so," he said at last.

Runs with the Sky, Horse's wife, led the other women from their tents. Horse thunder rumbled in the distance from the sound of blue-coats who rode around the camp. They were beyond counting, and they raised dust from their prancing about, which rose high into the still air.

Horse stood with the other warriors at the edge of the camp, encircling the women and children in a protective shield. Blue Dreams stood at Horse's shoulder, his younger head held proudly and defiant, his hands loosely holding the bow and notched arrow.

Sky Woman bent towards her son and whispered, "Whatever happens, stay close by my side."

Wolverine felt himself nod, although he said nothing to distract the older people from their tasks. He stared into the distance, watching horse soldiers ride endlessly around the camp at a safe distance, beyond the range of the strongest bow.

As he stared, Wolverine saw a break in the circle of soldiers. At an unseen signal, the soldiers stopped riding and turned their horses towards the syilx campsite. In moments, a silence hung over the scene, broken when a single horse and rider cantered through the break. Wolverine recognized the black robes of Father Kennedy, although the priest was taller and leaner than Wolverine remembered.

Father Kennedy rode towards the waiting line of syilx. His gaze never left the man at whom he stared. Horse waited patiently, his large angular face unreadable in the strong summer light.

Wolverine broke from the ranks of women and children and dashed forward to where his father stood. From behind Blue Dreams' solid form, Wolverine had a clear view of the priest as he rode to within an arm's length of Horse. In clear syilx language, Father Kennedy spoke to the entire camp.

"We mean you no harm. Our people wish to live on this land with you, and we will share everything we have with the syilx."

"What do you have that we want?" Horse asked.

In response, Father Kennedy reached into his saddlebag to pull out a blanket. He draped the small blanket over his left arm before turning his horse sideways to Horse. Steadying his horse with one rein, Father Kennedy leaned sideways and down so that his left arm was at Horse's eye-level.

"We bring you this blanket in good faith. It is a gift from us to you."

Father Kennedy smiled, and Wolverine stared into his black mouth as his bones grew cold. He tried to warn his grandfather, but his voice was gone, and he watched in horror as Horse smiled and reached for the blanket. At the same time, the priest's mouth widened, its blackness growing and growing until . . .

Wolverine woke up screaming without sound. His small body jerked as he fought to throw the invisible blanket away. He collapsed onto his sleeping pallet of tule, feeling the sweat pour from his body as his lungs heaved for precious air with which to speak. His mother Sky Woman lay beside him, her still form remaining in a deep sleep as her son struggled through his nightmare, alone.

Spring brought torrents of rain that fell for days, melting the snow and creating fields of mud. The syilx stayed close to their camp, venturing out only to gather firewood or fix one of the lodges. They kept a large fire burning in the middle of the camp. The older children were put in charge of keeping watch over the fire, stoking it when it needed to be rejuvenated, throwing wood on it when it grew low, and running around it to keep warm and to play their games of chase and catch.

The fire became the gathering place for the camp. Many times, Horse sat on an upended log, from which he talked with the other elders and headmen. The fire crackled and spiraled its sparks upward into the chill air. Horse often shifted on the log, turning to keep himself warm, the soft glow from the fire illuminating his dark eyes and long white hair.

Here, Blue Dreams came with his troubled visions, as well as those of his son. Horse would watch his son walk from his lodge, and note how Blue Dreams' shoulders were hunched against more than spring winds. Blue Dreams taught his father as much anglaise as Horse requested, but Horse showed scant interest in learning the strange tongue. Horse told the other elders about the language and its focus on possessive words, words related to the person more than the community.

Horse considered Blue Dreams' words, and found that they made his head ache. He talked with Wolverine, who every day grew more foreign from anything Horse knew. It wasn't just Wolverine's ability with English; it was also Wolverine's long trips into the land, which he continued despite the cold that kept the other syilx within their lodges. Wolverine talked with the animals, of this Horse was certain, and yet the boy kept what he learned to himself, and shared them only upon Horse's prodding.

Horse felt his world splitting, pulling him in different directions, taxing him against his will. The other elders and headmen felt it, too, but no one could decide what to do about it. They thought of Wolverine as an omen of the times. He confused them at a time when they struggled to make sense of the priest's strange messages.

Wolverine felt this confusion, and his walks into the land became longer and longer. Blue Dreams talked with him, but the boy silently waited for his father to finish before soundlessly returning to his own path.

Horse was sitting on his log after a spring rain when Wolverine came and sat next to him. Horse looked down at the boy's small frame. Wolverine looked up into Horse's large eyes, and smiled.

Horse nodded greetings at Wolverine. "Whi."

"Whi."

Wolverine looked away, into the flames of the fire. As Horse watched, he shivered, and his hunched shoulders reminded Horse of Blue Dreams.

"They say that Sn-klip begins to wake from his winter dreams at this time of year."

Wolverine looked up into the sullen skies. "No, Coyote is still asleep."

"You haven't seen him?"

"Maybe he's still with Mole."

"Maybe." Horse sounded skeptical. "The winter was hard, but not that hard."

As Wolverine looked up with a puzzled look on his face, Horse chortled to himself. He still found it hard to talk to Wolverine as an adult. The boy barely stood at Horse's waist, and yet he spoke of things many elders hadn't or couldn't speak about. Wolverine stirred a puddle with the long stick he always carried these days. His eyes studied the ripples the stick created. Horse waited, knowing that the boy had more to say.

"Father Kennedy is thinking about leaving."

Horse nodded. It was what he wanted to hear, and he felt surprised that he also felt a passing regret.

"Father Kennedy speaks our language well. He calls us Okandada, after the Lakota's word for looking for a place."

"Father Kennedy is wrong. We have always known where we are. Always."

Wolverine looked keenly at his grandfather. He had to tell Horse, but he didn't know how. His brow was furrowed in thought, as he studied Horse's worn features. He knew every wrinkle in Horse's face, and treasured the way his grandfather frowned when confusion led his mind. It was the frown that Wolverine copied for himself. That, and all of Horse's other expressions.

The fire hissed when Horse stooped to throw another log into it. The pale sun tried to break through the patchy grey skies. A headman walked by on his way to his lodge, but neither Horse not Wolverine saw the man shudder as he glanced at the two beside the fire.

"There are other sha-mas here."

Wolverine felt the cold wind bite. "Others?"

"Yes. Farther down the Valley, towards the lake."

"You have seen them?"

"Yes, they rode on a strange thing made of wood. They've been here for two days."

"Two days. What have they done?"

Wolverine shook his head. "Strange things. They took four pieces of wood and stuck them into the ground in four different places. They've been gathering wood and clearing stones from between those four poles."

"Clearing stones? Why would someone want to clear stones from the land?"

"They have two children with them."

"Sha-mas?"

"All of them."

"The children are small. Like me. And they talk a lot."

"Their anglaise makes them talk like that. It is a language to fill silences with sounds."

"Father Kennedy says that the Bible has all the answers we need to grow up with."

"Perhaps it's a good thing that he's leaving. This Bible is the thing that he reads from?"

"Yes. He reads from it every chance he can get."

"Do you know why Black Robes is leaving us at the start of spring?"

"My father may know. He was there when Father Kennedy told us."

Later, Horse prepared for the night by packing wood to dry in his lodge. Blue Dreams came from his own lodge, walking around the fire towards Horse. Horse carefully placed the last piece of wood onto the waist-high pile and then straightened from his stoop.

"My son spoke to you earlier about Father Kennedy?"

"He said that the priest is leaving, but not why."

Blue Dreams entered Horse's lodge. Horse closed the flap to

cut down on the wind that swept through the camp. Blue Dreams sat on a flat sheet of leaves and hide. The central fireplace filled the lodge with a soft glow. Blue smoke rose through the hole in the lodge's center. For a time, Blue Dreams watched as his father moved around the lodge. Horse moved slowly, his figure moving with the familiarity of the place. Seldom did Horse look closely at where he was in the lodge, or what he did. Instead, he sang a song under his breath as he went about his chores.

The lodge was bare of anything but the essentials. Horse kept most of his clothing stacked along the back of his lodge. He was conscientious in airing his clothes and keeping them clean. Blue Dreams remembered the many times he had watched his father by the creek, doing his own washing, something he insisted on ever since Horse's first wife (Runs with the Sky's cousin) had gone off into the hills to die when Blue Dreams was still a boy.

Blue Dreams still remembered his mother's kind face marred by pain. She had become sick, and coughed up blood near the end. One morning, as quietly as possible, she had risen and walked away from the camp forever. Horse went with her to keep her company. Two days later, he returned, his own face divided between grief and joy, grief for her passing away, and joy for his last hours with her, when he watched her for the final time slip into a peaceful sleep away from her pain.

Finally, when Horse was certain that everything was in its rightful spot, he sat beside his son. He gave Blue Dreams a piece of deer meat on which to chew. His eyes twinkled as he gnawed on his own piece of dried meat.

"I remember when you were young, how you used to watch us."

"It seems so long ago."

"Not long. Maybe thirty winters. Your mother and I talked often about you. You were so full of curiosity. And you learned quickly."

"Aiieee! Not quickly enough," Blue Dreams patted his own bum as he spoke. Horse smiled at the memories this evoked.

"The priest speaks of his own home tribe more often. He wants to return there."

"And this is why he leaves us?"

"It is one reason. He does not speak to us from his heart unless it is about his god, this one he speaks of from the black book he carries."

Horse shook his head. "Black Robes talks much of life. He speaks much about what we as syilx should think. Yet he has no woman, no children. He is unbalanced."

Blue Dreams thought about Black Robes from how his father saw him. "He says that the Jesus who instructs him from the black book had no women or children."

"Perhaps the Jesus should have had women and children. A man needs the other half that is in woman before he knows what there is to know about living. Otherwise, it is just words."

"I said the same thing to Father Kennedy. He said that I was being untrue to the words in the black book. He called me a heethen, or something like that."

"A heethen?"

"It's an anglaise word for anyone who doesn't believe in the black book and its words."

"The sha-mas are so strange."

"My son needs guidance."

Horse felt it all fit together, and wondered why he hadn't thought of it before. He nodded and stooped to stoke the fire. "Wolverine is close to our cousins in the hills. Closer than he is to boys of his own age. And he learns anglaise well."

Blue Dreams shook his head. "The boys in our camp fear going into the wilderness. Where once it was a sign of growing, now boys consider the priest's words, and say that there is no need to practice the old ways. Only Wolverine is comfortable spending time away from our camp."

"Your son is different; the rest of the boys his age are afraid of him. He is something they no longer believe in."

"Is it too late then?"

"No. But he needs different guidance. I need to show him the Old People. He may be the only one who can carry the stories and ways of our people beyond the time you and I are in this world."

Blue Dreams stared at his father. When Horse remained silent, Blue Dreams asked the question on his mind. "I thought the Old People no longer walk in this world."

"They don't. But they have left behind things that will be shown in time, when the syilx are ready to hear their voices again."

"The Old People." Blue Dreams felt the power in the words, and quickly looked away from the fire, as if it could speak. "What do the other headmen and elders say?"

Horse shrugged. "They need to know about Wolverine. His spirit is powerful, and dangerous. The Old People will know what he is."

"When does this happen?"

"Tomorrow. I need Wolverine tomorrow morning."

The dreams wrapped Horse within their blanket. He felt the tree roots beneath his lean-to shift with his dreams. He saw Badger for the second time in his life. The Old Person snuffled and rooted towards the spot where Horse waited. When Badger saw Horse, she became a New Person, her short hair revealing ears that heard everything. Without a word, she extended her hands to Horse, leading him uphill to a steep cliff overlooking the lake. She paused at the edge of the clearing where the cliff loomed, and Horse saw the familiar remains of logs that lay scattered in odd patterns on the ground.

Badger turned away from the clearing and began climbing

upwards, following the almost invisible path that wove its way in a criss-cross pattern over the cliff's face. Halfway between the third and fourth turns, Badger stopped at a large slab of rock. A crack ran vertically along the rock's face. At the spot where they stood, the crack was just wide enough for them to slip sideways into it.

Horse followed Badger as she scrambled into the crack. His breath became labored as he squeezed himself inside, and then slowly inched deeper into the crack, following Badger's quick lead.

After an endless time, the way became easier, and soon Horse found himself emerging into a dimly lit cave. He couldn't see to the far wall, but saw clearly enough to make his way over the rough terrain to a flat smooth spot where Badger waited along with several other Old People.

"You must bring the boy here. To the place where you buried the stone."

"Is the stone to be his?"

"The stone is no one's to own. Remember when your grandfather gave you the stone for safe keeping?"

Horse remembered his grandfather's story. Several versions of it had been passed through the generations by different families. His grandfather's story, the one he told his grandson in preparation for Wolverine's initiation, went thus.

The young man stood on the western side of the lake. His name was lost in time but, as in any story, later storytellers gave him names ranging from Elk Runner to Three Paws, none of them his actual name, but that never stops a story from happening. The last snows had been gone for a full moon now, and the air was warm. A breeze stirred the waist-high grass behind the man and, in the distance, a mile across the lake on the hillsides opposite of where he stood, the man saw a herd of elk grazing along the lush slopes. Bear scat fifty feet from where he stood told of a recent visit by a large bear, something the man determined by the size of the paw prints, the way a large swath of grass had been plowed by the massive form and the amount of scat left by the water.

But the grass was springing back, and some of the paw prints were dissolving in the soft dirt near the water's edge, so the young man knew that the bear had come and gone some time ago, enough time so that he had no fear of the bear being a danger. The man had traveled for three days, leaving the north tip of the lake behind as he walked south towards the Swah-netk'-qhu. He was in no hurry. Every night he was lulled to sleep by the sound of the waves lapping the shoreline. Each morning he woke to bathe in the cold water before continuing his journey.

The man had just crossed a small creek that emptied into the lake, wading across the narrow mouth just to enjoy the feel of the water washing around his ankles. On the other side he put his moccasins back on. The smell of the grass, the sound of the small waves breaking onto the shoreline, the sight of pale blue texture of the sky, the crunch of small stones as he walked, and the sharper scent of the pines filled his senses and he felt good enough to stop, letting the world complete his sense of happiness.

He heard a sound in the cliffs a quarter mile away and turned as a boulder slowly heeled forward and tumbled from its perch to the ground a hundred feet below, shattering with a loud crack as it struck the shale which lay in a slide at the foot of the cliff. Only then did he finally hear the coyotes howling in midmorning, something they never did. From a nearby stand of pines a murder of crows lifted into the air, their raucous cries adding to the din, increased as a flock of swallows also bolted into the sky. Two hundred feet away, the bear lumbered from the grass and ran past the young man before he could decide what to do.

A haze of dust in the distance and then instinct took over, and the man was running after the bear as it made for high ground. Half of the cliff in the distance crashed into the lake. But the lake was already moving, sudden whirlpools appearing everywhere, including a hundred-foot maelstrom near the lake's center. Then the young man heard something he had not thought possible, the sound of Mother Earth, Toom-Tem, groaning, a deep rumbling that shook him to the bone. He fell, got up, and fell again as the ground underfoot rolled in long quick ripples, so fast that the man thought his vision was blurred.

The third time he fell, the young man decided to lay flat. He gritted his teeth against the sound of the earth screaming. He wasn't surprised when the bear rolled past him, tumbling towards the lake. He clung to the ground, trying to dig his fingers into the soil. He dimly heard the bear splash into the water, but the trembling earth shrieked into his soul, shaking his firmly held belief in the strength of Mother Earth. The earth did not move. There was nothing in his understanding that allowed the world he knew to move the way it moved under him.

As the shaking subsided, he managed to sit up, noticing several things at once. The bear was still in the water, its bawling a sign of panic as it dog-paddled desperately for the shoreline. A whirlpool was pulling the bear, but it stopped as the man watched. The water along the beach began to pull back, by a few feet at first, and then more rapidly. Stranded trout flailed about in the mud. The bear was pulled by the tide until its large head was a tiny dot in the distance. The man also noticed that a large opening was now visible in the rock face where the cliff had broken during the earth shaking.

The retreating water played tricks with the young man's sight. It seemed to shimmer, then grow towards the sky. Through the soles of his moccasined feet the man felt the ground begin to tremble, far gentler than the first jolts, but increasing as the water reared into a single dark blue wall and moved forward. In the distance, it seemed to move majestically slow, but gathered speed. Only then did he realize that the wave might sweep him from the slope he sat on. He clambered to his feet and ran uphill. When he reached the top to stand a hundred feet above the water, he turned in time to see the wave sweep past the cliff, taking even more rocks down as it now roared north. The beach was once again covered with water which poured inland, washing past the spot where the man had just left. A fine mist from the wave bathed the man in a cold wash that made him shiver.

When the waters had subsided, stranding hundreds of fish a quarter mile inland, the Valley floor was a temporarily impassable quagmire of mud and debris. The young man headed south along the ridge until he reached the cliff, carefully making his way along unfamiliar terrain. Several times he slipped in the loose shale or gravel, catching his balance each time before he tumbled. He steadied himself by clinging to whatever he could grab onto, until finally he stood at a spot along the ridge that flanked the cliff fifty feet below the cliff top. From where he stood, the man could see a small horizontal break in the cliff along which, if he moved slowly, he could reach the opening he had seen from below during the first parts of the earth shake.

The young man had always enjoyed climbing cliffs, something he considered a personal challenge of his own strength and agility, so within a few minutes he stood at the entrance to what appeared to be a cave. Compared to the humid heat that filled the Valley, the wafts of air from inside the cave were cold gusts, which carried an odd scent or scents, nothing of which was familiar to the man. During the time he stood at the opening, shards of shale cracked down the face of the cliff, breaking apart as they fell, testimony to the instability of the newly exposed cliff face.

Still shaken by his recent experiences, somehow the young man gathered enough courage to move into the cave. He left the strong sunlight behind as he made his cautious way farther into the cave, whose ceiling was high enough in most parts for him to stand without stooping. The cave floor was littered with shards of granite, their sharp edges making it difficult to navi-

gate without slipping. Each footstep brought the sound of grating stone. The sunlight outside lit the first hundred feet or so,
but the winding tunnel took a sharp right and plunged the man
into darkness, which he thought was total. He paused, uncertain whether to keep going. As he hesitated, his sight grew used
to the dark, and he found the darkness not as total as he had
first thought.

After an endless time of fifteen minutes, the man found himself in a cavern, with running water a welcome sound. A ray of
indirect sunlight from an invisible opening filled the cavern with
a soft light, reflecting off the small pool of water and filling the
cave with dancing light. The man saw that water seeped into the
pool from a section of the opposite wall. How the pool drained
was unknown, but its texture was snow white, limestone making the water both undrinkable and radiant.

A sparkle drew the man's attention to a pile of rocks that
rimmed the pool. In several spots from within the depths of the
rocks, a pale blue reflected against the walls, adding to the mys-
tery of the entire cave. More startling were the strange drawings
on one dry wall surface, drawings for which the man had no
understanding. Someone had made those drawings, but when
and why would stay unknown. He walked to the nearest rocks,
stooping to take hold of the shard of blue that seemed the
largest, a stone not much larger than a pebble, but cold to the
touch. He held the stone up to the diffuse light, and blue irradi-
ated him. And something more, a cold wash of dread that froze
the hand that held the stone. A cold deeper than the fear that
had struck him when the ground moved beneath him pulled his
hand closed around the stone, which stayed cold.

By the time night fell he had set up a tule mat lean-to, eaten
some dried meat, and settled onto the bed of leaves and tall
grass. In the half-moon light he held the blue stone at arm's
length. Despite carrying it from the cave and having it next to
his body all day, the stone remained as cold to the touch as
when he first found it. In the moonlight, the stone deepened in

color, strange because the direct sunlight had turned the stone almost clear of all but the faintest of blue tinges. The young man fell asleep with the stone clutched in his fist. Once during the night he woke as another tremor rumbled through the valley. In the distance he heard falling stone, and the next morning, when he woke up, the cliff opening was gone, covered by tons of stone debris that had slid from farther up the mountain and all but obliterated the cliff.

On the third day of travel, Horse had his grandson help him build a raft. It took the better part of two hours to bind and tie the logs together, which Horse and Blue Dreams had gathered fourteen days before. As the two paddled the raft across the lake, Horse continued to tell stories of the Old People, stories he'd told no one else, stories that belonged to his successor. Wolverine was a quick study, and asked Horse questions that went to the heart of each story. And yet Horse also sensed the boy's inner hesitation by the way he asked his questions.

Owning a story in the syilx way meant not just memorizing a story, but knowing its center. Each story had its own heart, and stories could not be told unless the teller knew and understood the heart, and could use the heart to tell different listeners the same story using different words. Wolverine owned every story told to him, but a part of him proved reluctant to accept the stories for what they were: the center of the syilx world.

Horse could do nothing about this, and the closer they came to the cave of his dream, the more fearful Horse became. To his knowledge, never had an unbeliever entered the Old People's world. What would happen? Horse didn't know, but hoped that Wolverine wouldn't be hurt. Even this pained Horse, for it showed that he had doubts about his own dream, and doubts about the Old People's wisdom.

The cliff was as in Horse's dream and in the stories given to him. It loomed a hundred feet above the sloped ground that, in turn, angled towards the nearby lake. Trees and shrubs completely encircled the cliff's base, making the small clearing almost invisible from more than fifty feet away. The slide that had covered the cliff so many years ago had slowly eroded, although the opening to the mythic cavern was now hidden from direct sight behind a fold in the cliff. Horse spent some time studying the cliff's face, memorizing it from several different angles, noting every crevice and outcrop he could see from below. The cliff's location was a family heirloom. Given that innumerable cliffs were scattered on both sides of the eighty-mile long lake, you had to know where to look.

Wolverine found scattered and rotten logs strewn about the clearing. Some of the logs were half-buried in grass and peat moss, and crumbled to Wolverine's touch. He knelt near one log and looked up at the looming cliff. Its shadow covered the clearing, leaving them in shade that made the air chill. Behind him, he heard the water lap against their makeshift raft.

When Wolverine began climbing the cliff, Horse grunted with surprise. He followed Wolverine as fast as he could, but the young boy made him feel his years. By the time Horse reached the cliff opening, Wolverine was only a dim form that had vanished deep within the chasm. Horse slipped sideways and made his way along the narrow ledge beneath his feet. When he was some fifty feet in, Horse realized that the small air drafts that kept him cool came from deeper within the cliff.

His muscles cramping from the strain, Horse felt his way down the narrow tunnel and stumbled into the cave. He caught himself, and grimly noted that the cave was softly lit as in his dream and in the heirloom story passed to him by his father. Wolverine squatted near the cave's center. The boy reached into the small pile of stone shards. Wolverine cried out in astonishment as he pulled his hand from the pile. Something blue sparkled in his palm.

"What do you have?" Horse asked, hobbling towards him.

Wolverine extended his hand, palm upward. Cradled in them was a blue gem.

"It's beautiful!" Wolverine whispered. "The story is true."

Horse leaned against a cave wall. Wolverine looked around, noting how well the cave was like the story. As he turned the cold stone in his hands, he asked his grandfather, "In the story you said Mother Earth moved. How is this possible?"

"I know only that the stories are true, as true as that stone you hold in your hand. But you must leave the gem here. I have another, the first and only gem taken from here. Take this gem, and leave the one you have. The gem I have our great forefather took countless moons ago. He took it from here and promised that nothing else would be taken."

Horse extended the gem to his grandson, who took it into his small hands and carefully placed the other one back where he had found it.

"Tell me about the people who lived here."

"There is not much to tell. They lived in caves like this. No one knows what they looked like, or where they went. They were gone before the syilx came to the Valley. Many of their caves are hidden to this day. But they have power. You can feel it."

Wolverine looked around, studying the cave more closely. "Where's the air and light coming from?"

"I don't know. The people were wise, and knew how to live in ways we don't understand. What's missing here?"

Wolverine thought about the question. "If they lived here," he said, "and if there were many of them, there should be animal bones here. Signs of fire to keep them warm. Tools."

"Do you see any of those things? Any signs at all?"

"There are none."

"As I said, the people were wise."

"Then where are they?"

"Perhaps they moved south. But there are stories of them moving north and west to new lands before the great ice walls came to cover this Valley."

Wolverine held the blue gem up until it hovered between them, its deep blue surface sparkling. "And this?"

Horse felt lightheaded, and pulled his hand away from the gem. "It's yours. It has always been yours. You're the youngest syilx to visit this cave, and this gem was meant for you and your children."

"How did they know?"

"In the same way they saw the great ice coming. They knew the future as well as the past. They sent this gem from the stars." Horse felt weak. "Your time is here. Where you go, the syilx go. Leave me here for now. I must speak to the spirits here. Go below and prepare a fire for us. Look in my food bag if you become hungry."

Wolverine waited in the clearing. As night came, he prepared a fire before laying on his back to stare into the sky. Several times he stoked the fire to keep warm. Once, he watched as Sn-klip circled the fire's edge at a distance. Sn-klip paused once (a forepaw lifted) on the fire's opposite side, his red eyes staring at Wolverine. Wolverine smiled and said "Whi," before Sn-klip yipped once and went on his way.

Horse woke Wolverine an hour after sunrise. The fire was almost gone. As Wolverine rose, he heard Horse say, "I spoke with the spirits. I have a story to tell you that you must not tell to anyone except the one you give your blue gem to. Do you understand?"

"Yes. To no one."

"Here is the story."

•• • ••

The horse drums beat long into the night. Dust rose from many feet. The dust was good. The elders stared at the dust as it rose out of sight, its fine particles sometimes glowing orange and red through the firelight. On occasion, one of the elders would rise stiffly to join the dance. Years drained from them as they danced with the vigor of youth, remembrance bright in their eyes. Together with the younger ones, their heads moved with the rhythm of horses.

Horse rose last. As he moved to the center, the other dancers faded to the edge of the circle, where they formed a ring of one hundred people. They were family, and they chanted to Horse while he prepared himself.

Horse told his story, the cipcaptikwl. He spoke of his parents, and their parents. He spoke of the coming of the horse into the Valley, and of his awe. He spoke of the times he spent with his mother, the woman who taught him the ways of the people, the two-footed and four-footed, the ones who swam and the ones who flew.

Horse drew from his own past, the lonely years when he spent time searching for the wisdom to make right choices for the syilx. He spoke of the caves and isolated streams and lakes from where he stared at the night sky, its dome speckled with spirits removed from human contact. He remembered the animals who shuffled past his lean-to, their eyes momentarily pausing to study him before moving on.

"Times pass," Horse said. "Times pass, and with them go the old ways, the ways that no longer work. Once every ten generations the changes come. Ten generations ago the old ones from the tribes east and south of the Swah-netk'-qhu spoke of great winds from the east, winds filled with blood and sickness. Now those winds are here."

Horse paused to circle the fire with his eyes, staring at the members of his family and tribe. "The old ways are going, and what we do here we do for perhaps the last time in this way. We cannot turn back. Black Robes is only the first of many sha-mas. The ones who now live by the lake and who build their wood homes must be welcomed. What we do to them will be done to us by the others who follow."

"We color our past with stories. Now we must color the days

to come. The Creator will give us guidance through Wolverine."

The next day, after everyone had spoken their thoughts, the syilx agreed to have Wolverine brought up in the old ways, while learning what he could from the sha-mas and the Black Robes.

Wolverine heard this through the pain that gripped his stomach, sometimes making him double over. He tried to follow the words of his elders. He forced the pain away, gritting his teeth to keep his dreams from overwhelming him. The story his grandfather had told him after leaving the caves haunted him. The story was powerful, and he became confused about time itself. Two nights after returning from the cave, he had let the dreams in, and woke screaming from the black nightmare of spirits who mocked him, their words taunting him, teasing him about listening to old people like his grandfather.

"Their time is over," the dream spirits said. "They are old, and their ways are wrong. You must follow the words in the black book, the words in anglaise that carry the truths of the world. Forgiveness is everything. Bind yourself to the scriptures, or be damned to the hell Black Robes speaks of. Can you risk your soul on empty words? Does Horse speak for everyone, including you? Does an old man know better than you about life?"

These voices tore at Wolverine. "Horse's story, the story he told you about your people, cannot be shared with your family because his words are lies," the spirits whispered. "Lies. He wants your soul, and he will get it if you believe him."

"It's not that way," Wolverine shouted at the dream spirits. "He has shown me good things, spoken of good things. He knows things I don't know."

"Don't know. Don't know. Don't know," the spirits mocked. They knew him to be so young. They began to speak to one another, ignoring him. "So young to think he knows everything. Like his grandfather. So much pride. He thinks that what he thinks is the truth, the way others must follow. Yet he acts out of anger, fear, and hypocrisy. In telling others of the way it must be, he says all the right things, but he's wrong, for he acts out of his childhood, and thinks only of himself. He fears losing power, and of giving it to others. Power. Power. Power."

The sound of horse drums pounded into Wolverine' teeth, filling him with pain. His bright eyes stared fearfully into the fire, glittering in the shadow of his face, reddened by the sparks that flew skyward, scattering smoke to the winds.

The spirits turned to speak to Wolverine once again. "Power. Power. Power. Using the old ways, you pound messages home in the sha-ma-centerd belief that you're right, and others are wrong. Careful of using that power, young one. It always returns to its user. Always. Power creeps back in night dreams. Or it returns in the blood light of day, coloring everything until the user no longer knows himself, until power cleans the earth and returns to its uneasy and powerful rest."

Wolverine followed the dancers in the circle, the blue gem he had recently found in the cave burning against his skin. With each step he felt his power drain from him. By the end of his dance, Wolverine fought to stay on his feet, the campfire wavering before his eyes.

As the family elders sang, their clear high voices pierced Wolverine's world. His teeth hurt so badly that tears coursed down his cheeks to mingle with the dust that lay thick on Wolverine's neck. Just when he thought he could take no more, he saw the priest's pale face in the flames, and he fainted.

•• ● ••

"The people were comforted by your dance yesterday."

Wolverine nodded, afraid to speak, although he wanted to tell his father about the face that now stared at him from everywhere.

"You're afraid of the priest, aren't you?"

Wolverine nodded. He waited, but Blue Dreams stayed silent, watching the flames crackle along the wood.

"I'm afraid of Black Robe's words. He speaks of worlds beyond ours, worlds filled with fire to punish us for our sins."

Blue Dreams frowned. "You told me of these 'sins.' I don't understand what this means. It carries a strangeness that feels wrong. How can children be born into this thing he calls sin? Is their god so angry that he must punish children for what others do?"

"My grandfather asks that I learn of this world Black Robes comes from."

"I have thought about this since Horse spoke of it yesterday. Perhaps you need to speak to other sha-mas."

"The ones who have built that log kekuli by the lake?"

"Yes. They live alone, but not for long. Others are coming. The elders need to know more before deciding what to do. You're the one they've chosen for this task."

"I'm only a child."

"Wolverine, you were never a child. There's something in you that's very old, something we see only once every ten generations. Your trip with Horse to the caves gave you that stone you wear around your neck. You have been given power. As a child, you are harmless to the sha-mas. And you must learn how they think. Our people depend upon it."

"I dreamed of that power last night when I danced. It hurts."

Blue Dreams smiled and reached over to tousle Wolverine's long hair, something he seldom did. "We want you to go and learn about the sha-mas."

"Black Robes says that you and the elders are wrong to believe what you believe," Wolverine said. "He talks to us about worlds that are covered in flames. We will go there, he says, when we die, because we have sinned against their god."

"Perhaps Black Robes speaks only for a few," Blue Dreams tried to reassure his son. "The syilx need to know."

Wolverine looked into Blue Dreams' troubled eyes, and decided he wouldn't burden his father with the voices and faces that peered at him from everywhere now, voices that mocked him, faces that leered and laughed.

As a final gesture of acceptance, Wolverine clutched the blue stone. Its surface felt like ice to the touch, despite being close to his skin for so long. "I will try to learn the sha-mas' ways."

Blue Dreams heard the fear and bitterness in his son's voice, but said nothing. There was nothing he could do, and within himself he heard the keening song, the song of mourning, and he struggled to keep the song silenced, for his son needed his father to be strong. And for the first time Blue Dreams heard an inner voice that asked about the wisdom of what the syilx were about to do. A question for which he had no answer.

Storytelling: Part Two

•• ● ••

Service Berry Woman

Berry picking in July.
The stream runs by.
She is the berry woman,
the woman who faced down the grizzly,
Kee-lau-naw.
She was a girl then,
her cedar basket tied to the front of her waist
as she moved quickly along the creek,
following the women ahead.

See-yah, the service berry,
she grows best along this path
of bears, and the women
are usually careful, usually slow.

Today they are fast, and they move
as the deer moves, their talk low
and their paths the dust she breathes
and tries to please by hurrying
and not speaking.

The Woman in the Trees

She hums a song, mistress to no one.
She is young, and her ways
are young.

Her name is the name of a child.
She has already gone twice into the land
by herself, seeking the voices to guide her
for the rest of her life.

Her sister has the name given to her in a dream
and she is now different in her talk, in her manners,
in her play that no longer circles her sister.

She turns the corner
and the grizzly turns its head her way.
Ten body lengths on the other side of the bear
the women stand as stones, their mouths open;
their speaking, swallows that have spiraled skywards.

Her blood runs hot and she roars,
her voice as large as her waving arms.

The women leave the path, ghosts whose
shadows are the dry leaves. The bear rears onto its back paws
and looks down at this small person whose arms
are wider than the nearby boulders.

The girl roars again, and though the roar is young,
its spirit makes the bear's blood hot and it remembers its cubs
downstream.

Like the women, the bear is gone, its brown shadow a trundled
    nightmare
of speed along the path away from the girl.

The girl pauses at the edge of the world, at the edge of the heat
that shakes the distant land.

The world runs cold and she falls into a seated position
in dust that moves through the women who return
to the bear path.

The stories over the fire that night
give the name that the girl, the woman, now wears.

Service Berry Woman.
See-yah.

We All Have to Start Somewhere

Listen to the trees outside sway against your house. An old
woman rides those treetops, a woman older than my people, the
Okanagans (syilx or skelowh, in our language). She rides the
treetops, moving from branch to branch because she must. She
carries her children with her, and she must keep them safe.

The ground is not safe. Her people, the syilx, remained on the
ground, as a mist of white pocked their faces, burned their
lungs, and swept them into the river or hanging from tree
branches. The fur traders drifted into syilx territory before the
words bush loper were known.

Old Coyote knows the truth, but he says that he won't tell me
what that truth is.

We all have to start somewhere.

The past is the present is the future.

One time.

Winter Dance

The winter dance, it goes smooth, it goes fast. He spins around
the center pole, his dance the dance of the wolverine. Fast,

abrupt, snarling, vicious. His father Blue Dreams has told him to dance this one last time before he goes away forever from the ways of his people. It's not the same, though, for many young men are in the hills. They have chosen to hunt rather than attend the dance.

Wolverine's dance is stomped out to his wavering voice. He goes it alone, dancing until the sun has gone before he finally collapses. He is too young for the dance, but his people let him; it's the only gift they can give. More, the elders, those carriers of the past, of tradition, no longer believed completely in the old ways. Black Robes had turned some of them from their stories. Indeed, many elders were aware that Black Robes waits at the village edge to bring the children south with him to teach them the ways of the sha-ma. In the unusually warm weather, and with no snow, Horse cannot fight Black Robes' power. He tells his grandson to learn the white man's ways, and return to the syilx to relate his learnings in the cipcaptikwl.

Blue Dreams follows his son and begins his story thus.

"How long have we been here? We have been here since the first human was born. We have lived with this land and cared for it, but Coyote now tells us differently. He tells us to learn the ways of the sha-ma, the white man, before it is too late."

"We watch and we listen. Coyote is wise. We cannot fight the white man's disease. It has taken so many of us away into the next world. Once we were many, and we could have stopped the white man for a time. Enough time to keep more of our stories, more of our medicines, more of our ways. But the white fog fell on our people, and we are shadows in this world, shadows Coyote will keep alive until we can cast stronger visions once again."

"My son is going into the other world where people dig holes into Toom-Tem without thinking of making offerings. But I want him to learn their ways, their language. Other children from among you are also going with Black Robes."

"The Woman in the Trees, she who carried children under her arms, came to me in my dreams last night. She has seen Black

114

Robes, and tells me that he must have our children. They have the physical world ahead of them. She calls it dominion; dominion of this world at the cost of the other worlds."

"We do this also because the gathering of our people tells us this is the only way. People running from their past and running from their own tribes will know no boundaries in the world."

•• ● ••

She came as he stoked the fire. That morning, Horse had watched his grandson and the other children straggle from the camp, moving south a half-day's journey. Long after the children passed from view, the wails of the syilx filled the camp. The drums lamented, and only Horse's strong words kept the camp from complete despair. He reminded the people of their gatherings, of the struggles to reach the point of complete agreement.

He heard the Woman in the Trees approach in the way the pine trees stirred in the quiet. He continued stoking the fire as her warm voice broke the still air.

"Your grandson is safe, as are the other children."

As Horse completed his duties, she said to him, "Our people are so few."

"So few," Horse agreed. "But if your words are true, we are only starting a new river path to the stars."

"I once lost that voice."

"My voice?"

"No, the voice of storytelling. You have a way with words that are both you, and larger. The syilx voice. You all speak it."

"We sound alike, then?"

"There will be a time when this isn't so."

"The future you speak of, the times that are ahead of us."

"Your grandson will see those times."

For the first time, Horse looked at the woman's strong face. "Coyote has told me something of times to come. It is not my place to know such things. They do not make sense."

"You're wise in many ways."

"My wisdom is nothing in this world. It guides me down rivers full of sand."

"Sadness, yes. But I am here because of the choices you make. The sha-mas would say that your words are mystical, without practicality, without substance."

"And you say the same?"

"I say that your words are mute for many people."

Horse looked up into the cloudless sky, and held his pose for many minutes. When he turned his eyes to the fire, the Woman in the Trees was gone, her passing leaving a sense of loss. He thought on her words, reading them as he read deer signs, or as he pondered Coyote's dreams. The Woman in the Trees looked for something he couldn't give. He hadn't enough to give even his grandson, and this troubled his sleep that night as his wife nestled into him for comfort against the winds that blew in the rain and covered the stars.

Kettle Falls

In the month of chokecherries, Blue Dreams' family moved to Swah-netk'-qhu, Kettle Falls, to escape the priest. Wolverine, now thirteen, would be back at school next month, but his father wanted him to get away from Black Robes by traveling farther away than just to the foot of the Okanagan River. As they neared the falls, the sound of drums faded in and out against the torrent of water. Heat saturated the land. But as they swung around a corner along a narrow trail, the blast of cold, mist and wind struck Wolverine to the bones, sending a flood of relief through his bones as his body drank up the moisture.

Grey rocks loomed overhead. A rainbow arced over the thirty-foot falls. At this point, the sheer pressure of the entire river above the falls forced the water into a white arc that thundered into the rocks with such force that Wolverine felt the ground tremble from a distance of five hundred feet. A large rock sat in the middle of the river's path below the falls, creating a backwater of stillness. Where the water hit the bottom, and on either side of the great rock below, huge swirls of water boiled into whirlpools.

Blue Dreams moved his family to Lachin, the camp on the west side of the falls. Across from this campsite, on the other bank called Scalmachin, more families from other tribes could be seen, their men crouched on the log scaffolds that jutted into the river. These men were covered with mist that made their dark skins glisten, and they were intent on spearing fish.

Sky Woman began setting up their lodge of tule mats while Blue Dreams led his son to the edge of the river. He gave Wolverine the spear to hold and study, while he spoke with other syilx about the salmon run. Wolverine held the long wooden handle, and felt along the sharpened deer horn that formed the spearhead. Pine pitch held it in place, and the point was sharpened. A two-foot line was tied through the spearhead and attached to the wooden handle.

Wolverine's concentration was broken by his father's return. Blue Dreams pointed at the boiling water that gave the falls its name, and told him to watch. Blue Dreams then went out on one of the log scaffolds, where he braced himself by spreading his feet apart and lowering his body. He held his spear lightly in his right hand, while his left arm swung wide over his head. He watched the deep blue-green waters pouring under the scaffold. As Wolverine watched his father, he saw another man yell in triumph and begin to pull on his spear handle that bent with the weight of the salmon on the other end.

With one quick, smooth motion, Blue Dreams threw his spear down, the power of his shoulders behind the throw. The spear momentarily glistened in the sunlight before it disappeared into the river. Wolverine's gaze held as the line jerked, and the long handle began to bend with the weight of the salmon. Every muscle in his father's large arms stood out as Blue Dreams fought against the impaled salmon. At one point, the arrowhead loosened from its handle and the salmon, momentarily free, swam towards the falls. Blue Dreams yelled and leaned back as the spear handle bent. The line suddenly slackened as the salmon again let the current carry it downstream. And again it darted forward, picking up speed to hurl itself upward against the falls. The line snapped tight, and Blue Dreams braced himself by leaning back, letting the salmon's speed and weight hold him at a right angle to the ground.

The battle raged for a long time, but time was on Blue Dreams' side. In the end, he suddenly leaned down towards the water and then yanked hard on the line. The salmon spiraled into the air and landed not more than two spear lengths from where Wolverine stood. Wolverine hurried over and, dodging the salmon's flailing body, smashed the salmon's head with a heavy club, killing the fish with a single stroke.

Salmon Tyee, the divider, stood silently while Blue Dreams brought the huge salmon to the foot of the cliff, and threw it onto an already high pile of salmon caught by other syilx. As Blue Dreams turned to go, Salmon Tyee broke his silence.

"You did well, Blue Dreams. I saw you bring this salmon in. It was a good fight."

By mid-day Blue Dreams was tired, having caught six more salmon, each of which was large but not the size of the first catch of the day. Salmon Tyee called the men together and began to divide the salmon equally among them. Blue Dreams was given only three fish because some of the other syilx had not been as fortunate in their fishing. Satisfied, Blue Dreams had Wolverine carry one of the salmon, and they made their way back to where Sky Woman had a fire going. Already she had set up camp and had spent time gathering berries. Slicing up a salmon and cleaning it took minutes under her expert fingers, and she threw chunks of salmon into the mixture of boiling water and berries.

"How were the salmon?" she asked Wolverine.

"Plentiful. Their skins are thick this year."

Wolverine's mother nodded. Wolverine knew the next winter would be long and cold. The more dried salmon they could take with them, the better to survive the next few months.

Later, after a meal of boiled berries and salmon, Blue Dreams was back at the falls, where he managed to catch eight more salmon before he became too weary to continue. Salmon Tyee took the fish from Blue Dreams, who was too tired to speak or even to accept his share, which Salmon Tyee promised would be delivered to Blue Dreams' lodge.

Early the following morning, Blue Dreams left camp with several other hunters. They were gone most of the day, returning after bringing down two deer. Wolverine played by the falls with other youth of his age, running perilously close to the edge of the river bank and then scrambling up the steep cliff to the top of the falls. He was of the age where competition was fierce with the ferocity of boys coming of age. Yet it was also one of the rare times when Wolverine enjoyed the company of others, and he threw himself wholeheartedly into participating, hiding when hiding was required, running whenever he could, and dashing into the mists that roiled from the falls. The shouts of rough play were dim against the roar of the falls that filled the world as Coyote had said it would when he created them from the back of a huge fish, which he then banished to the great waters far to the west of where the syilx now camped.

As Wolverine played, he noticed his mother gathering shale from the cliff. She shaped these into scrapers with handles half of her own body length, fastening the fan-shaped rock with buckskin to the wood handle. When Blue Dreams and the other hunters brought the deer back, the hides were quickly immersed in water and held down by rocks. After the third day, when the hair was loose, firewood was heaped into two fire pits on either side of a wood frame where the hide was stretched, scraped, and dried. The work was hard, but the women enjoyed it, talking among themselves as they worked on each deer hide.

The first night of tanning hides, the men gathered around a

roaring fire that sent sparks high into the clear warm night air to mingle with the stars overhead. Blue Dreams began with a song for the salmon taken over the past week, and the other syilx joined in, their voices echoing against the cliffs above them.

Coyote Must Speak

"Where do we start?"

Coyote blinks. "Start anywhere. It's all the same story. The past is the present is the future."

"But people like linear stories — a beginning and an end."

"I was at the beginning, and no one knows the end." Coyote blinks again. "It's actually quite funny, the beginning. I could tell you fifty stories about the beginning, but it's only one story at the end."

"So you're telling me to start anywhere?"

"No, I'm telling you to start where you want to start. The others who tell the story will start from other places, other truths. It's the same story."

"So, in 1811 when David Stuart first moved up the Okanagan Lake . . ."

"No, no, no, no! Put some passion into it. Blood and guts. Let the characters change when they want to change."

"But that'll just confuse people. They won't read it."

"Some people won't read it. Lots of people won't read it. But throw everything into it. Give it lots of humor. I like that."

The room shifts hot and cold as he trots in. People gasp or try to ignore him; either way they move away. A few brave people approach, but he has his own hurricane eyes — fast moving, rotating, spinning, blowing east and west.

Ranchers take pot shots at his running form. He stops in the middle of fields to see who's shooting at him. Ears prick up and he shifts left, then right, then sits on his haunches and scratches for fleas. The curses are always the same. He was here before them, so he doesn't move unless he wants to move. He knows what happened when his people, the syilx, did move, and kept moving, first out of courtesy and welcome, then through necessity and force.

In the winter, he hunches down in his den, sometimes venturing out for food, and always trying to keep warm. He tells his children stories of the sha-mas, how they treat him like dirt or, in their words, like scavengers. He tells his children that they're a lot like him when it comes to scavenging. Then he laughs and tells them not to take the sha-mas seriously, because they do enough of that themselves.

He grins whenever he can, or sways left to see what people do. He's strong, a glint in his eyes saying "I've been there with your great grandmother and I know your great grandsons." He listens only when he wants to listen.

When he shape-shifted one time into a syilx, a sha-ma interviewed him about SPIRITUALITY. Sn-klip says this in a whisper, then giggles. SPIRITUALITY. The magic of words. Sn-klip describes the electronic machine that recorded the words he spoke. Once he got the hang of it, he made sure the machine recorded only what he wanted it to hear. All the time, the young sha-ma student sat across the desk from him, making notes, thinking of answers before Sn-klip could say the words the sha-ma wanted him to say.

The sha-ma was looking for answers, maybe even for THE ANSWER. Of course Sn-klip wouldn't oblige. No one was ready for THE ANSWER, but it was fun giving small answers that Sn-klip put little spins on, lobbing them at the machine that whirred and ticked, sometimes as if in amazement. The sha-ma couldn't even understand his own machine, or that it was speaking constantly at him. No one, this way, would get anywhere close to THE ANSWER. Sn-klip giggled when he thought of this. The sha-ma looked up from his notes, frowned, then began writing again, missing the point entirely, and missing Sn-klip's wide grin.

The Okanagans crowd the campsites to hear his stories. He created the world, or says he did, that is the same thing by now. No one touches his soul, and his price is the odd chicken.

The syilx watch his every gesture, mimic his pauses in their own re-tellings. The perked ears, the wide grin, the sneer, the laughter that raises neck hair, the stooped gait that breaks into a four-legged trot.

Through it all, old Sn-klip watches, always watches, sometime face on, sometimes from the corner of one eye as he weaves his stories. Stories that change, circle the audience, prodding here, snifflng there, twirling two-steps, round dances, grass songs, buffalo shuffles, three-chord disco chaos.

The story.

The story.

The story.

"Do things happen in threes, or fours?" Coyote asks his audience. Sometimes they say three, sometimes four, and once, someone, a kid, yelled "Seven" to wild laughter that Sn-klip made as large as the world.

Coyote says, "There are fifty ways to tell the beginning of everything, but only one ending. I was there when my people saw the first horse. I know because it was I who chased the horse from his hiding place."

They say, "Tell us your way."

He says, "My way has no straight path to anywhere. No easy river sand to throw into the wind."

They say, "Tell us of the world."

He says, "I will tell you a story or two about the syilx and the sha-mas."

They say, "When?"

He says, ""I have been telling it for two hundred years. No

one but the syilx listen. The others, the sha-mas, spin their own stories about us, and believe them."

•• ● ••

Low to the ground, four-paw all-season traction. He skids on ice and jumps around like pink feet on a hot tin plate. A tail to die for. Eyes the color of stars. A laugh that won't go away. Big ears that hear everything. A nose for trouble.

When he snags, he does it with style, dressed in shape-shifting clothes from Armani, slacks straight out of Friends, a look he knows will come back. The shirt, purple royalty, made of silk from the upper reaches of the Yangtze River, from worms fed on the finest mulberry leaves, gotten in trade with an eleventh-generation silkworm merchant who told Sn-klip to be careful who he shook paws with. Sn-klip's first snag taught him what the silk trader had warned him about.

She was slinky, short, with attitude he felt a mile away. In his purple royalty he went to shake hands with her, his name card in readiness. The hot dry breeze billowed his shirt and sent a spark leaping in the dusk light, jumping from his hand to hers in a crackle that lit her eyes, made her gasp, and straightened her spine. The way her eyes glinted at him as she never missed a beat in shaking his hand and palming his card; the way she moved in those high heels as though she were working in hay fields with feet close to Toom-Tem, Mother Earth; the way her arms moved with generations of treating hides and gathering berries; Old Coyote was lost the moment she turned her radiance to him. Her name was Mole.

Mole dressed to the nines, ready to move into the honky-tonk bar to do justice to the Red River jig taught to her by her grandfather. The way the cowboy hats moved aside for her as she led Old Coyote to the dance floor, two Indians in a bar the other side of the tracks from Indian country.

And they danced, sometimes slow, the sway and sound of Irish

Creek in their rhythm, sometimes blurred, the Six Mile stomp in every step, sometimes close, Polson Park spring camp in the looks they gave the cowboy hats.

That's how the stories started.

Old Coyote has seen it all. He's seen the skeptics, the believers, the ones who don't understand. He's heard them say, "It's just a dirty no-account Kie-Ute" like he was the bottom of a toilet. His own people keep their distance, for there's nothing he won't do to have them listen.

Mole keeps him busy these days. Fox, his brother, drops by sometimes to remind him of who really runs the family. But old Coyote forgets it the moment Fox leaves or puts down the phone.

The skeptics don't believe in animal spirits. Animals are dumb beasts. It's easier to kill them that way, have dominion over them. When Coyote watches frustrated ranchers and others taking pot shots at him, he's trying to tell them this. But they don't hear. Or they won't listen. Coyote isn't certain why that is.

It starts at the Big Bang, the Steady State Universe, the Quiet Whisper, all the names for when it started. He'll be there for the One Ending, and he'll be the one arguing for a New Start, because he does, after all, need his audience.

At the beginning, there was only water, Coyote, and the Great Spirit. Okay, so maybe things do happen in threes. Coyote wanted things different. He wanted the sun's name, then the moon's, then grizzly bear's syilx name (Kee-lau-naw), and, finally, even Fox's name. But the day the Great Spirit handed out names, Coyote slept in. By the time he showed up, everyone else had left with their own names, and the only two names left were

Sweat House and Coyote. Even Coyote saw the inevitable, and chose Sweat House. At that moment, the Great Spirit for the first time in eternity cracked up and laughed until She cried.

"Your name will be Sn-klip, and your gift to the world shall be laughter. You will teach all of my people what not to do. You will do this by being who you are, the one who breaks all the rules."

He's rude, he's crude, he's a joker. He mocks and he questions. He shuffles left when you turn right. He jumps when you run. You can't pin him down, but he becomes the center of his own mind. Nothing you can do about it except listen and put him back together when he falls apart, as he does so often.

His name is Sn-klip, and in one way, he is the story that follows, and every story that's told.

The Sha-mas

Three months after his last trip to Swah-netk'-qhu, each day at ten, before his Latin lessons, Wolverine sweeps the church. The whispers of the other syilx boys and girls are troubled. The spirits that they lived with cannot enter the House of God, nor are they welcome. The priest has withheld food from them when they speak their own language or tell their own stories. He has made them bow at the altar and genuflect before praying.

The language Black Robes speaks is rapid, hasty, challenging, centerd around the person speaking rather than the message being spoken. It cuts clean lines into the world, breaking things apart, stirring and shaking the land. Its power is terrifying in the way it is spoken from the book the priest calls the Bible. It tells things without showing.

The syilx who spend their winter months here feel the absence of the Winter Dance, the stories of their families, some of which could only be told at this time of year. They miss the laughter around Sn-klip's bold forays into bravery shading into foolishness. They miss the tug of the deer hide flaps in their winter homes, the crispness of their voices frosting through the snow-covered landscapes. They miss the soothing syilx tongue that thinks carefully and circles the world in speaking, making them part of everything around them.

The priest knows them well, and studies each one, probing, questioning, speaking, until the syilx tongue lapses increasingly into the language of the Bible. The children find themselves cutting clean lines into the world, breaking things apart, stirring and shaking the land. Their voices speak faster, and the word "I" centers them in the language.

•• • ••

The Holy Ghost casts its shadow over Wolverine. He hears it in the darkness of the sleeping room he shares with several other boys. He hears it when he pauses in the potato fields in the hot afternoon sun. He touches it in the stream as he bathes. The pine trees sing the spirit to him as he walks through the nearby forests that circle the small church. The spirit resonates in him, and draws agony with every breath.

Wolverine tosses at night, his dreams full of charred villages and kekulis shrouded in fog. His language floats into the background of his everyday life — the priest's English leaving no room for other ways of dreaming.

Each summer is a lifeline to his home life, when he tries to hide the pain from his family because he knows they also hurt, and that his people need to understand the sha-mas through his words and thoughts. He sees his father hide the pain through forced play and laughter, and the hesitation of his mother as she tries to comfort him, but not knowing how.

He watches other children sink into the other world, their spirits changing with each year, their words faster than his, although he knows he can speak that strange language twice as fast as any syilx. English turns him inwards, beating against his spirit in endless waves. His lifeline is in his memories, and his memories burn into him, hold him up against the heavy spirit of Christianity and English. He knows that the priest thinks in straight lines, cannot cross the circle or wait for the end.

Time is measured in a way that changes the land itself, measuring it in the rise and fall of each and every sunrise, regardless of weather or animal spirit behaviour or texture of the soil.

The priest challenges Wolverine.

"Your words are dust in the eyes of God. You must speak English and Latin, the words of the Book itself. How will you know God otherwise? Are you listening?"

Wolverine learns how to use his body and face to express the interest the priest seeks, although that syilx part of him draws a bear path to fend off the priest's caustic language. It would have been otherwise — Wolverine would have been like the other children, sinking out of sight — were it not that the priest delights in making him the object of many of his lessons. In converting the other children, the priest holds Wolverine in the syilx world without realizing it.

The others listen from the row of benches as the priest talks at them through Wolverine. "The Holy Spirit is the messenger of God. The Holy Trinity is the sign of God, and the Bible is the Word of God. Everywhere you go, the Holy Spirit fills the land."

Wolverine sits beside the other syilx children, his mind at Swah-netk'-qhu in the month of salmon fishing, the roar of the water separating him from the spirits that moved around the priest, so close to his physical body. He hears the stories of Sn-klip as the priest spins the story of Joseph and his brothers. The two become one, and Joseph lifts his head in those hot nights to listen to the strange keening of a dog he has never heard before.

Wolverine misses the jumps that Sn-klip's stories make, the way his own mind stretched trying to follow those jumps. The Bible doesn't jump. Its stories follow a single path, ever inwards to the Trinity the priest speaks of at every chance. The language is strong, creating power that cleaves the syilx world just as an untended fire fades from red into darkness, spitting odd sparks ever less frequently.

The other children now laugh at Wolverine, along with the priest. His short, stout body intimidates them, but they lash out at his spirit which weaves and sways like a pine tree in the wind, stirring but ever-rooted to a single spot.

Eventually the priest understands what Wolverine is doing, but he has won the other children, and leaves Wolverine as the target that distracts them from what the priest wants: their souls. He is also careful to keep Wolverine's temper at bay. He has watched the power of Wolverine in drawing the other children to him in the first years of coming to the Church to work, get schooling, and praying. He wants none of the children to emulate the defiance found in Wolverine's obstinate spirit. That he has the other children becomes clearer with each passing month. The priest is satisfied, and spends his energies tightening his hold on the Indian children in his care, one watchful eye always on Wolverine, keeping him at bay, ridiculing him in small ways while being careful not to drive the other children away.

At sixteen, Wolverine stands in the church in his school clothes. The priest speaks his sermon and the altar boys recite their Latin words back to the priest. Their inflections are impeccable, their genuflections synchronized. Wolverine knows his father waits outside, waits with the rest of his family. Horse will be there, as will everyone Wolverine grew up with.

The clean smell of wood and soap whooshes through the church. On the left side of the church, an open window, brought at great expense from Fort Okanagan, lets air into the warm interior. The priest's voice drones to the sparse congregation of eight, but that is a quarter of the population, so the priest doesn't complain. The clapboard floors creak whenever someone chooses to shift their position on the uncomfortable benches, or when they stiffly stand up after kneeling for portions of the mass.

The priest has many times explained the English translations of the Latin mass, but Wolverine finds it pleasant to respond to the sound of the spoken words rather than to their meanings, some of which he still only understands in vague terms. The body and blood of Christ being consumed in this ceremony at first made him queasy. No syilx would think of such a thing, eating another human being. The priest's explanations still make no sense to Wolverine, but he has learned that continual questioning angers the priest, who takes it as an affront to Christianity rather than as a quest to understand.

The sermon is short. The priest is nervous, and his quick gestures tell Wolverine that the priest knows who waits outside. The priest is like this every spring. Wolverine understands now that the priest fears losing the other children, now young adults, to the syilx way each summer. He also knows that the priest no longer has to worry about most of the syilx under his tutelage; they are his.

A wasp spirals in quick loops over the congregation, sometimes buzzing around a boy or girl, and sometimes banging in rapid succession against the window on the right side of the church, like the tapping of a cane on the floor.

The congregation launches into a quavering attempt to sing a psalm. Harmony is mixed into the singular voices of eight rough, untrained voices, some low, some high, some squeaky, some bass. The wasp continues to spiral around the small church, once threatening to attack a small girl who swats at it several times before it hurls itself against the window pane. Why doesn't it find the open window, Wolverine wonders? What keeps it in here for hours, banging into glass endlessly like water hitting against a rock?

The song and the mass end, and the priest, knowing of

Wolverine's excitement, holds him back to clean the small altar. The priest calls it spiritual cleansing. Wolverine watches as the congregation follows the priest out the front door into the bright sunlight. The priest stops at one side of the entrance to greet his parishioners as they shuffle out.

Wolverine cradles the chalice in his stocky hands. The gold sheen of the cup colors his palm a lighter color. He uses a bucket of water next to the altar to wash the chalice and the gold plate. This draws the wasp, which circles the water, its wings an angry buzz. Wolverine carefully places the chalice and plate upside down, on the cloth that drapes the top of the flat altar box. The wasp makes a quick dive to Wolverine's hand, and then there is the tap of it once again striking against the window pane ten feet away. Wolverine feels anger well up, and then he is looking at the wasp crushed against the window. His right hand swells with the sting.

Wolverine changes clothes and proudly straightens them before he steps out onto the front porch. His hand throbs, but he carefully keeps it low and turned away from the family who waits. His short, stocky frame draws the syilx's attention at the same moment as he sees them.

They see.

A short man in clothes that are too small for his body, and too tight for hunting or gathering. His hair is cut short. The pallor of his skin says that he has not been out in the sun for a long while. The sound of his feet draw their eyes to shoes that are not made of deerskin, but of cowhide. One hand is hidden behind his back.

He sees.

A group of Indians dressed in clothes that he can smell from where he stands. Animal clothes. Long hair that is dressed in bear grease. Dark skin that wrinkles as they frown.

For ten heartbeats, no one moves. Then, as laughter begins to ripple through the family, Blue Dreams steps forward to greet his son.

Wolverine holds his breath as his father hugs him. His father's odors almost overwhelm Wolverine, who finally gasps and pulls back. His father sees his son's expression, but before either can respond further, the rest of the family sweep Wolverine into their midst.

•• • ••

Blue Dreams listened as his son spun his stories of the years past. On his other visits Blue Dreams felt uncomfortable under the watchful eyes of Black Robes. Now he felt uncomfortable at the rapid pace of his son's words. Several times he asked his son to slow down, to think of what he spoke. Each time, his son had started slowly and then his words had multiplied to a speed that made Blue Dreams' head hurt.

At one point, Blue Dreams spoke of Wolverine's future wife, one chosen by Blue Dreams from a southern syilx family. Service Berry Woman was famous among the syilx for an incident involving a bear. But Wolverine didn't seem to hear Blue Dreams that night, so Blue Dreams took to listening to his son. Sky Woman had treated the wasp sting with a small poultice of leaves and grass, ignoring her son's weak protests.

Horse had left the two alone some time ago. The fire was dying down when Blue Dreams stopped his son in the middle of talking.

"I would like to hear more from you. But I am tired and so must you be. Leave the fire. It will last for the night."

Under his deer blanket, Blue Dreams could not sleep. His son's words wove their staccato beat into his thoughts. His wife stirred beside him, but her sleep was deep and untroubled. His son's words were both strange, and discomforting. Earlier, when the entire village circled the fire, Wolverine spoke of the white man, the sha-ma, of how many lived in the direction of the rising sun — so many that they were like the ants in the fields. He spoke of the Indians, the word given to the sylix and all others who lived on the land before the sha-mas were here. He spoke of how many had tried to stop the sha-mas' endless migrations, and of how now so many of them were gone from the face of Toom-Tem, leaving behind burnt-out villages or villages wasted by illness. There was no stopping them, no halting of the tide of people coming into the Valley.

Horse then spoke of how once his people were ten times what they were now. Of how syilx filled the Valley floors and the mountains. Of how great they had been. He spoke of the white fog he had seen in his youth, of the village filled with the rotting corpses of syilx who died in horrible pain. He spoke of the syilx who lay face down in the water, drowning themselves to cool the fire in their blood.

Wolverine spoke of the British, of those who traded for furs. And through it all, the syilx in the village listened to the sound of the fire burning their world away. Blue Dreams saw it, as did Horse, but they could do nothing. The words, faster than any syilx had spoken before, ripped the curtains away from their security, striking at their ears with an unseen terror, which Wolverine sowed without understanding, without knowing.

Now, as Blue Dreams lay awake, he thought of his son, and wondered how he could have sent him to the sha-mas, and thereby lose him. His son was more than syilx, and less than. He moved and spoke in the ways Black Robes had taught him. Black Robes had once talked of leaving, but the need to mold the Indian boys had kept him in the Valley. Now Wolverine and the others spread their stories through many camps. He wondered how Wolverine's future wife would live in the world in which Wolverine now moved.

The syilx could not go back. But they would not be the same. Ever.

●●●●●

In the way of the syilx, Wolverine at twenty-one was shorter then than he was before the story, and taller than he was after the story. Coyote doesn't explain this because it isn't important to the story, and what isn't important can be changed any time.

Wolverine also walked with a limp gotten from the time two years before when he had been thrown from his horse. This was important, for his wife often laughed at him. Wolverine tried to ignore her laugh, for he loved her very much. Service Berry Woman was quick, tall, and her brown eyes sparkled when she talked. His people said that she had spirit.

When Wolverine had returned to the syilx from Black Robes' school, his parents planned the marriage to Service Berry Woman. The syilx who lived in the village near the confluence of the Okanagan River and the Swah-netk'-qhu, the Columbia River, thought this marriage to one of their daughters would hasten Wolverine's spiritual return to the syilx ways rather than have him continue being the strange person he had become. Service Berry Woman, chaperoned by her older sister, had met her betrothed a year after his return. Wolverine had stammered, his poise withering before her physical beauty, and Service Berry Woman had looked at him, scorn in her gaze.

That scorn increased when, on their wedding night, Wolverine had seen her naked form and come too soon, his seed spilling before he could enter her. Service Berry Woman slept with her back to him on that night, and every night since.

Wolverine sometimes crouched by the fire and watched as she made deer leggings, or stirred the mix of berries in preparation for winter. Service Berry Woman brushed her long hair and pulled it up on each side of her head without pausing in what she did. Her long, slim fingers surprised Wolverine, for although his wife worked as hard as any other woman in the camp, her fingers, like her arms and legs, stayed slim, light, smooth. She often hummed as she worked, although she never put words to her songs. Her singing was something Wolverine looked forward to when he returned from his hunts. Wolverine was happy, but he sometimes worried about his wife's beauty. She stirred dark feelings of anger in him when she would look at others the way she often looked at him, her slightly mocking grin piercing him like the winter winds.

Wolverine's hunting was methodical, for his short legs made him cautious and careful. He couldn't run as fast or as long as some of his younger cousins, but he always succeeded in tracking something down, relying greatly on his keen smell to make up for his poor eyesight. This, too, he did because he had promised himself that never would he return home empty-handed and without food for his wife. He promised himself that he would be a good provider, whatever sexual shortcomings his wife attributed to him since that disastrous wedding night.

Sometimes Service Berry Woman told him stories, and laughed in the end, waiting for him to understand what she had said. Sometimes he couldn't see the story the way she could and he turned red as her laughter filled their home. His brother told him to be patient, for she was a gift, something the family had not seen in generations.

Still, it was hard.

In the early winter in the third year of their marriage, Wolverine spent two weeks in the hills, tracking a four-point buck he had tried to catch the previous spring. He had time to worry about his wife. Lately she had taken to leaving their home for long periods of time, returning at night with a glow in her face she only got when they made love together. And she had stopped singing to her husband, even though she seemed happier than she had ever been before. Wolverine's brother said that she was in love with someone else, but when Wolverine pressed him for more details he had to admit that he had none to tell.

So it was that Wolverine returned with the four-point buck given to him by the spirit world. As he neared the camp he almost ran into his brother, who was crouched behind a bush and watching the nearby lake. Wolverine was about to greet his brother and invite him for a feast when his brother waved at him to crouch down. Wolverine, puzzled, did as his brother asked, and then he heard the singing. Almost invisible against the lake was his wife, seated on the sand and running her hands gently along the surface of the water.

There was something different this time, and it took Wolverine some moments to understand what it was. Service Berry Woman was singing and there were words to her song. Against his brother's wishes, he was about to stand when a form appeared on the lake. It moved quickly and soundlessly forward. As it drew near the shoreline, Wolverine recognized the shape of a canoe. Three people sat in it, two women and a man whose red hair marked him as a bush loper, a fur trader.

The man was tall, his long red hair glinting in the sun and his skin as dark as any syilx from the long years outdoors. He jumped from the canoe as it touched the beach and then Wolverine's wife was in his arms. For long moments they kissed. As rage tore at Wolverine, the young trader was back in the canoe with Wolverine's wife happily in his strong arms. The two other women pushed off from shore, and then the canoe was gone as quickly as it had come, gliding into the night.

Two nights later, Wolverine woke up in the middle of the night to find his wife lying beside him, her tall frame cold from wherever she had been. As she felt him stir, Service Berry Woman whispered into Wolverine's ear, "My husband is strong. I heard that you caught your deer."

Heart-broken but strong, Wolverine swallowed hard before he spoke. "My wife wasn't home when I returned."

She laughed softly into his ear. "Of course not, silly. I went to my mother's camp down the valley. I became lonely and needed company."

In the next few days, Wolverine's wife seemed to be in another world. She hummed continually now, and her appetite shrank as her body grew thinner. Wolverine's brother told him to wait, for she would come back to him because she loved him very much. It hurt to say this, for in his heart Wolverine's brother knew this not to be true.

The next week, as the two brothers returned from a hunting trip. Wolverine hurried to his lodge. As he neared his home, he called out to Service Berry Woman. There was no answer. Entering the lodge, Wolverine noticed first how cold it was; the ashes in the middle of the floor told him that the fire had gone out some time ago. And his wife's favorite sleeping robe was gone, together with some other articles of clothing. Wolverine sat down on the ashes and wept, pain filling his world, pain and something darker than the pain, something that in other times would have frightened him.

Wolverine's whole family tried to comfort him in the next few days, but Wolverine felt his spirit shrink into a cold, hard circle of rage and grief. He took to walking along the shoreline of the lake. And one day, as he watched from the shoreline, the bush loper's canoe streaked through the water, driven by the paddles of the two women who were with him on that first awful night when Wolverine lost his world.

Wolverine hid before they saw him, and his brother was suddenly at his side. They watched as the two women beached their canoe and moved quickly up the shore into Wolverine's lodge.

Wolverine wanted to attack then and there, but his brother held him back until the two women crept silently out of the lodge, their arms full with dried meat and some of the belongings of his wife. Wolverine stopped the two women as they neared their canoe.

"Where is my wife? What has he done with her?"

The two women laughed at the short man, mistaking his small size for his strength. They said nothing until Wolverine pulled his hunting knife out and they saw the glint of moonlight on flint. Frightened for the first time, the younger of the two sisters said, "It will do you no good, so I will tell you. Your former wife now lives at the Fort three days travel south of us. My brother lives beside the Fort and he fears no one, and not someone of your size."

The small dark center at the core of Wolverine's heart took over. When he recovered his senses, the two women lay on the beach, their still forms filled with death's shadow.

As angered as Wolverine was, he knew better than to leave the two dead women unburied for their souls to take revenge, so he and his brother spent the rest of the night ensuring that they were properly buried under a shale rockslide farther into the hills. As daylight came, they took their leave from the camp and set out in the women's canoe. They also donned the two women's long robes, whose hoods hid their faces in shadow.

"Let me do the speaking," Wolverine's brother said as they traveled. "The sha-mas live in a strange place, and they live differently than us. I have been there before so I am somewhat more prepared than you are." Wolverine readily agreed, for all he wanted was the return of his wife. "Keep to the shadows as well, for you are not as tall as the woman whose clothes you wear."

As they neared Fort Okanagan, Wolverine could smell the sha-ma world from some distance away. The Fort was more trading post than military site, and the two brothers immediately recognized their cousin Two Moles who had come down to the Fort with her husband in the late fall to do some trading.

Two Moles waved them in and then laughed as Wolverine almost fell flat into the river, barely catching himself in time. Wolverine's brother secured the canoe as Two Moles giggled and swept around Wolverine in a giddy dance that spun her face-to-face with Wolverine. "Cousin Wolverine, you almost fell into the river. Splash, and then you would have been in some trouble."

A nearby group of fur traders overheard Two Moles. "What did you say?" one of them yelled at her.

Two Moles, realizing her mistake, denied she had said anything, but one of the men persisted. "You said that Wolverine almost fell into the river."

"I did not," Two Moles insisted. "I said to watch out and don't fall into the river."

"Ah, leave her alone," another fur trader said. "You know how she goes on. Can't trust a word she says, not to mention what a thief she is. She's into everything."

"That's true," another trader said. "Last week I caught her trying to steal my cooking kettle. Beat her to within an inch of her life, but it doesn't stop her. Let's go get something to drink."

The men disappeared while the three cousins unloaded the canoe of trading goods, including packs of dried meats and berries, favorites of the fur traders on their trips. The two brothers had further darkened their faces with an ochre that made them more unrecognizable. They made their way with Two Mole's help to the lodge of the fur trader who had taken Wolverine's wife. Inside the small log cabin, Two Moles introduced the two brothers as her cousins from the Swah-netk'-qhu.

The trader was drunk, and grunted as he paid attention only to his beautiful captive. Service Berry Woman hummed as she began to eat her first real meal in several days, all but ignoring the two forms that had seated themselves in a shadowed corner of the single room.

The trader and Service Berry Woman soon fell asleep, and Wolverine and his brother came out of hiding. Wolverine moved quickly and with two long, deep cuts took the trader's head off. As he did this, his brother threw Wolverine's wife over his shoulder and made a dash for the canoe. Wolverine was not far behind. They were almost at the canoe when several traders by a fire pit saw them and sounded the alarm. Wolverine clambered into the canoe. With a single, great push from his short but strong legs, the canoe shot far out into the water. The two brothers began to paddle, knowing that no one would be able to give chase in the dark. Once they were well away from the Fort, Wolverine took the trader's head and asked the waters of the river to accept it and clean its spirits. He then swung the head in an arc backward, then forward. When he let go, the head sailed into darkness.

Wolverine's wife soon settled back into her own life, thinking of the trader as she would a dream. But since that time, the syilx and the sha-mas have always stayed apart in their own villages, fearful of one another and the spirits that were let loose in those times.

And the years passed. When Service Berry Woman felt ready, she walked into the woods. She built a small platform in a large tree above the reach of any wandering scavenger, and laid down for the final time in her life. Alone, she sang her spirit song, the song of the bear she had faced down so many years before. When the final dream time came, she saw the bush loper's face. She smiled as she drifted into final sleep, her right hand clutching a strand of red hair that she had hidden throughout her marriage. They found her body three days later.

When they led the white-haired Wolverine to her body, he saw the glint of red in his wife's hand. A dull ache filled his heart where once a love had burned. He stared at the smiling face one final time, then turned his back forever on her and on the syilx.

Ivan Patriloney reined his horses in. He blinked, but the fence line ahead remained broken along a thirty-yard stretch. A tuft of horse hair wavered in the breeze.

"Damn horses," Ivan muttered under his breath. "Goddamn horses!"

Ivan swung down from the buggy, being careful of his bum knee. Even so, he winced when his left foot reached the dirt road. Should have listened to Pa, he thought. The old man was right.

Ranching was goddamn hard work. Especially when it came to horses. The damn animals were near to uncontrollable, what with that rogue roan no one had managed to break.

As Ivan limped forward past his two buggy horses, the lead horse pricked its ears forward and stomped the ground. Ivan felt its hot breath along the nape of his neck. "I didn't mean you," he said. "Ain't no call to get riled up like that. I ain't after your hide."

Ivan plodded on towards the broken fence. Dust rose with each short step. Ivan paused halfway, taking the time to study the lay of the land. Moist hoof-prints still marked the spot where the horses had milled about before breaking through. Judging by the signs, Ivan figured they couldn't have gotten far, maybe half an hour in this heat.

Ivan shaded his eyes from the sun and scanned the hillsides. In the distance he saw smoke from the new homesteader's place. A rise in the slope hid the cabin from Ivan's eyes, but he heard the steady thunk of an axe and knew that his new neighbor was clearing land. Maybe later he'd drop by, but right now he had to track down his horses.

Hoof-prints led away from the broken fence line. The prints ran some hundred yards along the flat surface and then veered sharply right to run parallel to the fence, heading west into the low hills.

"Damn horses getting smarter every year." But Ivan knew where they were headed. He smiled. They might be smart, but they couldn't fool him.

Ivan rode the buckboard the two miles to his small house. A hundred yards from the house, the steel-blue lake shimmered. Heat waves bent the opposite hills into twisted brown and dark green shapes.

Ivan unhitched the horses and led them to their stables in the cool barn. Not for the first time did he thank his father for building the barn next to the creek where it was shaded by thick clumps of fir trees. Ivan gave each horse its allotment of hay and filled the water troughs. He then wiped the buckboard seats before making his way into his home.

Adriana kissed him as he walked into the house. He looked down at her and pulled her closer, wondering at the worry lines that creased her otherwise smooth face.

"Is it that obvious?" Adriana laughed.

Ivan combed a strand of hair away from her eyes. "Is he acting up again?"

"He scares me when he goes off like that."

"It's his people. He misses them."

"Then why doesn't he go back to them?"

Ivan kissed her, then pulled away. "He only likes to visits them. Goddamn, it's hot in here."

"It's hot everywhere. I couldn't tend the garden anymore. I sent Cathy to play along the creek where it's cooler."

"How's my little bear doing today?"

"She bawled me out for not waking her in time to go to town with you."

Ivan sat down at the small table where the family ate their meals. "The new railroad line is running down the valley on time. They say it'll be finished within a month."

"That railroad will change everything."

"It already has. On my way back, I saw at least three more new stakes."

Adriana wiped a bead of perspiration from her face. "More people is nice. But the Indians, what will they think of so many white people?"

Ivan shrugged. "There's not a whole lot they can do. A lot of them are sick. I hear four more died last weekend."

Adriana's face looked pained. "So many. I lie awake at nights sometimes, thinking of the mothers who can't do anything about it. Ivan, we brought our sicknesses with us."

"Can't blame us. None of us knew better. Besides, the priests were the first here. Seems to me it all started with them."

"Ivan! Don't even think that! Father Tomlinson is such a nice man."

"To us he's nice. I don't think he's so nice to the Indians."

"He's doing his job. The Indians here aren't even Christians."

"Seems to me there's a lot of people in this world ain't Christian."

Adriana sighed. "No use arguing. We've already talked about this."

"Yes, we have. The Indians have their priest to look after them. None of our business, really. Let's get down to the creek. This damn heat is killing me."

As they neared the creek, they heard their daughter's cries of joy fill the clearing, and then a small body hurled itself at them from its resting spot on a large flat rock that angled into the creek. "Daddy! Daddy! You're home!"

Ivan caught his daughter as she jumped up at him. Adriana had tied Cathy's dark hair into two ponytails to keep it out of harm's way. Ivan spun his daughter around, tossing her into the air to catch her. Cathy quickly wrapped her arms around her father's bull neck. Then she twisted out of his arms and bolted to the creek, where she plunged in up to her knees. "It's so cold!" Cathy squealed in delight. She splashed around while her parents settled down on the banks.

"The horses got out again."

"The roan?"

"Damn horse has a mind like a man's."

"When are you going?"

"Later this afternoon, before it cools down. The horses will be trying to stay out of the sun, and I know where they are."

"Wolverine said he saw a large brown bear up in the hills yesterday. Be careful."

"Is Wolverine coming back?"

Adriana nodded. "He said he'd be back by mid-afternoon."

"Good. He can help me track the horses down."

"I worry about him."

"Don't. He's got family. I'm sure that's where he's gone today."

Cathy returned. "Daddy, where does this creek come from?"

Ivan smiled at his wife. "Darling, it comes from those hills you see northeast of us."

Cathy turned to follow his pointing finger. "How far, Daddy?"

"Miles. You can't see most of it for the hills, but there's an underground lake somewhere up there."

Cathy frowned. "An underground lake? How can a lake be underground?"

"No one knows how, dear. But some say that the Okanagan Lake has many hidden tunnels leading into the hills around it."

"Will the lake ever dry up? It's so hot!"

Ivan laughed. "No, not in our lifetimes. That lake is here to stay."

"I'm glad!"

Cathy hesitated. Ivan saw his daughter pause and asked, "What is it?"

"Can you read to me again? That story about the woman with snakes in her hair?"

"That's a little scary, don't you think?"

Cathy shivered, her black eyes widening. "Yes, it's scary, isn't it, Daddy?"

Ivan let out a whoop, but the roan twisted away and ran down the slope, the rest of the horses trailing behind. Ivan swore and kicked his horse into a run. Down the slope they went. Ivan felt vertigo take hold as he gave his horse free rein to follow the thundering herd below them. He barely saw the small creek; his eyes darted along the slippery slopes. He had to trust his horse, but it took all he had not to grab control through the reins.

The roan looked up at horse and rider. It tossed its head in challenge and veered, plunging down the slope and crossing the small stream. Dust blew up-slope, sweeping over Ivan as he felt his horse twist to follow the herd, catching Ivan off-guard.

The air went out of Ivan's lungs as he hit the ground. Earth and sky cartwheeled for long moments. Ivan knew better than to fight, and felt himself spin downhill until he hit the bottom after a hundred foot roll.

For long moments Ivan lay still, his eyes gazing skyward as he gasped for air. The dust quickly blew away, leaving him looking at small puffs of clouds that raced across the pale blue sky.

"Goddamn horses!" he thought. Pain lanced through his left ankle. At first he thought the ankle was broken. "Just what I need. A broken ankle to go with the bum knee. Damn, it hurts!"

For several minutes Ivan continued to heave for air. He lay still as he felt his body tighten from the pain and shock. "Wonder if Cathy is swimming in the creek still?" he thought. "Hope Adriana has supper ready when we get home."

The sky stopped spinning enough for Ivan to sit up. He did so slowly, the pain in his ankles making him groan. He reached down with both hands to feel his left ankle. His boot felt tight, which meant his ankle was swelling. He clenched his jaws and probed. The pain swept through him, but almost immediately he knew his ankle wasn't broken.

Ivan gave himself a few more minutes, then forced himself to stand up. He began to walk in circles, trying to work his ankle back into shape. Twice he almost collapsed, but both times he refused to fall, leaning on a tree stump until the pain subsided.

He was eyeing the creek, thinking about dipping his swollen ankle in the cold water, when he heard the horse approach. He turned as Wolverine swung into view, riding easily despite his old age.

"Find the damn horses?" Ivan asked.

"Yes. I calmed the roan down. I've got him tied down."

"Ought to shoot the damn horse."

"You might get him mad if you did that," Wolverine joked.

Ivan saw the glint in Wolverine's dark brown eyes, and he laughed. "Yeah, it might at that, eh?"

"Is the ankle bad?"

"Bruised, but it ain't broken."

Wolverine leaned over to take a closer look, and Ivan marveled that Wolverine could remain mounted while doing so.

"Looks like you can ride."

"I c'n ride, all right. Just get my horse."

Wolverine nodded as he straightened up. He turned his horse around and trotted out of sight. Only then did Ivan wipe the sweat from his face. He turned back and hobbled to the creek, where he dipped in his foot, boot and all. The cold swept through Ivan, making him grunt in pain. "Oughta take the swelling down," he thought. It was all he could do to keep his ankle immersed. The cold made him feel faint. His hearing faded as he struggled to keep upright against the urge to faint.

". . . horse was just over the rise."

"What?" Ivan looked up, his face a blank registry of pain.

"I said that your horse wasn't far."

Wolverine dismounted and helped Ivan onto his horse. Ivan barely cleared his right leg over the horse's back. The pressure on his left ankle made Ivan grunt and break into another sweat.

Wolverine looked up into Ivan's face. "You can make it back on your own. I'll get the horses settled in for the evening, then catch up. Just give the horse its head. It knows the way back."

Ivan clung onto the horse as it moved forward. Wolverine was right. His horse turned a semi-circle and, when Ivan gave it no lead, it began to walk southwest. Ivan barely remembered the next hour. He fought to stay mounted on the horse. His ankle became the focal point of his world. Each stride of the horse irritated the swollen joint. "Going to lose a good pair of boots," Ivan muttered to himself. From the feel in his ankles, the boot would have to be cut off.

Halfway home, Ivan heard the drumbeat of an approaching horse. Wolverine was quickly by his side. Taking a look at Ivan's ankle, Wolverine smiled gravely. "Looks bad. A lot of swelling. Hold tight and I'll lead your horse. You can manage, can't you?"

Ivan nodded, and then held on as Wolverine took his horse's reins and broke into a canter that swiftly ate up the distance to home. Against his better judgment, Ivan swung his left leg out to keep his ankle away from the horse's side. He wasn't sure whether it helped any, but at least his ankle didn't strike the horse's side.

Cathy ran towards them as soon as they rounded the bend for home. She bounced and skipped, singing in a low voice that faded as soon as she saw her father's unnatural posture. Then she broke into a flat-out run.

"Daddy, are you all right? What's wrong?"

Ivan forced a smile. "Nothin', sweetheart. Just twisted my ankle bad."

Cathy ran alongside the horse and studied Ivan's outstretched leg. Her eyes went wide, but she said nothing. Ivan saw Adriana come out of the house. Wolverine stopped at the low porch and dismounted to help Adriana as they eased Ivan down from his horse.

"He was thrown," Wolverine explained as they supported Ivan into the house. Adriana muttered something about the roan that the men couldn't quite hear. The tone told them everything and, despite his pain, Ivan grinned at Wolverine, who nodded in agreement.

Adriana touched the boot at the point where it met the ankle. Ivan's grimace told her everything she needed to know. Wolverine went to get some water, taking Cathy with him to the creek. While they were gone, Adriana carefully cut along the boot's seam on the side away from the bruising. Ivan held out as long as he could, but by the time Wolverine returned with a bucket of water, Ivan had passed out on the bed. Adriana soaked several long strips of cloth. Wolverine ground some leaves into a paste and slathered on the swollen ankle. Adriana then wrapped the ankle with the soaked strips of cloth.

Evening was upon them by this time, and Adriana served the meal she had cooked earlier. Wolverine ate in silence, but both she and Cathy were used to this. Only after they had finished eating did Wolverine tell them what happened earlier.

"Where are the horses now?"

"I secured them along the north bench. The roan can't go anywhere, and neither can the rest of the herd."

Adriana stared at Wolverine's dark face. "I hate that roan. It's caused us nothing but trouble."

Wolverine shook his head. "That's the smartest horse I've seen in a long time. My grandfather had a horse that smart."

Adriana was surprised, for Wolverine seldom volunteered information. Cathy jumped in before she could say anything.

"How smart was your grandpa's horse?"

Wolverine looked at the small frame in front of him. Adriana couldn't tell what Wolverine thought, but she saw the stocky Indian gather his story together. Wolverine leaned towards the rapt child, much as he'd done with Adriana when she'd first met him six years ago.

"My grandfather's horse was smart. Let me tell you about the roan, though. Your mother and father know this story well."

The wagon pulled up at the house. Adriana paused as she started to climb down from her seat. The house was what she'd expected, a small wood-framed structure from which a thin white curl of smoke rose from the chimney towards the back of the house.

The barn loomed fifty yards from the house. It was shaded by a clump of trees. In the still air, Adriana heard the creek behind it. A corral made of wood beams jutted from the barn's west wall. To get to the barn doors, a person would have to go through the corral. Adriana admired the simplicity, for no horse could escape, even if it managed to get out of the barn.

In the middle of this corral a horse stood motionless. Upon first glancing at it as she entered the yard, Adriana thought the horse was alone. Now, as she glanced at its light brown form, she saw the human legs that, by a trick in perspective, seemed to protrude from the horse's stomach. A hand reached around the horse's neck, and Adriana heard someone singing in a low voice, using a language she knew was Indian.

Ivan saw her hesitation. "That's Wolverine."

"Wolverine? Isn't Wolverine an animal?"

Ivan grinned. "Maybe, but I wouldn't say that to his face."

Adriana let herself be lifted down by her new husband. As her feet hit the dry dirt, Adriana stared at the corral. "I take it this Wolverine is a ranch hand?"

Ivan spoke as he lifted her belongings from the wagon. "Wolverine lives up in the hills by himself. He keeps an eye out on the place, and helps me when I need it."

"How does he know when that is?"

Ivan looked towards the corral. "I don't know. My parents knew him when he went to the mission school. He's an odd duck, that one. He comes and goes as he pleases."

"Is he from around here?"

"Near as I can tell, he's from one of the families around here. They seem to hold him in some regard, but he don't live with them, neither."

Adriana reached down to lift her clothes box. Ivan opened the front door for her. A few hours later, after they had christened the house as newlyweds, Adriana was heating water for coffee. She heard a soft knock on the thick wooden door.

The man who stood on the other side was no taller than she was, although she was tall for a woman. His dark face was smooth for his age. Adriana guessed that he was somewhere in his late fifties or early sixties. From what she had heard in the two weeks traveling to this valley, a sixty-year-old Indian was rare. Most had not lived through the white man's diseases to reach Wolverine's age.

"You must be Wolverine."

Wolverine nodded. "You're Ivan's new wife."

Adriana felt the humor in Wolverine's voice, and took an instant liking to the man. "Well, I know I'm not his old wife."

"May I come in, ma'am? I need to talk to Ivan."

Adriana nodded, and stepped aside to let the stocky man in. Ivan came out of the bedroom, tucking his shirt into his pants as he did so. Wolverine stopped half a dozen steps into the house.

"What is it?" Ivan asked.

"Your horse just gave birth."

Ivan grinned, his smile creasing his already wrinkled face. "That's wonderful." He looked towards his wife as he followed Wolverine outdoors. "Honey, do you want t'see our new colt?"

Adriana shooed them out, saying, "I'll be there. I'm just making coffee."

Ten minutes later Adriana walked into the corral. She swung the gate closed behind her, and then studied the corral more closely. A water trough stood on the inside railing a dozen feet away from the barn. The corral itself consisted of three sets of rails that made a barrier six feet high. Adriana knew the structure was sturdy, for it hadn't shaken at all when she'd closed the gate.

One of the two barn doors was half-open, and Adriana walked through into semi-darkness. The smell of damp hay, dry dust, and horse manure struck her at once. Adriana felt surprised that the odor, far from being unpleasant, gave her a sense of comfort and security. At that moment, she knew she was home at last.

Ivan and Wolverine were inside the largest of four stables. Adriana walked around the wagon towards their muffled voices. Neither looked up as she entered the stable, but Wolverine, whose back was towards her, moved to the side as Adriana neared.

The colt was between the two men. Ivan stroked its back as it wobbled on its legs. The colt's red skin was marked by white patches. Adriana watched as Ivan spoke to the colt. Wolverine looked up at her.

"It's a roan."

"It's beautiful."

"The skin will darken with age. But I've never seen such bright colors before."

The colt reared its head at Adriana's approach. Its eyes met hers, and Adriana felt its intelligence as it studied her for a moment. Then it suddenly lurched forward, surprising Ivan. Before the three of them could stop it, it was out of the barn into the corral. Wolverine ran after it as Ivan picked himself up from the floor. He dusted himself off and smiled at Adriana.

"Smart horse. Is coffee ready?"

Although Wolverine had told the story many times, Cathy always laughed, as she did now, whenever Wolverine got to this part.

"And was Daddy dirty?"

"Very. Your mother had to wash his pants because he'd fallen into a pile of manure."

Cathy giggled, and Adriana smiled at the memory of her husband's sheepish grin as he pretended not to notice the smell coming from his clothes.

"God watches us twenty-four hours a day. He watches us when we eat, when we sleep, when we go about our daily tasks." Father Tomlinson leaned forward to rest his elbows on the pulpit. His grey eyes swept over the people in the crowded church. They returned his gaze. Some shifted uncomfortably on the hard benches. Body heat made the church warm enough to be a distraction.

From outside came the snicker of a horse. Faint voices drifted in from people who waited patiently for the service to finish.

Although their voices were respectfully low, Father Tomlinson wished they'd either keep quiet or come in.

Children in their Sunday best lined the front rows. Sometimes a giggle or a gasp would tell Father Tomlinson they were acting up, but he chose to ignore them. Instead, he weighed how he would finish his sermon. He pulled himself to his full six-feet-two-inch height and absent-mindedly brushed a fly from the sleeve of his robe.

"Now I know that there's talk in the town about the Indians. Talk about how they were unfairly placed in the next valley. Talk even about how the Church was involved with setting up the reservation."

"Well, let me tell you all here and now, that's all it is — talk. God watches us all. He particularly watches those of us who carry out His works and words. He knows that the Indians are His children too. He knows that they must hear His words. But they cannot hear him if they are deafened by other voices, other beliefs, Satan's words."

A low murmur filled the silence that Father Tomlinson created as he again paused. He had their attention again, and he made them flinch as he suddenly boomed out, "I said Satan's words! Heathen practices. Is there a man or woman among you who believes that we should allow the Indians to continue their ungodly practices? One man or woman who thinks that the Church is too harsh in the way we treat our brown brethren?"

"Every day we see new people come into the valley. People of God. Christians who want to make a new start in a new land. Can we then allow ourselves to be stopped by people who don't even believe in the Father, the Son, and the Holy Ghost? Who believe that animals talk? Who worship trees? Who weren't even using the land in the way it should be used?"

Father Tomlinson struck a defiant pose, his shoulders drawn back and his posture to its full height. "Blasphemy. Christ died for our sins. It is my God-given task to bring His message of love and faith to the Indians of Priest Valley. It is a hard task, but God doesn't allow his messengers to shirk their duty. And I will not shirk mine. Let us pray."

After the mass, Father Tomlinson stood at the doors. A hot breeze rustled through the tall dry grass at the bottom of the stairs. He glanced west over the growing town. Beyond, a small mountain swept upwards, its slopes brown and dark green in the haze that shimmered from the valley floor. South of that small mountain, another one snaked southwest into the distance. If he strained his eyes, Father Tomlinson could see the thin blue band of the lake five miles away.

As each family left the church, they greeted the priest. He spoke a few kind words to each. Ivan Patriloney shook Father Tomlinson's large hands.

"I hear that you have a new neighbor."

"A farmer. Italian."

"I'm sorry that he isn't here to hear God's words."

Ivan shrugged. "I'm not sure the man is a church-goer."

"I see. Well, I'll have to drop by one of these days."

Adriana, who shooed her daughter down the stairs to play with the other children, turned to the priest. "We'd like that, Father."

Father Tomlinson smiled. "It's been too long since I've had the pleasure of your cooking, Mrs. Patriloney."

Adriana felt heat rise to her face. "You flatter me, Father."

"Nonsense. This is no time for modesty. You're an excellent cook."

Father Tomlinson watched the couple walk down the stairs, wondering about the rumours he'd heard about them using Wolverine for some of their ranch work. He frowned at the thought of Wolverine. Such a disappointment. One of his predecessors, Father Kennedy, the one they called Black Robes, had spent years teaching the boy, only to have the young man return to his people. Apparently Wolverine was too odd for the Indians, and now he lived alone, up in the hills. Darker rumors said that something Wolverine had done in the past had changed the way his own people treated him.

Father Tomlinson wondered what the Indians saw in the old man. Wolverine seldom ventured into town, and his visits to his family were just as rare. Yet whenever Father Tomlinson mentioned Wolverine's name to his people, they talked of him with a strange hesitation. Not respect or fear, but something different.

Father Tomlinson quickly forgot about the Patriloneys and their helper as he set about preparing to travel the ten miles to the head of the lake. By tonight, he thought, he'd be at the newly built church at the head of the lake. The thought made him feel giddy. So much work to undo the teachings the Indian elders continued to practice.

Later that morning, Father Tomlinson was cinching his saddle. As he finished, he heard the growl. His horse shied away. Father Tomlinson grabbed the bridle and used his considerable strength to keep his horse in place. He glanced over his shoulder. A coyote stood at the edge of the nearby trees, higher up the slope. It studied the man and horse. Before the priest could do anything more than settle his horse, the coyote silently turned to trot back into the trees.

•• • ••

Walking along the street towards Westminster Abbey, Pietro Rosselli clung to his father. Hawkers peddling wares filled the air with their sales pitches. Smoke from numerous open pits dimmed the overhead sun. Pietro smelled the mixture of food, clothing, wood cabinets, oils, candles, beer, wine, shoes, and unwashed bodies. He felt sick.

The walk seemed endless. His father pushed through the crowds, shoving his way through the crowd without excusing himself as he had done when they first left Victoria Station. Pietro followed blindly, clutching his father's right hand. When he stumbled, as he did many times, his father merely growled and kept going, half-dragging the young boy through the streets.

Pietro knew better than to complain. He tried to make up stories about what he saw, but soon the people and their voices became a blur. Pietro found it hard to keep his attention on what was going on around him. He lost track of time and became as grim as his father, wondering if the crowds would ever end.

Once Pietro's father stopped long enough to buy some fruit. Pietro clutched at his apple and gleefully bit into its smooth surface as the two began their trek once more. His father muttered words Pietro hardly understood or heard: "It'll be a joyful day when they pull these slums down."

When the smoke cleared enough to sweep the great block towers into view, Pietro at first thought he was dreaming that he had fallen asleep. He was convinced of this when the crowds suddenly thinned and the Abbey heaved into view. Pietro felt dizzy. The towers should have swept into the sky, but instead they seemed to squat low, despite their height. Pietro immediately thought of a toad brooding over its pond.

They entered the Abbey through its central doors. The nave towered far overhead. Along the north wall, tall glass windows swept to the ceilings. In each of the central windows, a man with a crown stood next to an abbot. The thin frames that held each window gave the nave the appearance of a tall, skinny room of great size.

Pietro's father leaned over to whisper in his son's ear, "Those men you see are kings of England. Next to each of them are the abbots who ruled this building during their lifetime. Damn church was into everything even back then."

Pietro nodded dumbly, his eyes fixed to the ceiling a hundred feet above. Visions of giant spiders weaving strands of web from the ceiling overcame Pietro. He imagined their large bodies as they swung from window to window. Each time they did so, their shadows darkened the windows. Their low chattering to one another lent an atmosphere of dreadful secrecy to the cavernous nave. Their intentions were clear; they wanted to cover the bold kings in webs to hide them forever from sight.

"Quite the sight, eh, Pietro? Every king and queen of England got their bastard start here. They were as bad as the Popes in those days. Intrigues, inbreeding, incest, and corruption. The slums you saw outside are the result of their doings. Every rich man needs a thousand poor men to feed and work for his habits. Every carriage they ride on was made of the bodies of a thousand dead men. Long live the Empire."

"But Da, it's so big."

"Ah, that it is, my boy. We're standing on the graves of two former churches. Those two weren't big enough for the likes of the British monarchy, so they tore the first one down and built on its bones. Then another king came along and knocked the second church down to build a bigger monument to the Church and King."

Pietro's eyes swept upwards once again. The shadow spiders continued to weave their invisible threads high overhead. Pietro shivered, although the air in the Abbey lay still and heavy in the afternoon heat.

•••••

The service droned on, the dean's voice empty of passion. Each word struck Pietro like cold bricks. He winced and shifted on the uncomfortable bench. Often he wondered why his father had brought him to this loveless place. He missed his mother, but Da said she was dead. Pietro guessed that this meant she would not come back to wrap him in her warm arms, her breath soft along the top of his head.

"My boy, no need to cry. The service is almost over."

"I'm not crying!"

His father shrugged and returned his attention to the dean at the front of the church. Pietro felt a hot fury choke him. He wanted to yell at the dean, tell him to shut up, to get out, to stop talking useless words. His father looked down at his quiet son, and he wondered at the boy's flushed face. Perhaps the boy was ill. He promised to take him home as soon as the service was over. The trip to London had proven to be a wasted trip. The man he was to meet yesterday had been killed in an accident with a horse and carriage, and there was nothing he could do about it. He would have to return to Italy, back to his vineyards, and hope for the best. The dead man had been the best man anywhere when it came to grapes, and now there was no looking back.

"Apples, Pietro. The answer is apples. You've worked for me for twenty years. What are you going to do when I die?"

Pietro looked at the old man. The heaths rolled to the horizon behind McDougall, shrinking the old man's large frame. For a moment Pietro saw the shadow of a spider framed in the blue haze of the hills behind McDougall. McDougall studied the tall, thin man before him. He knew the look in Pietro's eyes as well as those of his own sons.

"You're a dreamer, Pietro. But you know apples better than my own sons. I never thought an Italian would have this gift."

McDougall tossed an apple at Pietro, who easily caught it in his left hand. Pietro looked down at the small apple, turning it in his hand, his long fingers running familiarly over the apple's dark red surface.

"What's wrong with that apple?"

"Nothing, sir. It looks like a fine apple."

"You don't lie well. That apple is the finest of the crop, wouldn't you say?"

"It's certainly among the best I've seen this year."

"There's the problem."

"I don't understand, sir."

"That apple is fine for us, but it isn't a great apple."

Pietro studied the inert surface, but couldn't see McDougall's point.

"Walk with me," McDougall commanded. Pietro shrugged and tied the cart horses to a small apple tree. The horses began cropping the wizened grass around the tree's base. Pietro followed McDougall as the old man walked slowly down the gentle slope. Below them, Pietro saw the house nestled at the foot of the hill. A white wisp of smoke curled upwards in the still air. Rows of small apple trees filled the orchard.

Forty feet downhill from the cart, McDougall stopped at a tree. Its limbs were laden with a bountiful crop, and hadn't yet been picked as most of the other trees had been. McDougall reached up to pull an apple from a limb. The apple snapped from its branch, which swayed for several seconds before settling down in the warm still air.

"See this apple? It's like the others. Nothing like it in the valley. But it's small. Smaller than it should be. Look around you. That's the reason we have small apples."

Pietro looked at the lush landscape, the green that marked almost every part of the valley. In the warm air he heard voices from a mile away.

"It's too fertile here."

"I don't understand, sir."

"No, of course you wouldn't. The ground is just fine. But you see this apple, don't you?"

McDougall held the apple up between the two of them. "This apple needs heat, lots of it. And it needs dry air. And it needs grafting."

"Grafting, sir?"

"Grafting. Look, Pietro, I won't lie to you. When I'm gone, my orchards and land will go to my sons. The house will be theirs as well. My daughters are married into other clans. You and I know that I haven't been able to pay you what I should. You'll have two choices when I die. Stay here to work for my sons, or leave to make it on your own."

"I can't tell you what to do. But I do know you're damned good with apples. The only reason these apples are this healthy is because of you. You have a gift with them. I want to do one thing for you before I'm gone. Send you to Edinburgh."

"What would I do in Edinburgh?"

"There's a new man down there, a scientist. He's been studying the art of grafting, among other things. I've heard good things about him. I want you to spend some time with him. Listen to what he has to say. If you're going to spend the rest of your life growing apples, I want you to learn all you can about it. More than I can learn."

"But what about your sons?"

"Oh, they'll go, too. But it's more than facts and knowledge. You have the skills and talent. You have a feel for apples. No one else in this valley has what you have. Learn what you can, because when I'm gone you'll have only yourself to support."

He was hyper-kinetic, his small quick form tracing spirals on the lecture floor. White hair speckled his otherwise unkempt ink-black hair. Every so often the man stopped in his tracks to scribble some words or diagrams on the blackboard. Several broken pieces of chalk crunched underfoot whenever the man's boots ground down on them. The man was oblivious to the chalk as it became flakes and then dust on the wood floor.

His booming voice carried to the back row where Pietro sat with the McDougall boys. The three McDougalls were bored, and spent most of the time either writing notes back and forth or whispering to each other. Often, one or more of them would get up to leave the room, a pattern that they'd followed for the last three days. Sometimes they wouldn't return for an hour or more.

The lecturer ignored the McDougalls, as he ignored the several others who followed the same habits. His excited voice was for those who listened raptly to his every word. Pietro could hardly keep up with note taking, and had filled more than sixty pages with notes and diagrams during the five-day series of talks the lecturer was completing today.

"So grafting is the new thing with these scientist types, is it?"

Pietro stuffed the rest of his note papers into the satchel before looking up at the oldest McDougall son. "That's where the future lies."

The four men walked across the campus. Green lawns stretched everywhere, and the inner courtyard itself was filled with students hurrying to and from classes. Pietro ignored the crowds, consisting mainly of young men and women half his age.

As they passed the church, the oldest McDougall pointed to the bell tower. "You can hear that bell ring for services from clear across the city."

Pietro shrugged. "Bells are bells. They distract from what people have to do."

"I keep forgetting about you seeing Westminster Abbey a long time ago."

"Not that long ago. Just before they cleaned up the slums to make way for Victoria Street reaching Victoria Station."

"That's around the same time as they remodelled the high altar, wasn't it?"

"After. The work was done when I saw the Abbey."

"Our father isn't well, you know."

"I know."

The oldest McDougall squinted at the taller Pietro. "What do you plan to do when our father's gone?"

"Expect I'll move on. Maybe see the new world. Rupert's Land, New Caledonia maybe."

"Why not the United States? I heard there's plenty of adventures and fortunes to be made there."

"Too much excitement for me. Besides, New Caledonia has seasons just like Scotland. Rugged land there. Maybe I'll find somewhere where I can grow apples. My own orchards."

The oldest McDougall extended a hand, stopping Pietro. "I wish you luck, Pietro. Rupert's Land is cold in the winter, colder than Scotland, I hear."

"I hear that too. But a man's got to do what he's got to do."

"Bobby Burns?"

"No, I think Shakespeare."

"You see, Pietro, that I'm not as dumb as you sometimes think."

"I never doubted you."

"Well, let's go home. I'm not looking forward to the next five days, but a man's got to do what he's got to do, eh, Pietro?"

"We'll be coming into sight of land soon."

Pietro Rosselli looked west. The waves had subsided to five-foot swells, lifting and carrying the boat closer to landfall. Pietro shivered and sank deeper into his large fur coat. The Hudson's Bay winds tousled Pietro's long hair. Day had come seven hours ago, but the grey overcast hid the sun. The dark black waters through which the *Madrigal* plowed foamed into white streaks behind the ship, leaving a wake half a mile long.

A gull squalled and bickered above the mainmast. It sometimes roosted on the maintop before sweeping up and away from the ship. Every so often it swooped down to hover over the deck, where stale bread was sometimes thrown into its voracious beak.

The deck itself was slick with water and seaweed tossed aboard during yesterday's storm. Most of the passengers stayed below deck, many of them green with the seasickness brought on by ten-foot swells that had rocked the *Madrigal* for the past thirty hours. Pietro was one of only three passengers well enough to hang onto the railings of the main deck. From his vantage point, he watched the ship's crew scurry about in their duties, the captain's voice sometimes hollering from above. The commands were few, for the seasoned crew members each knew their duties better than the captain.

Pietro heard the snap whenever a sail caught a crosswind. The ship's decks shuddered whenever this happened. Pietro felt the twists as the ship plunged ahead, leaning slightly to starboard as the captain maintained his heading towards York Factory.

Pietro never heard the captain's approach, only the whiskey voice from five feet away.

"Well, boy, what do ya think o' the Bay? Grand, ain't it the truth?"

"Wild, sir. Wild."

"Boy, you ain't never seen the Bay wild. What we passed through, that weren't nothin' more 'n a good blow. You want t'see the wild seas, you's gotta be on the seas for longer'n two months. Twenty years, and then you'll know the wild seas."

The captain's small wiry frame reminded Pietro of the McDougalls half a year behind. "I'll grant you that I've never seen a truly wild sea, but this was wild enough."

The captain stared at Pietro for a moment, then broke into a gap-toothed grin. "Boy, you'se'll do fine in this god-forsaken land. Jest fine. Put hair on yer chest, this Rupert's Land will. Put some starch into ya."

Pietro watched the captain's small back as he broke into a sea shanty, his whiskey voice out of all proportion to his size, as he made his way up the stairs to his post. Although Pietro couldn't see him from where he stood on the main deck, between songs the captain's voice soon began bellowing orders with enough starch in them to stiffen Pietro's spine.

Pietro returned to staring at the black waters. He kept a tight grip with both hands on the thick wood rail as he leaned over to watch the water hiss by, churned into white froth by the boat as it slid through the cold. How long he stood there he didn't know, but the grey skies were darkening when he heard the captain's voice bellow, "Land ho!"

Due west of the ship, a thin strip of darkness rose above the surface. With each passing minute the wedge widened and deepened, until distant hills could be distinguished from the breakers. The crew became more frantic as the ship neared the coast. The more hardy passengers ventured onto deck, careful to keep out of the way of the crewmen.

Most of the passengers didn't last long on deck, for the sight of the water streaming past the ship churned their stomachs. Several didn't make it below deck before they were violently ill, throwing up while sailors cursed and the captain yelled for them to clean up their own messes, damned if his men were maids.

By the time they were eight miles out from the Factory, everything was in hand. Sailors manning their posts made the occasional shift of sails, but the captain's steering was swift and assured.

"Five Fathom Hole ahead. Take the wheel, mate!"

"Aye, captain."

Within moments the captain's small body seemed to hurl itself from the command post, scarcely touching the ladder to the main deck. Pietro fought a sensation of vertigo as the captain scuttled over towards his quarters. At first, Pietro thought the captain would pass him by, but the captain stopped two feet from Pietro, close enough to seize his left arm.

"What d'you think, mister? Would you take the *Madrigal* into a storm with me? Cut through a white squall? Spit into a typhoon's heart and laugh? We're on a good ship, mister. Ain't many like her, is there?"

"None that I've seen, sir."

The captain looked at Pietro for a moment, then grinned ear to ear. "Boy, you'll go far in this here Rupert's Land. New country like her, she's beggin' for peoples like you."

The captain stared landward and shivered. "Ain't nothin' out there for me. Land's too treacherous, boy. Can't read her like you can the sea. Too many moods. She can smile at you while kicking you in the plumbs."

"I'll be careful."

"Won't matter, boy. When she wants you, she'll get you comin' or goin'. Keep travellin' west is my thoughts. You'll know where t'stop when you gets there."

"West?"

"West. Far as you can take it, boy. West."

As the captain turned and made his way to his quarters, Pietro watched in awed silence as the *Madrigal* slid to a halt and anchor was weighed. Rupert's Land waited for him, and it would take Pietro five hard months to get to New Caledonia on the west coast of the continent.

The Indian rode down the slope. He rode his horse with assurance born of long times in the saddle. He skirted around Pietro's fence line until he reached the small gate leading into Pietro's yard. Pietro leaned on his hoe as the Indian rode up and dismounted.

"Hot day."

Pietro nodded in agreement, and waited.

"You're new to these parts." The Indian's flat tones drew Pietro's curiosity. He'd never heard an Indian talk fluent English.

Pietro frowned as the Indian's small, stocky body moved towards him. At first Pietro wondered about why the Indian struck him as odd. Then he realized that the Indian walked in a way most horsemen didn't, straight-legged and without any roll in his steps. Instead of answering the Indian, Pietro chose to wait. The Indian met Pietro's reluctance with a small grin. At the time Pietro had no way of knowing how different this was from other white men Wolverine had met.

"I'm looking for stray horses. Seen any?"

"No."

The Indian extended his right hand. "Wolverine."

Pietro shifted his hoe to his left hand and returned Wolverine's handshake. Wolverine's small hands, wrinkled by age and calluses, had the texture of bark.

"Pietro Rosselli."

Wolverine frowned. "Italian, isn't it?"

"Yes."

"Figures. I read something about Rome once. Something called an empire."

"That was a long time ago."

"Guess that's why I couldn't finish the book."

"Read much?"

Wolverine's dark eyes studied Pietro for several seconds. "Not much call for it at home."

"You come just to ask me about strays?"

"No. I've been watching you. You're not a farmer or a rancher."

"Planting apple trees."

"Apple trees. What are apples?"

"Men have been growing apples since Eden."

"Ah. Those apples."

"You know the Bible?"

"When I was a boy."

"Read it any more?"

"Not much use for it."

"You and me both."

"Learned English from it. Lost my people doing it."

"Lost your people?"

"The old ones sent me to learn from a priest called Kennedy. By the time I got back, the younger ones had moved in. They didn't have much use for me. Thought I was an outcast."

"Too bad."

Wolverine smiled again. "Should have saw it coming. They taught me English, but they didn't teach me to be smarter."

Pietro laughed. "The Bible has done many things, but making people smarter isn't one of them."

"So how are you planning to water your trees?"

Pietro gestured towards the hill looming over them. "There's a stream — a creek — on the other side. I found a place where I can dam it. If I dig a ditch, the water ought to do fine down here."

Wolverine knew the stream, and shook his head. "That stream leads to the lake. Goes past Ivan's place."

"Ivan?"

"Man I sometimes work for. He sets a lot of store in that creek."

"Does he use it for anything?"

"Mostly to water his horses. His girl loves the stream."

"My ditch shouldn't affect the stream that much. I need the water."

"Well, I hope you're right. Hate the thought of you two at odds. Ivan's a good rancher."

"And I'm a good apple grower."

Wolverine looked over Pietro's shoulders to the hills above. "I'd better get going. If you see a roan leading a pack of horses, leave them be. I'll find them."

As Wolverine walked back to his horse, Pietro called to him. "Drop by any time. We'll talk."

Wolverine mounted his horse and nodded. Within moments he disappeared, goading his horse into a trot that kicked dust into the air that floated gently into the grass and trees along the small dirt road.

Pietro, as he turned to his hoe, shook his head. "Strange fellow. Hope he comes back soon."

Wolverine rode to the top of the hill. He turned his horse to stare down at the man he'd just left. Pietro had returned to hoeing his garden. In the distance, over the lake, an eagle spiraled in the wind currents. Wolverine felt a pang of regret. "Not as many eagles as there once was," he thought.

The warm wind stirred Wolverine's long hair, grown white

over the years. He suddenly dismounted and tied his horse to a nearby tree just off the road. He sat on the dry grass, and watched as a buggy rode into view. It passed with a cloud of dust that drifted south. Wolverine recognized Ivan and his family, but they didn't see him from where he sat in a hollow beside the tree. Neither would they have heard Wolverine's horse, which placidly chewed on the grass beneath the tree.

Wolverine looked northwest. From where he sat the small mountain that reared above Pietro's hidden cabin arced west. Wolverine could see the small creek that looped around the hillside towards him before it bent sharply back to run down and west to the lake. In the sun, the creek sent splinters of light that made Wolverine blink. Wolverine decided to let Ivan find out about Pietro on his own. He had a roan to catch, and for the first time Wolverine felt pleased that he had the roan as a diversion.

"Am I worried about nothing?" he thought, as he untied his horse and moved north again. A vague unease troubled him, an unease that left when his horse shook its head, bringing his mind from Pietro to the task at hand. Pietro seemed to be a fine man. He and Ivan would make natural friends. With that, Wolverine kicked his horse into a trot, quickly disappearing into the trees that sloped to the top of the low mountain.

Ivan reined in his horse. Movement far down the valley caught his attention. Ivan remembered Wolverine's advice. Don't move and no one will see you. He felt the first cold winds of winter in the air. The trees had turned colors and their leaves blew into piles along the trail in front of him. Without the sound of his horse, Ivan heard the wind blow through the pine trees. They swayed in the wind, dropping cones that rattled to the ground.

The movement down the valley continued unabated; clearly the man moving about was unaware of Ivan, or had chosen to ignore him. Ivan thought it was the former, for the man was a stranger to the valley, and would not know the sounds the valley made naturally from those made by other people.

Ivan studied the situation. He hadn't ridden through this spot in over three months. In that time, a small log cabin had appeared along the sloping ground. A half-acre of soil had been turned over and fresh green leaves marked where a vegetable garden had been started. At first glance, the cabin looked like any other homestead in the area.

However, above the log house and encircled by the fence line, rows of dirt had been dug. From this distance Ivan could only see the flash of light from water as it trickled through these ruts.

The tall, thin man was younger than Ivan, and the way he walked puzzled the rancher. The man had obviously spent a long time in the saddle, yet his walk wasn't quite that of a horseman's. Nor was the way the man studied the steep slopes before him the familiar gaze of a rancher. Instead of eyeing the trees and brush, the man seemed intent on gazing at the flat open spaces.

As Ivan watched, the man drove in the fourth of a series of posts, closing in some forty acres of land. He paused after the post was set, took his hat off, and wiped his brow. The hat wasn't the range hat Ivan and the other ranchers in the valley wore. It looked more eastern, something a few of the townspeople had taken to wearing.

"Heard you coming," the man said as Ivan rode into the clearing. "What do you think?"

"I don't know. What should I ought'a think?"

The tall man leaned on his sledgehammer and looked up at the horseman's face. "I've staked out some property here. My name's Pietro Rosselli."

"Name's Ivan Patriloney." Ivan leaned over to shake Pietro's extended left hand. Pietro's handgrip was strong, surprisingly strong. Ivan had expected a city folk's handshake.

"I got here nine weeks ago. I didn't see you around until an hour ago."

"You saw me studyin' you?"

"Couldn't miss it."

Ivan straightened in his saddle and tipped his hat to keep the falling sun from his eyes. "I was roundin' up the cattle until yesterday. Lookin' for strays now. The rest're on the low bench a mile from my house."

"Well, Ivan, I guess I'm your new neighbor."

"Saw you plantin' them poles to stake out property."

"Yes, I had the surveyor come over to mark the land. I don't want to intrude on anyone else's property."

"A surveyor, eh? Expensive, ain't they?"

"They sure are. But they're worth it in case of any disputes."

"I guess so. I was here before they was. Know my land like my hand."

"Yes, I don't doubt it." Pietro's grey-blue eyes gazed steadily at Ivan, and Ivan looked up and away after returning Pietro's gaze for several seconds.

"Nice ditch you have there. Where's the water coming from?"

"There's a creek on the other side of the rise. I tapped into it."

Ivan suddenly remembered Cathy complaining that the creek was slower and lower than usual. At the time he had thought it due to the heat. Now he wasn't too sure.

"There's people who depend on the water for their animals."

Pietro shrugged. "Thought you knew already. I met Wolverine a while back. Told him."

"Never heard about it."

"Can't help it if you don't talk to your hands."

"Wolverine isn't my hand. He's free to come and go as he pleases."

Pietro was surprised at Ivan's sharp tone. "Sorry for any misunderstanding. I need the water for my orchard."

"Orchard?"

"Apple orchard. Just planted the last of the seeds a week ago."

"Your fence line is right on the path my horses take."

"Haven't seen any horses come this way. Wolverine was looking for them last time I saw him."

Ivan stared at the rivulets of water that flowed along the small furrows between each row of trees. "Your ditches are taking my creek water."

"I didn't know it was your water. The surveyor who mapped out my land said the water in the creek was public, to be used by anyone."

"Well, your surveyor was wrong. I've had claim to that water since my father's days."

"That's not what my title says."

"Title? You got title?"

"Of course. A man would have to be a fool not to have title to his land."

"You calling me a fool?"

"You mean you don't have title to your land?"

Ivan felt the heat color his face red. He stared at Pietro — at the groomed appearance, so fastidious, so angular. When Pietro smiled, his teeth gleaming in the sunlight, Ivan knew that he was going to be a problem. He needed time to think about Pietro's plot of land placed so carefully not quite in Ivan's way, and not quite out of it.

Ivan nodded at the dark man. "Got to go now," he said, turning his horse around to ride away before Pietro could bid him farewell. Pietro studied the rancher's receding form for several seconds. Before Ivan had reached the bend in the trail, Pietro turned his back on him and looked up the hill at the two most distant posts marking the edge of his land.

That Sunday, Ivan was passing the cut-off road to Pietro's log house when Adriana poked him in the ribs. "Dear, let's be neighborly!"

"After what I told you about that robber?"

"Oh, Ivan, I told you a hundred times to get title. Now you're blaming our new neighbor for something you didn't do."

"It ain't fair that the man can take our water just like that."

"Maybe you can work it out with him. Ivan, we've got to try. It's the Christian thing to do."

Ivan swore under his breath, but turned the buckboard onto the narrow dirt road leading to Pietro's house. Pietro lowered a fence pole into place before he turned to greet his neighbors. His upper torso was bare and tanned. Adriana tried to ignore this as she shook his hand.

"I'm Ivan's wife. My name is Adriana. I hear yours is Pietro Rosselli."

"Pleased to meet you, Mrs. Patriloney."

"My husband and I were going into town for church services. Would you like to accompany us?"

A shadow passed over Pietro's face, a quick frown that marred his smooth, dirt-laden skin and then was gone. Pietro smiled and shook his head. "No thank you, Mrs. Patriloney. I'm trying to get my house and fence line done before the winter gets here."

"You're not a rancher, are you, Mr. Rosselli?"

"No, Mrs. Patriloney, I'm not."

Pietro's continued use of Adriana's surname brought a faint blush to her cheeks. Ivan continued to stare straight ahead, as if not hearing anything that was being said. When Pietro volunteered no further information, Adriana's blush deepened. "Well, just what do you plan to do, Mr. Rosselli?"

"I grow apples, Mrs. Patriloney."

"Your name suggests you're Italian, but you have a curious accent."

"That'd be my Scottish brogue. I spent some time there."

"It's a long way from Scotland, Mr. Rosselli."

"Aye, that it be. I learned to grow apples there."

"Apples? A peculiar occupation."

"I hope not. I spent a year traveling to get here."

"And you plan to grow apples here?"

"It does sound incredible, doesn't it, Mrs. Patriloney?"

"We've got to go," Ivan's clipped voice made Adriana turn to him. Pietro smiled.

"I hope you have a good service."

"Join us some day, Mr. Rosselli."

Pietro shrugged wordlessly and watched the buckboard rattle its way down the short lane that led to the main dirt road into town. Cathy, who had been quiet during the previous conversation, waved at Pietro from the back of the buckboard where she lay on some blankets. Pietro waved back before returning to his tasks.

Wolverine nodded at the row of barely visible trees — trees that were really small plants being constantly fed by the crudely effective lines of water ditches. "Heard you were making trouble," Wolverine said to Pietro.

"You've met Ivan, then?"

"Ivan and me, we go back years."

"Is there going to be a problem?"

"None that I know of. Ivan was one of the first ranchers here. He's set in his ways, and he doesn't like change."

Pietro grunted but said nothing as he watched Wolverine ride away. There was no doubt — the Indian was an odd man. Odd and old. Pietro had studied Wolverine's face, but the man could have been anything from forty to seventy for all Pietro could tell.

"Wasting time on nothing," Pietro thought. He made his way into his cabin and shut the door against the wind chill. Seating himself at the table, Pietro dipped a quill pen into the inkwell. The sheets of paper lay where he had left them after the last entry made four days ago. He knew what he'd written, but the sight of the words gave him comfort. Pietro drew the pen from its holder and let the extra ink drip back into the inkwell. Satisfied that the pen wouldn't smudge his paper, Pietro carefully wrote the date: "October 7, 1890."

Without pausing, Pietro busied himself writing for the next quarter hour. The furrows in his forehead smoothed out with each passing minute. As always, his writing was swift and assured. Pietro had acquired the habit of thinking about what to write every day well before he actually sat down at the small table.

October 7, 1890

Leaves turning colors still. There's a row of them just above my fence line. On my morning walk I stopped to pick one of the bright red ones. It's on the table in front of me. The Indian stopped by an hour ago. Not sure if he's trying to spy, be friendly, or checking up on me for his boss. Can't say that Ivan's his boss, but the two of them are close.

My trees have taken to the soil. In the past four months, only five of a hundred needed much work. The others seem to like the land. Can't say as I blame them. I've noticed I'm beginning to sound like the ranchers around here. Haven't seen much of them, but their words and expressions have a way of sticking to you.

The Indian says that the local priest wants to drop in on me sometime. Haven't got much use for priests, but maybe the man will be tolerable. If not, I guess I can be civil for an hour or so.

The Indian tells me that it ought to be a mild winter. Says there's a thirty-year cycle between the mild and the hard ones. Have no reason to doubt him, but I'll keep an eye out on his friend. Ivan every so often studies me. I feel his eyes on me from up on the slopes out of sight. Twice now I've had to rebuild parts of my ditches. I don't like guns, but if this keeps up I may have to get one for protection.

Pietro looked at his entry. Satisfied that he'd said everything that needed to be said, Pietro carefully added the page he'd written to a growing pile of paper sitting in the center of the table.

Outside it was still light. Squaring his shoulders against the cold, Pietro decided to take a final walk into the hills above his home. No telling how much longer he'd have these chances, what with winter coming on. The walk would give him time to plan and think ahead for what he needed to do before the first snows fell.

●●●●●

Ivan stared below to where the Italian toiled in his orchard. The warm spring air ruffled Ivan's shoulder-length hair, reminding him of the bitter winter that had killed many of his horses. Wolverine was nowhere to be found, so Ivan went about the tiring task of rounding up what horses he could. He knew that the roan hid from him, and with it were more horses than Ivan had found over the last two weeks.

He had been riding the ridge towards his cabin, looking forward to a home-cooked meal. He hadn't given Pietro much thought over the last months; neither had he planned to drop by this day. The man had stolen Ivan's creek water, and for that he nursed a silent grudge. But Ivan remembered his priest's words, and kept his anger hidden, to be dealt with at a later time.

The glint of water first drew Ivan's attention down the slopes. Almost at the same moment he heard the strong, distant singing. The voice drifted in strength and pitch, but its tone clearly contained the same joy that struck the church choir on rare occasions. Ivan reined his horse in, and listened to the strange words that were carried easily over the winds that blew north towards him.

> And by the moon the reaper weary
> Piling sheaves in uplands airy
> Listening, whispers, "'Tis the fairy
> *Lady of Shalott.*"

Despite the warm air, Ivan felt spooked. The words ghosted him — and so did Pietro. The man had built a wooden eave through which water flowed the quarter mile from the creek to Pietro's orchards, there to split into a dozen trickles of water through the rows of apple trees.

Ivan was about to ride down and try to be civil to his neighbor when he saw the horse and rider trot into view. He knew the rider as soon as he saw him, and checked his horse. What could Wolverine want with Pietro?

•• ● ••

"Whi."

Ivan recognized the Indian greeting word, as did Pietro, who returned Wolverine's hello by stopping his work. Wolverine stopped his horse at the edge of the first row of small trees.

"Haven't seen you in some time." Pietro's voice held a sense of caution.

"Went down the Valley for a dance. Family gathering at the Falls."

Pietro walked through a row of trees and stopped a dozen feet from Wolverine. Wolverine stared at the trails of water.

"Looks like you've been busy."

"I need the water for my trees. Someone's been blocking the water from time to time. Know anything about it?"

Wolverine shook his head. "As I said, I've been away for awhile."

Pietro grinned. "But you wouldn't say if you knew, would you?"

Wolverine didn't take the bait. "Clear your water with Ivan yet?"

"Don't have to. The water's public. That's what the local people say. Nobody owns it."

"Ivan and his family were here before most of the locals were."

"That may be, but Ivan doesn't make the laws."

"Heard you singing back there when I was coming this way."

Pietro closed the short distance to Wolverine's horse. "Song was a poem by a man named Tennyson. Big name in England when I left. Why don't you get off of your horse for a spell and talk."

"I'm not taking you away from your apples, am I?"

"I've been working without a break for most of the day. Looking forward to chatting for a spell." Wolverine dismounted and the two men disappeared into Pietro's small home.

Ivan turned his horse and continued his way home along the ridge, letting his horse take the lead. Since when had Wolverine the time to be so friendly with Pietro? The Indian hardly spoke to anyone, and Ivan had never seen him keep company with a white man other than himself.

That night, Ivan hardly heard Adriana, who talked as she sewed a new dress for Cathy's ever-growing figure. Cathy sat on the floor, holding a book in her small hands, her eyes moving slowly, lovingly, over the black text. Adriana noticed Ivan's distance, but kept her peace. Ivan would tell her when he was ready. He was as stubborn as she was when it came to thinking things through. Later, after Cathy had been put to sleep in her small bed, Ivan stared at the wood beams over their own bed.

"What is it?"

Ivan's eyes glinted in the dark. "Saw Wolverine today."

"Wolverine? Oh, good. I was worried about you being up on the range by yourself. There's a cougar killing cows and dogs."

"I didn't talk to him. It was an accident. I was on my way home when I decided to stop at the Italian's place. Wolverine got there before me."

"Mr. Rosselli's? But I don't understand. Doesn't Wolverine work for you? What's he doing with Mr. Rosselli?"

"I don't know. I'm worried." Ivan thought of the song. "That Italian's a strange man."

•• ● ••

Early the next morning, Wolverine rode into the yard. Ivan finished feeding his horses and then sauntered to the corral rails. Wolverine nodded, and was about to speak when Cathy's small figure dashed across the yard.

"Wolverine," the slim girl shouted as she jumped up and down in front of Wolverine's horse.

"Why, if it isn't Cathy! You're growing!"

"I'm four feet tall!"

"Better watch out or you'll be taller than me."

"No one is taller than you, Wolverine."

"I wish that was true," Wolverine smiled down at the excited girl.

"You just get back?"

Wolverine looked sharply at Ivan, but the rancher's face was unreadable.

"Spent time down at Kettle Falls. Winter dances."

"That must have been so much fun," Cathy's large eyes mirrored her excitement.

"One day I'll take you."

Ivan interjected, "Girl's got enough to do without trouncing around the country."

"Something bothering you, Mr. Patriloney?"

"Nothing to speak of. Are you able to help me this spring?"

"Already have. On my way here today, I spotted some of your horses. They were in the hay fields along the north bench. Rounded them up."

"I suppose I should say thanks."

"Nothing to it. Glad to help any time."

Ivan eased himself into a seated position on the top rail of the corral. From where he sat, he was at eye level with Wolverine, who hadn't dismounted.

Cathy took a last look at Wolverine before she dashed towards the house to tell her mother he was here.

"Growing to be a fine young lady."

"Cathy isn't your concern. I need your help. The roan has a bunch of my horses somewhere up on the range."

For the first time since he rode into the yard, Wolverine smiled, the wrinkles around his dark brown eyes more marked than Ivan remembered them from four months before.

"That roan means something to you in the spirit world."

"Don't know about the spirit world much, but it does seem to be something," Ivan laughed.

"My father told me a story about how spirits latch on to people they know from former lives. The one he told me about was Sn-klip, Coyote."

"I know one thing, Wolverine; that roan ain't no coyote spirit. I don't know anything about former lives. Imagine the priest would have trouble with that idea."

"Imagine he would."

"You never told me much about your father."

Wolverine dismounted and hitched his horse to the fence railings. The two men watched the horse as it dipped its neck to drink from the trough.

"My father passed away this winter."

"Sorry to hear about it."

"Don't be. He died like a warrior should. Chose the time and place. One day I woke up and he was gone. Blue Dreams taught me what I know. We did a mourning dance for him."

The horse looked up as if it understood the men, its eyes studying Wolverine for a moment before it returned to drinking water.

"Have you eaten yet?"

"No. I was going to check on my kekuli."

"Have a bite to eat before you go."

"Gladly."

"Did you see anything else on your way here?"

"Like what?"

"Anything I need to worry about."

"Nothing to worry about."

The last rains of spring came through the valley with a whisper. The area formed its own weather, bleeding the moist coastal air two hundred miles west into the dry dust that lay over the valley in an age-old blanket. The valley shaped its creatures in the same way, the animals here being smaller, leaner, and more ferocious than their coastal cousins. Survival meant foraging for hours to get to the rich patch of grass hidden under the fallen stumps of trees near water tables.

The land had its memories of water thick at the valley floor, stretching for twice the length of the relatively small lake that now arced north-south between the two immense plateaus that cradled the valley. Those memories shifted through the valley this year, woken by the unusual amount of rainfall that had swollen the creeks and filled the ravines. The brown stubble that completed every open patch of earth made way for the bright green of grass and the yellow shine of dandelions. The hills hummed and blazed with the sound of harvesting bees. Foraging bears raided the hives to find honey in abundance, so much so that they quickly settled out of their early spring testiness into a state bordering on complacence.

Deer flourished in large herds that wandered and bolted along the slopes leading to the lake below. For once they didn't have to wander over distances to find food. Food was everywhere. Trees bloomed, their limbs bowing under the weight of their thick leaves, making nibbling easy.

Over the spring, rain dripped continually onto the ground

from countless pine needles and leaves. The thirsty earth slurped up the water and gave back the kind of grass that sprouted like this once every twenty to thirty years, in a cycle only the valley controlled.

On the upper benches, Ivan had finished branding the last of the late spring calves. The two-day task had left him tired and sullen. He felt his age, although he tried to hide it from Wolverine. At nine years of age, Cathy was a five-foot tall, slim arrow filled with boundless energy. She helped where she could in the branding, by stoking the fire and keeping the branding irons hot. She helped corral reluctant calves so that Ivan or Wolverine could wrestle the bawling animal to the slippery earth. She kept the ropes free of knots and entanglements, draping them within easy reach of the two men.

Despite this, Ivan felt uneasy in letting a girl do this kind of work. He knew better than to make Cathy stay inside with her mother, but he also hoped that Cathy would grow out of her need to be "one of the boys." What man would look twice at such an independent woman?

At nights, around the campfire, Wolverine enthralled Cathy with tales of the coyote, Sn-Klip, of the bear, Kee-lau-naw, of the deer, Stla-chain-um. Their spirits were constantly reflected in Cathy's blue eyes, filling her with a desire to hear more and more.

When they weren't branding or rounding up strays, Ivan patrolled the range and patched the several corrals he had built over the past year. He preferred to do this alone, for it gave him time to think and to enjoy the lay of the land, his land. During these times, Wolverine took Cathy into the hills to teach her about the medicines and foods that grew in abundance even during the drier years. He taught her the rudiments of building shelters, of making fires that wouldn't sputter and die out from the constant spring rains, of hunting small animals by building snares. At first Ivan tried to stop this, concerned that his daughter was misbehaving, but his need for her help outweighed his parental worries, and eventually his protests stopped in an uneasy truce.

The more Cathy learned, the more she wanted to know. Ivan frowned at this, but he couldn't see his way clear to dampening Cathy's enthusiasm. The energy that would take more than Ivan had to give, so he watched and listened at a distance as Wolverine, his old and tough frame seemingly energized by Cathy's genuine interest, spoke increasingly in the Indian language. At her age, Cathy easily learned the words of this language in which each syllable carried a different weight and meaning within the context of larger phrases.

Just when Cathy started speaking Okanagan slipped past Ivan that spring. He didn't know until Adriana asked him about Wolverine one day. "Ivan, can we talk?"

"Of course, dear. What is it?"

"What do Wolverine and Cathy do when she's with you on the range?"

"They help me a lot. You know how helpful Wolverine is."

"Do they spend time together, away from you?"

"Sometimes. Cathy likes Wolverine."

"I'm worried."

"Don't worry," Ivan laughed. "I've thought about this, too. It's a growing phase. Maybe every girl goes through it."

"Cathy spoke to me last night. I couldn't understand her. She caught herself and changed her words."

"Changed her words. What do you mean?"

"I think she was speaking Indian."

Ivan thought about this for a minute as he absently continued looping his rope. "Now that you mention it, I've noticed her talking to Wolverine over the campfire."

"Dear, Cathy isn't Indian. Learning their language will make it hard on her later on."

"The two of them are talking, that's all. Wolverine teaches her how to survive. I don't see anything wrong in that."

"I'm worried."

"I'll speak to her."

Somehow, with all the tasks before him, Ivan never got around to speaking to Cathy. And now, as the three rode home from the spring roundup, Ivan hunched forward in his saddle, the light rain dripping from his broad-rimmed hat. The rain parka, although of heavy canvas, warded off the worst of the weather, but small trickles of moisture sometimes trickled down Ivan's back.

Cathy seemed oblivious to the rain, her long black hair tightly bound in a pony tail. The horses crossed the swollen creek and made their way cautiously up the steep slopes. The three riders knew enough to give their horses the lead. As the terrain opened up below them, Ivan stole an odd glance at the landscape. The creek's flow made it hard to speak, so the three rode in silence, although Cathy had asked Wolverine countless questions before they rounded a slope and the creek's roar struck them dumb.

The trail looped in a wavy line from the creek to beyond the spot where Ivan had fallen over a year ago. In parts, the trail was invisible under the green tufts of grass, but the horses knew their way, and progress was steady, if slow.

The roan reared out of nowhere, its tail flashing before them. Ivan, who had the lead, cursed as his horse threatened to bolt. As he fought to control his horse, the roan whinnied and pawed the ground with its left foreleg. It shook its head and mane before it turned and ran ahead of them. A stream of other horses followed, and Ivan shouted over his shoulder, "I've had enough of that damn roan. I'm going after it." Without waiting for a response, Ivan kicked his horse into a run.

"Dad, don't!" Cathy screamed, her voice drowned out by the pounding hooves and the constant roar of the stream below them. Ivan's back was to them, and he was halfway to the first bend in the trail before Cathy and Wolverine could stop him.

Cathy, as experienced as she was, let Wolverine break the trail ahead of her. The two quickly had their horses into a half-run, the fastest they dared to go on the thick wet grass. Around the bend, Cathy felt giddy with the realization of the danger below them, but she somehow had the feeling that this was familiar ground.

Ivan had made up half the distance between himself and the trailing horse. They were all going at a full gallop, but Cathy could do nothing except pray. Even as she watched, the roan twisted and plunged straight down the steep slope towards the creek. The other horses in the herd followed suit, churning the ground into a mass of rocks and dirt that flowed under, around, and behind them. Ivan knew this move well, and was already following suit.

Cathy was the first to see the man stand up at the creek's edge. And then she recognized the wooden troughs that diverted a part of the creek towards Pietro's orchards a quarter mile away. Pietro had dropped the chutes to slow the flow of water into his troughs. Cathy screamed, but knew that Pietro couldn't hear her. The roan was only a dozen yards away from the creek's edge when Pietro stood to see what the commotion was about. Pietro was directly in the path of the charging herd. His mouth opened in a silent cry, whether of help or of surprise Cathy never knew.

In slow motion Cathy saw the roan desperately twist its body to avoid the man. At the same time Ivan whooped, a call so loud Cathy heard it over the sound of the horses and water. Wolverine spurred his horse into a full run.

The roan brushed Pietro, enough to send him spinning. The herd that followed, startled by Ivan's whoop, had paused for a split second, enough to momentarily slow them down, but not enough to keep them from plowing into the creek. Pietro disappeared under a surge of water and horses.

Ivan whooped again, and the roan turned at the other side of the creek. It reared on its hind legs, snorted, and then took off at a dead run up the other side of the ravine. The herd, which milled about in confusion, hiding Pietro under their churning hooves, saw their leader bolt. They followed suit.

Ivan reached the water and was off his horse in one motion. Wolverine was moments behind. By the time Cathy reached the other side of the creek, the two men were pulling Pietro's limp body from the water.

"Is he dead?" Cathy heard herself scream over the water.

The two men were bent over Pietro's still form, and neither took time to answer Cathy as she unmounted and dashed to them.

Wolverine's small, stubby fingers were running along Pietro's body, pressing here and there in movements quicker than any Cathy had ever seen him make.

Wolverine looked up at Cathy and shook his head. "I don't understand it. Only a broken . . . "

Before he finished, Pietro's eyes opened to stare at the face between him and the grey skies. His eyes cleared, and the hatred that poured from them was a force that made Cathy gasp.

"You. You planned this."

As he said this to Ivan, Pietro struggled to a sitting position, grunting from the pain that shot along his right leg. His eyes widened and Cathy turned to follow his gaze.

The last of the rocks — which had been kicked up by the horses a minute before — rolled and settled in the creek bed. Even as they watched, the water was backing up against the rockslide.

Pietro turned to Ivan. "You must think it funny to keep blocking my water this way. Well, now I know. You and your damn horses, you're doing this to me. Get off my land now."

Ivan was about to protest his innocence, his mind still confused by the rapid turn of events, when Pietro hissed, "My land borders the creek on this side. Your land is on the other side of the creek. Get off of my land. Now! If I ever see you on my land again, I'll have you arrested."

Ivan felt his cheeks flush. "Keep your damned water. I was tryin' to help you, you old fool."

Pietro pointed to the creek. "Off of my land, now, or I'll show you who the fool is, broken bones or not."

Cathy and Ivan remounted their horses. As they rode across the creek, Cathy turned to see Wolverine busy stripping the cloth from Pietro's right leg. The white skin underneath the clothes flashed in stark contrast to the dark muddy waters and rain-soaked landscape that filled Cathy's vision. She turned to follow her father, whose silent rage built as they rode away from the creek.

•• ● ••

Pietro was in his orchard thinning apples when he sensed someone behind him. "Shouldn't you be trying to catch Ivan's roan?"

"Can't be caught unless he wants to be caught. That chestnut color means he can hide most anywhere."

"So why'd you come over here?"

"Need to talk to you about Mr. Patriloney."

"Nothing wrong with him, is there?"

"Nothing. He's as stubborn as you. Thinks you're the cause of his water problems."

Pietro grabbed the jug at the base of the tree and took a big swig of water. "Man tried to kill me and you tell me he has water problems. He's the one that's been damming the creek. My orchard will do poorly, and it's all Ivan's doing."

Wolverine sat on his haunches and watched as Pietro thinned the apple trees. Pietro's motions were smooth and quick. Only when he walked did Wolverine notice the limp from the broken ankle.

"Last time we spoke, you were willing to talk to Ivan about the creek."

"Last time I spoke, Ivan hadn't tried to kill me in a stampede."

"Mr. Patriloney's family came from Russia many years ago. He's been here longer than almost anyone except us Indians and the old fur traders."

"That doesn't give him the right to kill people."

As Wolverine stood up, the shine of blue caught Pietro's eye. "What's that around your neck?"

Wolverine pulled the stone from underneath his shirt. He looped the leather that held the stone over his head and handed the necklace to Pietro. Holding the cold stone sent a chill down Pietro's neck.

"What is it?"

"My grandfather gave it to me. Said it came from the stars."

"The stars?"

"It was in a cave. It's been passed down through my family for untold winters now."

Pietro moved his hand up and down. "The stone seems quite heavy for its size."

Wolverine smiled. "Most times it's very light."

"Not today it isn't."

Pietro held the stone in the sunlight. The light blue color recalled the stained glass image of Mary Immaculate from a church a lifetime away.

"Stone like that would buy you a large part of this Valley."

Wolverine laughed. "Indians can't buy land like you can. Government won't let us."

"Heard about it. One day that'll change."

Wolverine shook his head. "Not in our lifetime."

Pietro gave Wolverine a hard look. "At your age that could mean real soon."

Wolverine looked into the orchard. "Could be many years from now. Many."

"Right. Listen, I have work to do."

Wolverine took the stone back and wrapped it around his neck, the blue sparkles a contrast against his dark skin. "Think about Mr. Patriloney, okay?"

"Already have. Man owes me an apology. Nothing more to be said."

Pietro stopped thinning two minutes later to watch Wolverine riding down the road into a grove of trees. He thought of the Scottish family he had known many years ago, and then thought of that captain who had brought him to these shores. The sun felt hot, and Pietro decided that he would call it an afternoon.

Ivan heard Wolverine riding down the dirt road long before he saw him. He kept working at fixing the railing to his corral. Her heard his daughter running down the road to greet Wolverine. Soon the two rounded the barn corner, Cathy jumping up and down as she ran alongside the horse. Her long hair was tied in a pony tail.

"Wolverine's here," she shouted to no one in particular. "Wolverine's here!"

Adriana came out of the main house. She wiped her hands on her faded apron and walked down the steps towards the corral where her daughter and Wolverine were heading. Wolverine jumped from his horse and Cathy quickly took the saddle made of buckskin sacks filled with deer hair in the Indian style.

Ivan saw the saddle and grinned. "Imagine you'll have to change your saddle before you see your kin. Looks like you've come from a distance."

Wolverine, who hadn't seen Ivan for two weeks, not since the horse incident with Pietro, shrugged. "My family knows where I go. It doesn't seem to worry them."

"I've seen the Nez Perce use that type of saddle."

"They probably do. Had a talk with Mr. Rosselli a while back."

"Got nothing to say about that man. He's trespassing. I asked the justice to look into the matter."

Wolverine watched Cathy throw the saddle onto the top rail and lead his horse to the water trough, where she tied it to a hitching rail. She ran her hands along the horse's flank and said, "You've been running this horse."

Wolverine said nothing. Adriana stepped into the void. "Supper's ready. You're welcome to stay and eat."

Wolverine was about to decline when he saw Cathy's bright eyes. "I guess I can stay awhile. I'll wash up. I've been on the road for a week."

After supper Cathy wanted to follow the two men onto the porch, but Adriana insisted that she help wash the dishes and clear the table. By the time Cathy ran onto the porch, the two men were deep into a discussion.

"Mr. Rosselli wants you to apologize."

"The man is going to have to wait for a long time for that to happen."

"He's not well."

"Not surprising given what he's been up to. Got to wear on his spirit some, stealing my water like that."

Wolverine smiled. "You two talk the same way."

"More like that old fool talks like us ranchers. Bad enough the gold miners ripped off so many of us down south; now the apple-growers are coming in."

"I like Mr. Rosselli," Cathy volunteered.

Her father's anger made his voice loud. "Don't go questioning your father like that. You're still young enough for a whipping."

Cathy sank into a sullen quiet. Wolverine watched the sun setting. finally he broke the silence. "Let me tell you a story about a great chief."

Cathy brightened, her cheeks coloring as she leaned forward in the rocking chair. "Is this the Indian you called Walking Grizzly Bear? He sounds so exciting."

"Old Coyote tells the story better. He told me once that all stories are the same. If you tell them enough they even sound the same."

"I don't care. Walking Grizzly Bear sounds brave."

"Do you want to hear the story?"

Cathy instantly sank into silence to listen to Wolverine's story of Walking Grizzly Bear:

All stories are the same story, just told by different people. This is my story of how Walking Grizzly Bear stopped a war against the whites, the sha-mas, back when I was still a child.

At that time, Cumcloups was ruled by a sha-ma called John MacLeod. Macleod worked for the Hudson Bay Company in the year following the great merger between the Bay and the Northwest Company. He was a busy man. Cumcloups was the center of the fur trade for the Indians. Being so busy, MacLeod one day saw Walking Grizzly Bear, a young man with a group of warriors, and thought the man was looking for trouble. Having no time for such nonsense, MacLeod told the young warrior to return home to Nkamaplex, the Head of the Lake.

Walking Grizzly Bear left the fort, but promised himself that he'd return. Only after he had gone was MacLeod informed as to whom he had asked to leave. For several days he fretted, but when nothing came of it MacLeod became busy arranging for a brigade of horses laden with the winter's gathering of furs to send to Fort Okanagan.

One morning MacLeod was awakened by a sound of alarm. He hurried to dress and left his sleeping quarters to find out what the fuss was about. At the gates to the fort he was greeted by the same young warrior whom he now recognized as the chief they called Walking Grizzly Bear. He apologized profusely, perhaps because behind Walking Grizzly Bear were a hundred of his warriors bedecked for either war or peace.

Walking Grizzly Bear accepted the apology, and the gifts MacLeod had brought out, with these words:

"It is well that you do honour to my people. We mean to cause no trouble but we are not ready to lay our honour down. My father was slain by the Lillooets three moons ago, and for

*this I am still mourning, but that does not mean that I am
weak. One day the Lilloets will find this out. I accept your gifts
of tobacco, powder, and flint. I will give these to the two
headmen who have come with me, and to the ones who have
chosen to come with me today."*

Cathy waited, but when Wolverine stopped and stared into
the gathering night, she couldn't contain herself. "The story
isn't finished. What happened to MacLeod? What happened to
Walking Grizzly Bear? You have to finish the story."

Cathy's father also watched the gathering nightfall, but by the
way his head was tilted sideways, Cathy knew he was also listening. Wolverine used his left hand to move his silver hair over
his shoulder.

Cathy began to think that Wolverine hadn't heard her questions, and was about to speak again when Wolverine turned
towards her father.

"Hatred is a strange animal, stranger than Coyote. It gathers
its own strength. Perhaps Walking Grizzly Bear saw this, and
knew that he could not go there, could not lead his people down
a path where they would not survive."

"What do you know of hate?" Ivan asked, his voice curious
rather than hard.

"I killed once. I am not proud of what I did, but it had to be
done. Some would say that hate is enough, that treachery calls
for punishment. I used to be among those who thought this. The
thing is, I didn't use a rifle. I cut a man's throat. I still feel the
weight of the knife in my fist. Now I see what Walking Grizzly
Bear was trying to teach all of us. Perhaps Old Coyote will
return one day, but his voice is like the Woman in the Trees. It
belongs to another world, a spirit world I can't find anywhere
these days."

"If you're talking about Rosselli, he makes his own world. I
don't have to agree to it, and I won't. The man is stealing my
water."

Cathy protested. "I don't know what you two are talking about. I want to hear the end of the story."

Even her father laughed at her petulant voice.

"Stories don't end. They go on and on. Everything you do leads to something else. Old Coyote keeps telling his stories over and over because he knows this to be true."

"But that's not what they teach us in school."

"No, it isn't what they teach in your schools. If you want those kind of stories, perhaps your mother can tell you about them. I don't know them, not any outside of the Bible, anyway."

"I don't like it when you get like that," Cathy tried to get the last word in.

Ivan and Wolverine looked at her and chuckled. Her mother came out and called Cathy in. The final words she heard that night from the men were from her father. "Old Rosselli owes me. Nothing you can do about that. Maybe you're right and we"ll go on like this for the rest of our lives but, dammit, the man owes me. Where I come from, that means something."

"I think we're getting to the end of this, right?" Coyote shuffles nervously back and forth on the carpet. His question is rhetorical, so I continue to stare at the computer screen, a slave to its blinking cursor.

"What I don't get," Coyote continues when I don't say a word, "What I don't get is why you spend so much time on that rancher and orchardist. It's like the syilx don't exist to those two."

"What's your point?"

"My point is that you've marginalized the syilx."

"I repeat, what's your point?"

Coyote stops pacing and looks at me, his eyes brighten. "Oh, now I get it. That's damned clever of you."

"Let me continue writing. I need to wind this up."

"Make it different. I want to see Wolverine do something. Throw everything in. Let the readers decide what to read or not."

• • ● • •

Wolverine knew the storm was coming from the way the grasshoppers hushed in the afternoon air. A distant rumble and a quick stir of some nearby leaves made Wolverine scan the skies above. To the southwest, clouds billowed white and black over one of the mountains of peace where vision quests happened to those syilx apprenticing as shamans, now so few and so ridiculed by the growing Christian community.

His mind cast back to his wife of long ago. His people had been of two minds when the story of his killing at Fort Okanagan became known. A few supported his actions, the actions that would have been supported just twenty winters before. But most began to avoid him. No one spoke to the sha-mas; an unwritten uneasy silence instead settled between Wolverine and every syilx except the closest of his family. Service Berry Woman had lived with him the rest of her life, but there were times she woke from dreams, and Wolverine knew in his heart that her dreams were not of him. He loved her despite this, and he still missed her, his heart feeling the void her death created.

Such feelings swept over Wolverine as he stared into the distance. How long he saw the horse he didn't know, not until another growl of thunder brought his pain back to the present. The horse was watching him from a hundred yards away. It stood at the edge of the treeline overlooking Wolverine's small lodge. When it felt Wolverine's eyes on it, it snorted and walked along the treeline as though Wolverine wasn't there. A string of other wild horses followed in single file behind their leader.

"I knew you when you were so different," Wolverine whispered.

The horse stopped for a second and looked down at the

human again, raised and lowered its head almost as though it were saying yes, then continued walking along the slope down-hill towards Pietro's orchards, far below. The apples beckoned the herd, and this irritated Pietro no end. Ivan chortled when-ever he heard news about another horse raid on the orchard. "Serves the man right. This ain't no place for damn apples. Takes up too much of my water."

Wolverine watched the herd disappear. On a whim, he got onto his horse and followed the herd, letting his own take its lead. His horse followed the thin trail downhill. Often Wolver-ine had to lean forward, flat on the horse's back, to avoid the low branches that overhung the way down. Although Wolver-ine was familiar with this hill, he was amazed that his horse led him through parts he couldn't recall seeing before. Once, horse and rider plunged into a deep ravine that Wolverine had passed on many occasions but never noticed because its entrance lay hidden by a large Saskatoon bush.

After an hour, the two emerged onto the valley floor next to the creek that wound towards both Pietro's orchards and Ivan's grazing fields. Far ahead of them the herd continued its steady way towards the orchards. Wolverine had become so engrossed in the ride, and the new places visited, that only a sharp rumble woke him to the threatening clouds overhead. He stared up through the tree limbs and felt a gust of warm air whip past him towards the ravine behind.

His horse became skittish with the changing atmosphere. Humidity came in waves of heated air that gusted in random directions, picking up speed and force with every moment. Wolverine felt his sweat cake his shirt to his body. The swollen air made Wolverine dizzy. He pressed on through the thickening build-up, having nowhere to go but forward. He would never reach home safely. His only chance was to try to reach Pietro's home before the storm broke. He pushed his horse into a quick trot.

The herd ahead broke into a gallop, running for the shelter of trees a quarter mile from Pietro's place. Wolverine remembered the area. Cathy often played there, and Wolverine hoped she wasn't there still, or she would be trapped by the storm. For a second he hesitated, then turned his horse towards the grove. He couldn't take the chance of leaving the young woman alone in a storm he knew would be extremely vicious. He followed the creek south to the pool.

•• ● ••

To escape the growing humidity, Cathy swam in the small pond. Her strokes easily pulled her through the warm water. At fourteen, her long body was larger than most girls of her age. Cathy was proud of how she towered above the other schoolgirls, and made full use of her height and weight to lord it over them. She felt they were silly for paying so much attention to the boys. Most of the boys were from ranching or farming families from all over the upper Okanagan Lake, and their awkward attempts at book reading and writing left her shaking her head. Boys could be so stupid.

Still, there was one boy who was different. He sat at the back of the classroom. He came from below the new border between the Americans and Canadians, but was staying with cousins from the nearby reservation. He never spoke up, but his deep brown eyes probed everything he looked at with a clarity that sent shivers down Cathy's spine, especially when those eyes turned her way. His hair was longer and darker than hers. Sometimes when she caught him looking at her from an angle, he reminded her of Wolverine.

The day came when she found herself caught alone with him in the school yard. He was shorter than she was, so she stared down at him, trying to play him like she did with the other boys. He sat on the plank steps leading into the two-room school. Nearby several girls watched her, giggling and poking one another. But they kept their distance, so Cathy ignored them.

"What's your name?"

The Indian looked up at her, and she shivered.

"I asked you what your name was. Are you always this rude?"

The Indian looked down at his open book again, then flipped the page to continue reading. Cathy was about to knock the book from his hands when he looked up again. His smile made her catch her breath.

"You want to knock my book away, don't you?"

Cathy took a small step back and glared at him. "You don't know what I think. You should go back to the reservation where you came from. You're just a silly American Indian."

The Indian looked at her, never losing his smile. "Roger. My name's Roger."

It took Cathy several seconds to shift gear. Before she could speak, Roger stared into her eyes, not a hard look, but a look of bemusement and tolerance. For no reason she could fathom, Cathy was defensive.

"I know Wolverine, you know. He's the only good Indian there is from around here. He helps my dad a lot."

Roger laughed, and closed his book with a snap that made Cathy start. "I know Wolverine, too. Everyone knows him."

"Well, you don't have to be so stuck up about it." Cathy turned her back and returned to the nearby group of girls.

Now, a week later, as Cathy swam through the water, she thought of Roger. When she next saw Wolverine she would ask him who Roger was. For the moment, she enjoyed the smooth feeling of the water flowing over her athletic body. The fierce sound of the pines swaying in a hot wind drew Cathy's attention skyward, and for the first time she saw the storm clouds coming over the nearby mountain to her west.

The next thing Cathy watched, helpless to prevent, was her horse being struck on the rear by a falling branch. While the branch wasn't large enough to hurt her horse, it did panic the beast. It broke free from its tether and ran for home, quickly disappearing as Cathy began a frantic swim for shore.

Ivan slowed his horse to a walk. The humidity was unlike any-thing he had known in this Valley, and he was worried. When the streams of hot wet air hit him from different directions from time to time, he broke into an instant sweat. He wasn't worried about himself so much as he thought of Adriana and Cathy. Adriana would be out looking for Cathy in this type of weather, and that worried Ivan more than anything. But he couldn't force his tired mount into a trot, not in this type of heat. His horse would drop in less than a half of a mile. So despite what he wanted to do, Ivan kept an even pace towards his house three miles away. His horse kept pricking its ears forward, sensing the changes that were coming. Every so often a deep low growl from the west echoed through the hills.

His worst fears rose to the fore when he heard the sound of a running horse. Although he couldn't see it through the trees, he knew it was Cathy's from the way it ran, and he also knew it was running from the pond where Cathy liked to swim.

Pietro tapped in the final wood spike to hold the water trough together. The line was now a hundred yards down from the hill where the stream turned away from his orchard. The sound of distant thunder drew Pietro's eyes towards the peace mountain to the west. Black and white met his gaze, and he knew the storm would be big from the way the bottoms of the approach-ing clouds turned from midnight black to a curious grey swirl.

A running horse emerged from the nearby tree line. It raced towards Ivan's ranch home. Although it was riderless, Pietro noticed the makeshift saddle and knew it to be Cathy's. Pietro stood up from his crouch and looked towards the hillside. "Where could Ivan's daughter be?" he wondered. Then, on an age-old instinct, he walked up into the tree line in search of Cathy. "This is no weather for a young girl like Cathy to be out in, especially if the storm broke before she could find shelter," Pietro thought.

Moving south at a steady pace, Wolverine saw steam rising from numerous places along the hillside. The creek itself twisted and fell towards the Okanagan Lake three miles away, but Wolverine couldn't see more than two hundred feet in any direction. The pine trees around him swayed as the winds roared south, east, north, west, always hot and growing stronger by the minute. The rumbling approach of the storm led Wolverine to throw caution away as he kicked his mount into a quick gallop. As he rounded the final turn before the pond Wolverine felt a stab of fear clutch at his heart as a new wind, cold and hard, thundered through the trees, breaking limbs as it roared uphill. Was this the Woman in the Trees coming for him, coming for the girl now within his reach?

Pietro stopped to stare at the sky. Black had turned to pea soup grey, the clouds spinning in an odd circular pattern as they neared. Before he could stop it, his hat flew into a scorching blast of humid air that both bent the trees all around him, and sent what Pietro could swear was steam or mist from the ground, as though everything around him was boiling. He knew he had little time, so he reached the top of the small ridge and ran as fast as he dared towards the pond where he felt certain Ivan's girl swam. A gust of wind almost swept him from his feet, and then a cold blast of air turned him half around and threw him from his feet. He was falling down the slope towards the pond, and he couldn't stop his roll.

•• ● ••

Ivan came over the ridge, urging his tired horse over this final hurdle. "Where is Cathy?" he wondered. A premonition of something awful darkened his sight for a moment, and he wiped his eyes with the back of his right hand, taking some of the sweat away. The winds were so great he knew it was useless to shout. For several long moments he simply sat on his horse and stared at the trees as they swayed like prairie grass, roaring with a sound he had never heard before. It was like a dream. He saw Wolverine emerge from below, racing for the pond. Lower down, along another ridge, Pietro was rolling head over heels towards it, too.

Something, impossibly a human figure, dropped from the skies. Ivan kicked his horse away from the oncoming object, his horse plunging downhill in a frantic race against something so strange he thought it would sweep him away if he stood in its way. And as he and his horse fell towards the distant pond, Ivan felt the cold blast of air twist around him, tearing through trees like straw.

Cathy made it to shore as the first lightning bolt cracked into a pine on the other side of the pond, the explosion sending blue streaks of heat into the sky. Cathy's hair stood on end from the static. She kept low and ran towards a ditch that Pietro had dug several years ago. As she threw herself into it, a movement caught her attention. Pietro was screaming as he tumbled into the pond. Ivan was a hundred yards away from her, riding hard. His horse looked every bit like Cathy imagined one of the horses of the Apocalypse would look like, its ears pinned back and its mouth foaming white in the hazy atmosphere. As she rose to meet her father, she was lifted off her feet by another blast of air that threw her farther from Ivan, knocking the breath from her. As she lay gasping, she found herself staring into Wolverine's face. He bent over her to hear above the storm.

"I thin . . . g's broken."

"Lay . . . We can't . . . anywhere . . . storm."

Ivan thundered up on his horse, barely reining it to a stop before he was leaping onto the ground and running the short distance to where his daughter lay. For some strange reason, he turned once towards the slope he had come down, before he crouched down next to Wolverine. Wolverine glanced up the hillside but saw nothing that would draw Ivan's attention from his daughter. He then saw Pietro laying face up in the pool. Ivan was bent over Cathy, but what words she spoke Wolverine couldn't hear over the storm, which broke over them with a roar that made thinking straight hard to do.

The rain was like a solid body of water, and Wolverine looked around from his crouched position. They were on a flat surface, perhaps a foot above the pond. Twenty feet away, water poured down in a growing torrent from the mouth of a ravine. Wolverine grabbed at Ivan, shaking him to attention. Ivan looked up, rage almost taking him over the edge. He batted Wolverine's hands away as lightning bolts streaked everywhere, lighting the entire landscape every two to three seconds. The crack of thunder overwhelmed even the rain that poured endlessly from the dark clouds above.

Wolverine ran into the growing pond and dragged Pietro onto shore, mud caking both of them. A huge blast of wind almost lifted Wolverine into the air. He kept dragging Pietro away from the water, hauling him up the same steep slope he had fallen from. Water made it hard for Wolverine to hold onto Pietro, and several times his grip slipped and Pietro tumbled down the slope. Each time Wolverine had to start over, his moccasins finding little traction in the mud and soaked earth. Yet Wolverine persevered and, finally, Pietro lay still. Wolverine collapsed onto the orchardist, draping over him to protect him from the storm.

Ivan lifted his daughter and was grateful the storm covered her screams. He hurried away from the mouth of the ravine for safer ground within a low depression higher up the same slope where

Wolverine now struggled to drag Pietro. His horse disappeared into the trees with the other mounts, but Ivan paid them no attention, as he paid the other men no attention save for the brief curse that crossed his mind about what the hell Pietro was doing around here at this time. Perhaps spying on his daughter. Well, Ivan would make sure that this would never happen again.

As dramatic as the storm started, it ended five minutes later. The winds stopped so suddenly that Ivan felt his ears pop from the change in air pressure. For the first time he could hear Cathy, and he told her to remain still while he searched for, and quickly found, two long straight branches amid the ruins of the nearby trees. He used strips of his shirt to bind his daughter's broken leg in a makeshift but effective splint. By the time he finished, Cathy had passed out, the best pain killer possible at the time. Ivan saw his horse at the edge of the tree line and, as he stood, the horse trotted to them.

When Wolverine came to, remnants of the storm were scuttling through the opening sky. Pietro stirred under him. Wolverine rolled over and sat up. Ivan had his daughter draped over the horse and was riding off. He looked back once, and Wolverine felt hatred pour from the rancher. Only then did Wolverine understand how it must look to Ivan. And he also knew better than to call for help, or to wave at Ivan. Wolverine turned to Pietro then, and began to look after the Italian's broken left arm, which hung limply at his side.

Storytelling: Part Three

•• ● ••

Mountain Goats

The heft and heave of goats scrambling up slopes
and cliffs of Lake Okanagan,
cloven hooves gripping granite ice.
We chased them — the mountain-goat caller,
his voice ringing the goats,
asking permission for the goats to give their lives.
Bolting up the rocks, the goats wavered
between the hunters at the base,
and those above —
bows drawn,
fingers knocked against the arrow shafts.
Calls broke rocks that spiraled into space,
sending the hunters scrambling for safety.
But the goats locked into line.
Finally, Stla-Chain-Um, she of the deer family,
her voice the voice of goats,
spoke through her throat, her gravel words
shaking the goats from their trance to continue their run
along the cliffs.
Goats for food,
stories for children and generations.
The hard scrape of flesh against red-streaked rocks,

broken bones mixed with the hunt's excitement.
Clutching for life onto rocks
rubbed smooth by generations of goats,
like the great buffalo stones of the plains.
We traded life for life.
Free fall, the abrupt loss of weight
for a few moments
of drift before everything switches off,
no gap between the whistle and impact,
no gap between life and death.
After,
the feast
and the red stars
bright with the pupils of goats.

Mourning Dove

Christine Quintasket walks into the room with the limp she picked thinning apples earlier in her life. She sits down without more than glancing at the wicker chair, shifts her weight to the right slightly, favoring her left knee. "Old Coyote said you were looking for me."

"I didn't know who else to ask. You don't seem surprised."

Christine gently moves the braid of hair on the left side of her head until it rests on her upper back. "Where I've been, nothing surprises me. You couldn't wait til you came over, eh?"

"I need to tell a story. A story about you."

Christine leans back farther into the wicker chair, causing it to creak. The red needle on my tape recorder jumps at the sound and eases back almost to zero. A matching string of beads — red, blue, and yellow — are entwined along the length of each braid of black and white hair. They click each time Christine moves her head.

"A story. A story about me." Christine's voice is flat, a statement rather than a question. She claps her hands together sharply, the sound making the needle jump to the end of the scale. Christine smiles for the first time.

"Old Coyote could have told you any story you wanted."

"Yes," I agree, "but I wanted a story from you. A story from your life."

"You've read Jay Miller's notes on me?"

"I've read them."

"You've read them, but they aren't me. No, they aren't me."

"He did a lot of editing."

Christine leans forward, her voice barely registering on the needle. "That's not me. There's a chest my family has. Now that's me. There are things there that would change this world. There are stories there whose sounds would shift the ground you walk on." Christine snorts as she leaned back. "But my family won't give the chest up. Don't blame them. Sometimes I wonder why I wrote them down, those stories. They aren't meant to be told for another hundred years, your time. Til then, they're safer locked away."

"What stories?"

Christine shakes her head. "Just one hint. Did you ever hear the story of those Spaniards who came into the Valley and took some of us as prisoners? Happened before the first priests came, a long time before the first fur traders."

"I've heard the story."

"Well, they didn't make it out after the winter. But I know where they're buried. Teequalt, Long Theresa, told me the story once. Said to write it down when I could and wait til the world was ready. Didn't say what to do in the meantime, so I had to think for myself."

"That's why the chest."

"That's why the chest."

I wait, and Christine waits. The needle goes to zero. Christine smiles, first at the recorder, then at me.

"What else do you need to say, if anything?"

"Just that the book I wrote is my story, but it's only one story of several, and each of us can tell the story again in different words. I must have rewritten that story a dozen times, but it's not the same as telling it. Not even close."

"People will accuse me of putting words in your mouth, of fictionalizing real events."

Christine gives a low, throaty chuckle. "Stories are stories. Like history, they aren't the real thing, so why pretend? But they can teach us a lot, entertain us a lot, and tell us who we are more than the white man's sciences can. You go ahead and tell this story, and tell them that the past, the present, and the future are one thing, and Old Coyote is another thing, another story."

"It's not an answer many people can live with."

Christine's voice lowers and she leans towards me. "Well, then, tell them that if I thought for one minute that you had all the answers, I'd have to stop you. Nobody has that right."

Old Coyote pads into the house, his tongue hanging out of his mouth. He sits down and looks at Christine. "Have you finished the story? I'm hot and I want to go back to the other side."

Christine nods and stands up slowly, her beads clicking as she sweeps her braids behind her ears with both hands. Old Coyote waits respectfully as Christine makes for the door, then turns to me.

"Did she tell you what you wanted?"

"She told me a story."

"That's all you'll get from her. That's all there is in this world. Stories. How's your story going?"

"It's coming along nicely. Another eight months and it'll be ready."

"Well, you know where I am if you need help. Next time I come back, I'll have a story for you that'll curdle your hair." Coyote looks at the top of my head and adds, "That is, what hair you have left. See you around."

"See you around," I say, and close the notebook.

Walking Grizzly Bear

●● ● ●●

1865

At the beginning of the end, Wolverine stood at the back of the half-circle of syilx. They were silent, a great crowd watching the sha-mas who sat behind a flat piece of wood. Long Bear was translating the sha-mas' language, a steady drone of words from a people who used so many to say so little. Although Wolverine knew the language from his priest school days, he felt his head ache, and every so often he left the circle to catch his breath.

August heat poured over the land, streaming into the gulleys and flatlands, its sign the chirr of grasshoppers. Three hundred paces south, the lake shimmered, its edges curled and waved in the sun.

The lead sha-ma said: "We come from the Great Mother. She asks her sons to make their marks on this paper where her words live. She asks you to do this so that all men can live together in peace. Our mother wishes her children of the Okanagan long and fruitful lives. She watches over you, and she is proud of her children that they honor her so."

Words. Wolverine hovered, waiting for the wind to stop, for the speakers to hear the grasshoppers, the children at play. But the wind of words blew steadily. Wolverine saw Walking Grizzly Bear's eyes close in sleep.

204

•• ● ••

The two traders grabbed their pistols as the Indian came from nowhere. One minute the edge of the trees had been clear. In the next, a short stocky man paused and then walked to the cabin. Trailing him was a horse laden with skins. From the way the man walked, William Pion immediately recognized the Indian he called Inquala. He knew enough of the man to tell his partner to lower his weapon.

The man, if he noticed the drawn weapons, never let on. He hitched his horse to the rails and smiled at the sha-mas. Pion made a shallow bow and told Inquala to wait. He quickly entered the cabin and returned in moments with a foot of tobacco.

Inquala smiled and sat on the bench the two sha-mas had vacated when they had watched his approach. They joined him, and for five easy minutes they sat in comfortable silence. Montigny studied the horse, his eyes calculating the cost of the furs Inquala brought.

Inquala feigned indifference but he shrewdly assessed the fact that Montigny's need to buy the furs would bring a good price, perhaps as much as a dollar a pound. The furs were good. His four wives had spent many days preparing and treating the hides until they were the best in syilx country.

Montigny's low voice brought Inquala out of his reveries. "My partner says you're a good hunter."

"Your partner knows me well."

"I'd like to go hunting with you someday."

Inquala gave Montigny a hard look. He noted the trader's spare yet well-kept clothes — clearly the man had pride in his appearance. Was there more than that?

"I was going into the hills today."

Montigny nodded. "I need the ride. Mind if I come with you?"

Inquala hid his surprise. "I thought you boat men didn't like horses."

"Horses have saved my life, and those of my crews, on many occasions. Nothing wrong with horses."

"I'll drop the furs off and we can leave."

Montigny looked at Pion. "Look after the post while I'm gone. I'll be back tomorrow."

Later, as their horses carried them up the steep slopes north of the post, Montigny spent time watching Inquala, who continued to feign indifference as he studied any tracks they came across. When they came across signs of deer, Inquala followed the trail, now paying no heed to the white man who followed. Montigny was expected to keep pace and he did this so naturally that Inquala, had he been attentive, would have been surprised.

They rode down a small gulley, and then Inquala was off his horse and into the trees in a single fluid motion. He notched an arrow in his short bow and walked swiftly for a thick clump of undergrowth deeper and lower in the gulley . The wind blew up the valley. Inquala stopped fifty feet from the undergrowth, paused for several heartbeats, then pulled his bow horizontal to shoulder height. Montigny heard the release of the arrow before he saw the deer at the edge of the undergrowth.

Inquala gave thanks to the creator and left a small offering from the deer for Toom-Tem. The rest, he and Montigny skinned and dressed. Montigny occasionally looked up into the face of the man who squatted two feet away. Inquala was quiet and efficient, his steel knife slicing easily into the carcass in a series of quick cuts.

Later, as the two made camp and washed their tools off to dry, Montigny kept his silence, following the Indian's lead. He gathered wood and with his flint he started a fire. Inquala watched from a crouched position, his eyes gleaming with interest. Montigny extended the flint to Inquala, who took the stone without comment, reached into his own travel bag and pulled out a small stone that gleamed gold in the low light.

Inquala turned the stone in his hand. Montigny knew enough to keep silent, his heart racing. Inquala turned the stone a final time against the fire and then gently tossed it in an arc towards Montigny, who caught the stone as though it were the most natural thing in the world. Montigny had only once before held gold in his hand, at Fort Okanagan seven days to the south.

"A trade for a trade," Inquala said casually. "Perhaps you could give me a gun or two when we get back to your place."

Montigny nodded as he carelessly pushed the small stone into a pocket. "I will see what I can do."

Inquala laughed then. "I hear that the sha-mas at the fort down south place some value on this type of stone."

"Some. Did you get this from around here?"

Inquala looked at the fire. "It's been some time. I think my father gave it to me."

"The fur traders would give much for this stone if they could find more."

Inquala shook his head. "My father once said that his father had told him some things can never be. So much died with the last white fog."

"White fog?"

"The fog that snatched our children and old ones away. My grandfather's people died, many of them burning up, their faces marked by running sores. Their breath carried in the wind, and took others with them. Entire families and villages were no more."

"We call it smallpox."

Inquala laughed. When he saw Montigny's puzzled look, he said, "You sha-mas have a strange humor. There was nothing small about the sickness."

"No, I suppose there wasn't."

"We will go back early tomorrow. I want to return to my people. The winter will be long and we haven't gathered enough berries and medicines this year because of the cold months."

Montigny thought about this for some time. Later, as they made their sleeping places by the fire, he spoke. "The stone you have given is worth many furs. I need to return to Fort Okanagan for the winter, and my partner will go with me. Someone needs to look after the cabin we made. It has some stock. I would be proud if you and your family would do this favor for us."

Inquala grinned. "I will speak to my family of this."

Montigny also grinned. "Sleep well."

"I will tell you a story," Walking Grizzly Bear said to his son Kesakailux at Douglas Lake. "It is a tale told by Coyote."

Kesakailux nodded and listened as his father told him of the Woman in the Trees, a story he never tired of. At the end of the story, Kesakailux thought of a question he had wanted to ask his father for some time. "Does this woman come to us in a dream?"

"No, she's real. We syilx who see her are not in our times when this happens, but she is as real as you and I."

"My uncle Horse says that only a few syilx ever see her. Why does she hide?"

"She doesn't hide. But she doesn't seek out everyone."

"She must be afraid of us. We are a strong people. How many horses and cattle do you have?"

Walking Grizzly Bear laughed. "You think we are strong? In my grandfather's time we were as the leaves of a tree. I have many horses, but the wealth was different then. We shared more. Now the fur trade takes all of our time, and there is less to hunt and fish."

"Horse told me about riding through a village once, and of all the dead syilx he found. So many he couldn't bury them."

"I know the village. No one goes there now. It is sacred ground. Only Coyote has the strength to travel through that land."

"The Woman in the Trees could go there, too."

"Yes," Walking Grizzly Bear admitted. "She could go there too."

"She must love those children fiercely to do what she did. I want to be like her. Loving someone to death."

Walking Grizzly Bear could not sleep that night. His son's words troubled him for reasons he couldn't know. The strength of the voice when it spoke was nothing he had trained his son to feel, and yet Kesakailux had spoken defiantly. More would follow from this, but Walking Grizzly Bear could not see what that might be.

●● ● ●●

Blue Dreams pulled his son from the path of Walking Grizzly Bear as the headman rode into camp with the young warriors. Walking Grizzly Bear rode to the center of the camp and dismounted near the fire pit, letting a young warrior lead his horse away.

Horse and the other elders waited for Walking Grizzly Bear, having been told of his coming several days before by one of the scouts. They knew why he came, of course, and they had agreed to provide him with thirty men from the village. Horse noted wryly that it wasn't as though they had a choice: Trying to stop the young men from going on this war party was like trying to stop snow from falling, the sun from rising, or Coyote from boasting.

Walking Grizzly Bear sensed acquiescence as soon as he arrived, and thanked the old ones for allowing him to speak. As his eyes swept the waiting group, for a second he lingered on Wolverine, and he smiled, sending a ripple of warmth through the boy.

Walking Grizzly Bear turned to Horse and the other elders. "I come to ask for your help in avenging my father's death. I ask that you help me in seeking out those who have so far escaped payment for such a deed."

"We have expected you, Walking Grizzly Bear. We have met in counsel way and we will give you thirty warriors. We ask one thing of you."

Walking Grizzly Bear stared at Horse, but kept his thoughts to himself. "Ask and I will see what I can do."

"We ask that you let Blue Dreams be part of your party. He is our best young hunter and warrior. You will not have to watch your back. Blue Dreams will be in charge of the warriors from our village."

Walking Grizzly Bear turned to where Blue Dreams stood. His next words were meant for both the circle of elders and Blue Dreams. "I have waited ten winters to do this. I have called in many favours, and have made many promises. Blue Dreams shall be in charge of your warriors, and he shall answer to me. I know Blue Dreams. I agree to your wish. We will stay here for two days and then we shall be gone."

That night the village gathered and celebrated the past victories of the warriors over the Secwepemc and Lillooets. Many more warriors from the Secwepemc and southern syilx joined the Head of the Lake warriors at the camp, setting up their small sleeping quarters at the village edge. Some stayed awake through the night, singing, dancing, and telling tales of past deeds, as they would over the next nights on the trail of war.

Walking Grizzly Bear greeted many of the incoming warriors by first name. This was impressive because in some cases it had been years since he had last been with them. Walking Grizzly Bear wasn't tall, but his bearing was unmistakable. Some said that he had walked up to the spirit for whom he was named and sat down beside the fearsome animal. The grizzly bear had given him a single look before returning to its foraging of berries. Other stories said that the bear was a mother, and her cubs had stood aside to let Walking Grizzly Bear walk by unimpeded. Walking Grizzly Bear had stocky shoulders and a barrel chest; he could outrun any warrior among the syilx, north or south. He could also out-wrestle men ten years his junior, and his arrows were the straightest in the land. He was the only one who could pull his bow to its fullest.

During the next several nights, his deeds were told around the fire pit. Women stared at him with obvious attraction, wondering whom he would next wed. He already had nine wives, and there were no signs of him slowing down. These marriages created a network of family relations throughout Secwepemc, Thompson, and syilx territory as far south as the Spokane peoples ten days' ride away.

Walking Grizzly Bear had fostered and cultivated these connections carefully, visiting each village within a huge territory many times over ten years of travel. As a hunter without peer, he often left generous gifts of deer, moose, or elk meat at each stop. His stories of bravery were crafted to place the growing number of warriors who followed him in their best light, strengthening his bonds. He also allowed his wives to spend time with their families. Although he had many wives, at any one time only two or three traveled with him for any length of time. The others were content to wait for him to travel through their village, which he did at least once each year.

Walking Grizzly Bear used his hunting skills to trap the animals whose fur the sha-mas from Fort Okanagan traded. He was the one who showed his syilx people how valuable such trade could be, and again he was careful to trade for goods that he knew would make impressive gifts to his growing number of followers.

It was also he who served by example in breaking down the resistance of the syilx to sha-ma contact. Wherever he went, Walking Grizzly Bear avoided criticizing the elders for their initial resistance to white contact. Instead, he impressed them with his quick grasp of the language the sha-mas spoke, and the ease with which he seemed able to turn huge profits for the furs they valued.

All the while, he remembered his father's death at the hands of the Lillooets, who had slain him when he threatened the fishing industry along the great canyons of the Fraser. Walking Grizzly Bear, who had been headman of the Head of the Lake band for ten years when Pelkamulox was slain, swore that he would avenge his father's death.

In his thirties by then, Walking Grizzly Bear was the most powerful syilx alive, and his friends were many. Thus, when he asked for help in gathering a war party to travel to the great canyons, the elders had difficulty in refusing him, and more difficulty in stopping the young men from the three nations bordering the canyons from joining him.

By the time Walking Grizzly Bear reached the Head of the Lake on his way to Secwepemc country, over three hundred warriors had declared they would follow him. It had been many years since a war of this scale had occurred. Only Walking Grizzly Bear had the following and influence to pull it off, against the wishes of the fur traders who saw the threat to their livelihood but also who knew how determined he could be. They turned a blind eye that year as Walking Grizzly Bear rode through towards the canyons of the Fraser River.

Blue Dreams said farewell to his family. Wolverine's eyes shone with the bright eagerness of a follower. He stood, as did many of the other children, on a small hill to watch Blue Dreams and his warriors race northward with Walking Grizzly Bear at their lead. In the distance, a hundred more warriors from the villages to the south waited respectfully for Walking Grizzly Bear to join them. In unison, the war party turned north and rode in a long line out of sight towards the lush lands along the Spallumcheen River half a day's ride north, where more warriors from the Secwepemc were rendezvousing with the party before they headed west towards the canyons.

The next days were memorable only in that Wolverine led the rest of the boys on mock raiding parties and extended war games that included archery contests and running games, which often took two days to play out. Everyone was nervous; the children from excitement and the adults from worry. Wolverine once caught his mother sitting alone in her lodge, staring vacantly at the opposite wall, the deer hide in her hands untended. Wolverine caught himself before he spoke, and his mother neither saw nor heard him as he quietly climbed out of the kekuli.

The games exhausted the boys, and soon they became as listless as their parents and grandparents. Wolverine caught himself doing what his mother did, sitting or standing with his mind churning with thoughts he never remembered. The pit of Wolverine's stomach knotted whenever he thought of his father, and for the first time he wondered about Walking Grizzly Bear's tactics. Could Walking Grizzly Bear prevail against a people as fierce as the canyon people? Could he win, or were they now limping back in defeat, their dead slung over their horses?

Although Wolverine had heard much of Walking Grizzly Bear's war prowess, he now recalled the stories Horse had told him of the canyon people — fierce fishermen who knew how to scramble up and down rocks that made Swah-netk'-qhu seem tame. Could anyone beat the Lillooets in their home territory? What would it cost? And the strongest fear, would Blue Dreams return alive to his family?

In the month of Saskatoon berries, the village broke up. Each family went its own way, to pick berries, to go hunting, or to begin the trek south to the river that flowed from the great lake. Salmon runs were starting in a moon's time, and it was critical for the syilx to get good sites at Kettle Falls, and at the confluence of the Okanagan and Columbia rivers. Trading would come later as the syilx returned to their winter camps.

Yet the people left sadly, their thoughts on the many young men who had gone on the war party to the west. Wolverine felt the first dreams of the Woman in the Trees at this point in his life. She came to him, facing him directly, her blue-green eyes tracing the outline of his small sturdy frame. The camp was sleeping. A single guard patrolled the edge of the camp, a concession to the anxiety everyone felt but didn't speak. If Walking Grizzly Bear was lost, nothing prevented the Lillooets from sweeping through syilx territory in a counter-attack. Horse insisted on having someone keep watch at all times.

One minute Wolverine had stared at the fire, and in the next, the moon shifted a quarter-way up the sky. The fire burnt low. At first, all Wolverine saw were sparks flying into the dark mat of the pines. He blinked, and then felt a shadow move against those trees, a tall figure with the grace and speed of a hunter. The hair along his arms rose and a chill made him tremble.

"Do not fear me."

The laughter came from the sound of pine needles rubbing each other. "You are the one."

Wolverine saw the eyes. "I am a boy."

"One day your grandfather will take you to a cave. There you will be given the stone that has been passed through the generations within your family."

Wolverine stared into the woman's blue-green eyes, and was enchanted by them, his fear draining as he felt her presence fill him with peace.

"My father speaks of you in his stories."

"I have heard the stories. They are peaceful. I mean my people no harm. You are my ancestor and my future."

"I miss my father."

The woman turned away. As her shape returned to the trees above, her voice sounded the winds. "There is little time. Your father will return tomorrow."

Walking Grizzly Bear returned the next day. His riders came into the village, over a hundred strong, flushed with both victory and pain. Several families started their songs of death as others joyfully greeted their warrior kinfolk. Blue Dreams almost fell from his horse, his wife helping him down. She saw the poultice on his right leg, an arrow wound. Blue Dreams grimaced as he sat heavily on the deer skin mat just inside their tule mat shelter.

"It was a clean shot. I broke the arrowhead off. It went through my leg without stopping. Pulling out the shaft was easier."

Wolverine was gathered into his father's arms while his mother worked to dress her husband's wound, cleaning it and applying new medicines. Only then did Wolverine ask timidly, "Did my father kill many enemies?"

Blue Dreams looked down into his son's brown eyes. "Killing people is never good. Perhaps there is justice, but no man should take pleasure in taking another man's life. When you kill as a warrior, that is the way you will die."

"I have a message for you."

Blue Dreams and his wife looked at their son. Wolverine never flinched. He had practiced bravery many times in front of the other children.

"The Woman in the Trees tells me we don't have much time."

Blue Dreams gave his son a perplexed look. "The Woman in the Trees. I have seen her only once in my life."

"She says she's family."

"Have you spoken to your grandfather about this?"

"She came last night. I haven't seen grandfather today. I think he's at the sweat house up the hill."

Blue Dreams looked at his wife again before speaking to his son. "I want you to keep this between you and me. Perhaps this is a sign. It means something. Something you need to do that no one else can do. The Woman in the Trees doesn't visit anyone unless she needs to warn them about something."

"She was a nice woman."

Blue Dreams tapped his son on the shoulder. "Leave your mother and me. Go play. I am tired and need rest. Tomorrow we will talk more about your vision."

Blue Dreams slept through the next day. At times he was feverish, but his wife patiently fed him broth. Some time during the second night, the medicines took hold in his wound, and the fever broke.

In the interim, stories filled the camp. The war party had

fought several pitched battles in the canyons. The first time, they thought they had beaten the Lillooets badly. In the end, it had only antagonized their enemies into a united front that harassed and worried at the flanks of the war party over many days, never directly confronting the larger group but slowly whittling away at their ranks. Finally, after a brief skirmish that had left Blue Dreams wounded, Walking Grizzly Bear had enough and pulled his warriors out for the long trek home.

Perhaps he would not have done this if it hadn't been for Blue Dreams. The attack had startled the horses, and one syilx fell but luckily grabbed onto a ledge, hanging a hundred feet above the raging river. Blue Dreams heard the call for help and, in turning, took an arrow in his upper thigh, The arrow head went through cleanly, and Blue Dreams tried to ignore the pain as he reached down, grabbed his comrade's wrists, and by sheer strength pulled the man up. The others from his village had formed a protective ring and fought off the Lillooets who were trying to finish off the two stricken syilx.

The fight lasted no more than fifty heartbeats, but in that time three more syilx and Secwepemc fell never to rise again. The Lillooets took their casualties, so no one knew how badly, if at all, the Lillooets had suffered. Walking Grizzly Bear made camp a mile outside the canyon and took stock. A man of plants pulled the arrow from Blue Dreams' leg and dressed the wound.

No one spoke to Walking Grizzly Bear as he made his rounds through the makeshift camp of tule mat lean-tos. The anger in their eyes told Walking Grizzly Bear that his warriors wanted to continue fighting, but he also knew that too many of his own party had fallen. It was time to leave, having shown the Lillooets that his father's death was now avenged.

As well as he knew that the fight was over, Walking Grizzly Bear also knew that his people would have broken camp back home. There was no other thing to do but to return and prepare for the winter. The other headmen agreed. Before they left, the syilx made a marker of stone, a warning to the Lillooets that they were not to be taken lightly ever again. Walking Grizzly Bear was the last one to leave. Along the rim of the canyon, the Lillooets emerged in a long line, not moving as they stared at this man who had come to their own territory and claimed it as his own. Truly, Pelkamulox had a worthy son. Bravely he stood alone as the Lillooets began moving towards him, and his own party moved away. Walking Grizzly Bear stood until the Lillooets were within arrow reach, then he turned his back to them and walked after his war party. And so ended the story of Pelkamulox's son.

It was happening again. Walking Grizzly Bear heard from his tenth wife of his son's rages, heard as she wept and asked Walking Grizzly Bear to stay at Douglas Lake. Walking Grizzly Bear sensed something beneath his wife's request but, since she would not speak it, he could not do anything. He promised to return in a moon's time. As he left the lodge, Kesakailux met him. His son held the ropes of the horse lightly, being a master rider.

"My wife worries when I leave. Can you tell me what bothers her?"

Kesakailux shrugged. "My mother worries about my wife. There is nothing to worry about."

Again, Walking Grizzly Bear sensed something, and again he could do nothing. "I will be back in a moon's time. Do nothing hasty."

Kesakailux handed his father the bridle. "What can happen in a moon's time? Be well, Father."

So formal. Walking Grizzly Bear almost decided to stay, then thought of what he could do to help the situation. "Remember, I ask that you treat your wife with care. Her family is strong."

Walking Grizzly Bear was at Head of the Lake when a rider

came into the village. He knew from the rider's grim look that his son had not paid heed to his words. Within the hour, Walking Grizzly Bear had prepared his travel gear and rode south along the west side of the lake, the Douglas Lake rider following without a word once he had told Walking Grizzly Bear of the situation.

Walking Grizzly Bear remembered Service Berry Woman and that strange young son of Blue Dreams. Wolverine had never taken another wife. As old as Walking Grizzly Bear felt, he was sad for Wolverine. A man shouldn't have to travel life alone.

At Douglas Lake, several days later, Walking Grizzly Bear walked slowly to the lodge where they kept his son under guard. Walking Grizzly Bear felt his bones ache from the heavy ride into the mountains onto the great plateau. He wanted nothing more than to sleep with his tenth wife, who would normally have everything prepared, but who was now grief stricken.

Walking Grizzly Bear heard the hushed comments. "Sha-ma lover." "The man who loves whites." "The Bear too good for his people." And the one that really hurt, "The man who gives nothing." He ignored them all as he limped to his son's jail.

Kesakailux stood as his father opened the flap and stooped to enter. Walking Grizzly Bear saw his wife on one side of the fire. On the other side was the headman of the village, along with the grieving families of Kesakailux's now-dead wife and lover. This would not be easy, Walking Grizzly Bear knew. The Okanagan alliance was a loose confederacy of villages and headmen with governance by cooperation and good will, not force.

Walking Grizzly Bear hugged first his son, then his wife, as he heard the stifled moans from the other side of the fire. His tenth wife whispered in his ear, "Be brave for our son," and Walking Grizzly Bear nodded as he gently stood away from his family and turned to the others.

"Your son has taken the lives of two people from our village."

"I know this. I grieve for their deaths." Walking Grizzly Bear knew better than to state the obvious. There was no place for that now. There was a way out, and it would cost him dearly, but he would pay the price. He knew this because he had thought of it every moment on his ride up here to the lake. He would not do the obvious.

The headman turned after staring at Walking Grizzly Bear for several long heartbeats. "In our custom, I would like the head of each family to say their words."

Over the next hour, Walking Grizzly Bear heard the story of how Kesakailux had returned early from a day-long hunt to catch his wife and her lover wrapped naked together in a deer hide blanket, the sweat from their lovemaking still on them. Walking Grizzly Bear heard how he had attacked their sleeping forms in a rage, not stopping until both were dead. Walking Grizzly Bear heard how Kesakailux had left the lodge long after the screams had died down, and fallen into the arms of the guards who had kept everyone at a distance. The village had known of the affair, but they could not stop it, as they could not stop the demands for justice from the families of the two who were slain.

In answer to the stories he heard, Walking Grizzly Bear took his son outside to the fire pit at the center of the village. There he, his wife, and his son danced a grieving song. Exhausted as he was, Walking Grizzly Bear stayed on his feet until the last drum beat sounded, then collapsed. No one helped him. A silence descended and then the headman's voice cut into the gathering night. "Inquala, what have you to say for your family, for your son who has taken two lives?"

Walking Grizzly Bear bowed his head to the elders who formed an inner ring around him. "I cannot bring back the dead. I cannot say that it didn't happen. My son loved his wife dearly, and for that he killed her. It was perhaps not the right way, but at the time it was the only way. Now the only way is not through more bloodshed. It is through making a peace. We are all related here. I have my wife here. Many of you have family staying in my village. It must always be that way. We must always share. And for that I give you all what I bring."

At the clap of his hands, the villagers were startled. They heard the sound of thunder approaching. Within moments a herd of horses poured around the corner of the ridge. Ten of Walking Grizzly Bear's finest warriors rode the horses into and through the village to the other side amidst the growing approval of the families. The herd was stopped twenty paces from where the villagers stood, and warriors led two magnificent horses to where Walking Grizzly Bear stood. One at a time, Walking Grizzly Bear took the reins of each horse and led it to the head of each of the grieving families. Each time he spoke the same words: "Take this in honour of those who have passed to the other world. When I give to you, I give myself."

To the headman of the Douglas Lake camp, Walking Grizzly Bear said, "My gift is for all of you. I make peace in the only way I can without taking blood that belongs to all of us."

And so Walking Grizzly Bear won his son back, and lost much of the power that now flowed around him to others.

His son-in-law came to Walking Grizzly Bear during the Winter dance among the stuwi'x. Walking Grizzly Bear felt poorly, and his dance was short. He watched the younger ones dance, and the voices continued to belittle him. The cost of his son's tribulations had drained Walking Grizzly Bear more than the payment itself. He had gone to Cumcloups later that summer and had been ridiculed by the new Chief Factor for the Bay, who told him he had never heard of Montigny's promises, nor did he think much of those who lived in the past, or who thought that the Pacific Fur Company was anything but a bunch of American ruffians and hooligans out to fleece everyone.

Word had spread of that meeting, and while the greetings were warm, the smiles were false or, worse, speculative. Some of his wives no longer waited for him, and he heard the stories of their unfaithfulness. His son tried to repay his father for what he had done, but Kesakailux was one man against a flood of those who saw the hesitations, the pauses between and during storytelling, the cipcaptikwl times of the animal people. That Walking Grizzly Bear could no longer dance all night was no one's concern. That he gave away gifts now in ever-increasing amounts, and without looking to whom he gave, caused bitter enmity among those whom a generation before would have held Walking Grizzly Bear in higher esteem. Even the elders said that times were changing, words that Walking Grizzly Bear took in with growing disbelief and sadness.

Tonasket saw his father as soon as he entered the great house. Walking Grizzly Bear was seated alone, with syilx on both sides who ignored him even as they pointedly talked about him. Tonasket walked up to his father as the assembly grew silent.

"Father, it is time. Your daughter and I can no longer wait. We have a second child on the way, and we cannot keep coming up here. You must do it now."

Walking Grizzly Bear looked down at the ground, flushed with shame; shame that his son knew no more than to do this. When he looked up into Tonasket's eyes, he saw anger. Beneath the anger, he saw shame of a different kind, a type of shame Walking Grizzly Bear could not understand because he had never felt its like before. He would give Tonasket what he wanted, but knew that it wasn't so easy as Tonasket thought.

Into the silence of the waiting assembly Walking Grizzly Bear spoke, glad that he still had some influence. "My son wishes to be the headman of the Sinkaietk, the syilx below Inkameep. He has many friends down there, many syilx who call themselves family. If it is the wish of the Sinkaietk that Tonasket be their headman, I will not stand in the way."

Walking Grizzly Bear continued watching his son. Tonasket smiled. In a low voice, Walking Grizzly Bear cautioned his son, "People will let you lead so long as they want. You cannot make it otherwise. In the way of all things, return favors when you can, not when you want. A headman both gives and receives favors. He gives favors when he can. He returns favors when others ask him, or when they need him. Sometimes this means doing things you do not want to do, or do not approve of, yet the ones who gave you the favors have perhaps done the same. It is not for you to reason out the justice of this, nor to hesitate when giving favors. Favors given reluctantly lead to resentment and anger. As a leader, if you decide to do something, do not look back."

Tonasket replied in the same low voice. "Father, my wife and I thank you. But do not tell me what to do as headman. I know what to do."

With that, Tonasket turned and whooped as he strode for the exit, where his wife and his followers waited. Walking Grizzly Bear felt the pain of watching his daughter stand from him and greet her husband without even coming in to see her father. "It is time," a voice whispered, and Walking Grizzly Bear nodded. It is time.

A final visit to Cumcloups, what the sha-mas called Fort Kamloops. From the many warriors who had once followed his every move, there were now three men. They sat quietly by the fire, each deep in the thought of the past. The route they took was the one they had taken many years ago on their way to Lillooet country, but now the fever no longer burned.

Walking Grizzly Bear knew she was waiting, and so after his meal he told the others to wait for him. He walked into the forest and after five minutes settled himself on a large flat rock at the base of a great old tree. The rock was slightly damp, but Walking Grizzly Bear felt peace flow through him, somehow heightened by the slight discomfort of the damp rock.

She came as silently as she had many years ago. Walking Grizzly Bear watched her move over the treetops, a white figure who stirred the branches as she approached. He sang his spirit song in honor of the woman who had come to him only once before, from the banks of a great river. She stood on the flat rock as Walking Grizzly Bear, moved by his own song, danced to the center of the small clearing, his voice quavering as he swayed in the wind under the stars. He grunted and shuffled as his bear spirit willed him to. When he finished, he was sweating and proud.

Enid hugged Walking Grizzly Bear. Then he said, "Let me tell you a story."

It happened this way. In the month of service berries, a group of sha-mas came up the valley. At the south end of our Okanagan Lake they found a supply of berries we had stored for the winter. They chased us away by shooting in our direction, and killing some of our dogs. Then they ate the berries and what they couldn't eat they spilled into the lake, sometimes falling in themselves because they were drinking alcohol.

We thought they had gone the next day and some of us went to see what we could save. But they were only waiting, and they killed many of us, and then continued traveling north along the lake. They took two Secwepemc on their way to Cumcloups, where I met them in the Fort. It was a sad day. My pride was not there, for it would have killed the Secwepemc.

I dressed as I thought they would like a great chief to dress. I wore their medals. I wore their uniform. I wore a stove pipe hat with feathers. I swallowed my pride, and in doing this, I saw my proudest day, for the sha-mas let the Secwepemc go, and ridiculed me. Had not my warriors been there, it would not have been a good day for me or for the Secwepemc. That is my story.

Enid pulled Walking Grizzly Bear to the flat rock and bade him sit. "Let me tell you a story," she said.

It happened this way. It was my first day on this world. My people told me to be careful, and I was. I knew where the camp of syilx was, and I walked from my camp to where the family was. On my way, I saw a sister and her brother lost on the great river. In the way of my people, I rescued the two and returned them to their parents. It was not the way I wanted, and I could not stay, for the family had seen me fly over the trees, and knew I was not of this world. I left before I could speak. That is my story.

"It is a good story," Walking Grizzly Bear said. "I remember that boy. He was not like me."

"Not then he wasn't. He was young and full of curiosity, full of questions. The man before me owns himself."

Thinking of his son, Walking Grizzly Bear said, "It may be all I own."

Enid laughed. "Where I come from, that is enough. It is all you have to take with you into the next world."

"It is time then."

"It is time."

In the first days of spring, in the month of buds, they came from everywhere. Spokanes, Secwepemc, Sinkaietk, syilx, and many others. They came and they surrounded the Fort. The songs of death and of celebration made the traders within the wall shiver. Drums filled the air with a rhythm bone deep and as old as Coyote himself.

The body was taken from its temporary home in Toom-Tem, wrapped in a great blanket made for the occasion, and placed on a litter. With his wives and children both in front of and behind him, Walking Grizzly Bear made his last journey home.

The huge procession swelled in the three days it took to travel the valley floors to Nkamaplex, the Head of the Lake. Every night people listened to the deeds of Walking Grizzly Bear, the one the sha-mas called Inquala. They spoke of his early days, of the hunts for the great buffalo, of the great war with the Lillooets, of the hunting trips now burnt into their memories.

The wives spoke of his love for them, of the gentle way he treated his children and grandchildren. They spoke of how he sometimes went berry picking with them, breaking an age-old custom and, in doing so, showing his wisdom. They spoke of his teachings of patience and of life, of what it meant to be a human being, one who could speak to Coyote without fear and one who, if the stories were true, had spent his last night speaking with the Woman in the Trees.

The bone games in his honor were magnificent, teams of warriors and families endlessly honoring the last of the great headmen by gambling with Coyote's spirit. The songs swelled from one end of the camp to the other in great waves of sorrow so deep it swelled the hearts and stilled the mind in a way never remembered before.

At Nkamaplex, the long procession was met by countless syilx whose songs could be heard five miles away. The procession sang as well, and the two sets of songs became as one. At the burial place, a hush fell over the enormous crowd and everyone heard the clear clean song of the meadowlark float into their hearts. An old coyote paused in a nearby field and sat to watch the ceremony. Tonasket, the headman of the Sinkaietk, laid Walking Grizzly Bear's medals alongside his body. As he turned to go, he felt thousands of eyes on him, and his spirit quailed in front of so many. Only then did he know what it was to want to be a part of such a gathering.

In 1959, on the hundredth anniversary of Walking Grizzly Bear's passing, a tombstone was placed over his grave:

No. 1 Okanagan
In loving Memory of
INQUALA
The Great Chief of the Indian Tribe of the Okanagan,
who was living and Ruling in 1838

That is my story.
There are ten thousand others waiting to be heard.
When I give to you, I give myself.

Printed in
September 2004
at Gauvin Press Ltd., Gatineau, Québec